In USA Today *bestselling author Sarah Fox's delicious new Pancake House Mystery, it's up to Marley McKinney to discover the waffle truth behind a rival's murder...*

Winter has come to Wildwood Cove, and riding in on the chill is Wally Fowler. Although he's been away for years, establishing his reputation as the self-proclaimed Waffle King, the wealthy blowhard has returned to the coastal community to make money, not friends—by pitting his hot and trendy Waffle Kingdom against Marley McKinney's cozy pancake house, The Flip Side. Wally doesn't see anything wrong in a little healthy competition, until he's murdered in his own state-of-the art kitchen.

Marley isn't surprised when the authorities sniff around The Flip Side for a motive, but it's her best friend, Lisa, who gets grilled, given her sticky history with the victim. When a second murder rocks the town, it makes it harder than ever for Marley to clear Lisa's name. Marley's afraid that she's next in line to die—and the way things are looking, the odds of surviving her investigation could be stacked against her.

Includes pancake recipes right from The Flip Side menu!

Books by Sarah Fox

The Pancake House Mystery Series

The Crêpes of Wrath

For Whom the Bread Rolls

Of Spice and Men

Yeast of Eden

The Music Lover's Mystery Series

Dead Ringer

Death in A Major

Deadly Overtures

YEAST OF EDEN

A Pancake House Mystery

Sarah Fox

LYRICAL PRESS
Kensington Publishing Corp.
www.kensingtonbooks.com

Lyrical Press books are published by
Kensington Publishing Corp. 119 West 40th Street New York, NY 10018

All Kensington titles, imprints, and distributed lines are available at special
quantity discounts for bulk purchases for sales promotion, premiums, fund-
raising, and educational or institutional use.

To the extent that the image or images on the cover of this book depict a
person or persons, such person or persons are merely models, and are not
intended to portray any character or characters featured in the book.

Special book excerpts or customized printings can also be created to fit
specific needs. For details, write or phone the office of the Kensington
Special Sales Manager:
Kensington Publishing Corp.
119 West 40th Street
New York, NY 10018
Attn. Special Sales Department. Phone: 1-800-221-2647.

Kensington and the K logo Reg. U.S. Pat. & TM Off.
LYRICAL PRESS Reg. U.S. Pat. & TM Off.
Lyrical Press and the L logo are trademarks of Kensington Publishing Corp.

First Electronic Edition: October 2018
eISBN-13: 978-1-5161-0774-2
eISBN-10: 1-5161-0774-8

First Print Edition: October 2018
ISBN-13: 978-1-5161-0777-3
ISBN-10: 1-5161-0777-2

Printed in the United States of America

Chapter 1

My car's headlights cut through the darkness, illuminating the driving rain. The windshield wipers swished back and forth in a rapid rhythm as I carefully navigated my way along the deserted streets of Wildwood Cove. Normally I preferred to walk to work each morning, trekking along the beach so I could listen to the crashing waves and smell the salty air. Lately, however, I'd been making more use of my blue hatchback. Over the past several days the weather had been less than inviting, drizzling with rain if not outright pouring, and chilly enough that the occasional glob of slush splattered against my windshield along with the pelting raindrops.

The rain was supposed to let up in the next day or so, according to the weather forecast, so I hoped it wouldn't be much longer before I could get back to enjoying my early morning walks along the shoreline. For the moment, though, I was grateful for the warmth and shelter of my car.

When I turned into the small parking lot behind The Flip Side pancake house, I pulled up next to the only other car in the lot—a baby-blue classic Volkswagen bug belonging to The Flip Side's chef, Ivan Kaminski. He arrived even earlier than I did each morning, as did his assistant, Tommy Park. It was barely six o'clock, but I knew the two of them would have been working for a good while already.

I shut off my car's engine and grabbed my tote bag off the passenger seat, steeling myself for the upcoming dash through the pouring rain to the back door of the pancake house. As soon as I climbed out into the rain, I slammed the car door, ducked my head, and made a beeline for the slim bit of shelter provided by the recessed doorway.

Despite having spent mere seconds exposed to the elements, I had damp hair and droplets of water running down my face. I wiped them away with my sleeve and jiggled my ring of keys until I found the right one. As I put the key into the door, I caught sight of something white from the corner of my eye. A flyer lay plastered against the pavement, waterlogged and with a muddy footprint stamped across it.

I darted out of the shelter of the doorway and peeled the soggy paper off the ground. When I was once again out of the rain, I peered at the flyer, the exterior light above my head providing me with enough illumination to read by.

When I took in the bold black words printed across the saturated paper, my former good mood did a nosedive. I'd seen the flyer before. I'd seen several them, in fact, plastered all over town on utility poles, signposts, and community notice boards. I'd also received one in the mail. That one had gone straight into the recycling bin. This one I crumpled up in my hand as I unlocked the door, the words *Wally's Waffle Kingdom* disappearing from sight as the paper scrunched up into a soggy ball.

Once inside, I unlocked the door to my office and tossed the scrunched flyer into the wastepaper basket. If I never saw another one, I'd be happy, although I knew the advertisement wasn't the real problem. That was the Waffle Kingdom itself. The Flip Side had become a fixture in the small seaside town of Wildwood Cove, with many faithful customers who returned again and again to enjoy Ivan's scrumptious breakfast creations. There were other restaurants and cafés around town, but none of them specialized in breakfast foods like The Flip Side did.

Up until a couple of weeks ago, I'd never really worried about competition. Then Wally Fowler had moved to town—moved *back* to town actually, since he'd grown up here—and my mind had remained unsettled ever since. I wasn't about to roll over and give up on the pancake house just because of some competition, but I couldn't keep my niggling concern at bay.

If the Waffle Kingdom's fare was as good as the flyer proclaimed (*the best waffles EVER!*) it wasn't unrealistic to think that The Flip Side would lose some of its business to the new establishment. In the summertime, when tourists flocked to the small town, that might not be such a problem. There would probably be enough business for both restaurants during those weeks. But during the rest of the year? That could be a definite issue.

I'd been hoping to give each of my three full-time employees a raise in the near future. Now I was keeping that plan to myself, unsure if I'd be able to follow through. I'd have to wait and see what happened once the waffle house opened. As Wally and his flyers had been announcing to the whole town for several days, the grand opening of the Waffle Kingdom would take place next week.

It would take time to know the full extent of the effect on The Flip Side, so I was determined to carry on as usual. I just wished I could get rid of that ever-present worry lingering at the back of my mind.

With the wet flyer in the trash and my jacket hung on the coat stand, I ran a hand through my damp curls and made my way into the dining area. I flipped on the lights, and immediately some of the tension that had crept into my shoulders fizzled away. There was something so comforting about the cozy pancake house. Like the beach and the charming town, The Flip Side had easily worked its way into my heart, becoming a second home away from my blue-and-white beachfront Victorian.

Smiling, I glanced out the large front windows, seeing nothing but inky darkness and rivulets of water running down the panes.

Well, almost nothing else.

I walked quickly across the room to the front door, bone-chilling damp air hitting me as soon as I pushed it open. Staying beneath the awning so I wouldn't get soaked, I approached the two white rectangles taped to one of the windows, spaced a couple of feet apart. When I got close enough to recognize them as two more Waffle Kingdom flyers, I let out a growl of annoyance.

Ripping the flyers off the glass, I stormed back into the pancake house. "Of all the nerve!"

Twenty-one-year-old Tommy Park poked his head out the pass-through window to the kitchen. "What's up?" he asked.

I waved the crumpled flyers. "Wally the Waffle King strikes again."

The kitchen door swung open and Ivan appeared. Tommy ducked away from the window and came through the door a second later.

"These were taped to the front window," I said, waving the flyers again.

Ivan grabbed one and glowered at the piece of paper. While an intimidating scowl was the chef's typical expression, this one was far darker than usual.

"He's rubbing your nose in it," he declared, crumpling the flyer as his large hand closed into a fist.

Tommy took the other flyer from me. "Totally not cool."

"It's one thing to open up a waffle house that will compete directly with us," I said, "but it's hitting a new low by plastering the ads all over the front of this place."

"He's trying to get under your skin." Ivan tossed the crumpled flyer toward the wastepaper basket, making a perfect shot.

"But why? Does he really think annoying us will get us to close up shop so all our business goes his way?"

"Not going to happen," Tommy said.

"Definitely not," I agreed. "But why else try to aggravate us?"

"Probably for fun," Ivan said. "Some people enjoy riling others up."

"That's true." I'd learned that firsthand several months back when a bitter and vengeful woman had tried to make my life miserable.

"And I hear Wally Fowler's a slimeball," Tommy said. "I'm not sure anyone in town actually likes him."

Ivan nodded his agreement. "Wildwood Cove would be better off without him."

If enough people believed that, maybe I had nothing to worry about. The townsfolk weren't likely to give the self-proclaimed Waffle King their business if they despised him.

"I guess it's best to ignore him and focus on keeping our customers happy, like we always do," I decided.

"Sounds like a plan." With a flick of his wrist, Tommy sent the second flyer arcing into the trash can.

He returned to the kitchen and Ivan followed after him, his scowl as dark as ever. Was he more worried about the new waffle house than he was letting on? With his bulging muscles, numerous tattoos, and dark, intense eyes, Ivan wasn't one to be easily fazed. But something in his face led me to believe he was taking the potential problem posed by Wally and his waffle house very seriously.

My worries tried to resurface, but I forced them back down, focusing on starting a fire in the stone fireplace to keep myself busy. The Flip Side would be fine, I told myself. It was a well-established restaurant, with a solid and loyal customer base that loved Ivan's cooking and the cozy atmosphere.

Surely it would take more than Wally the Waffle King to destroy what we had here. After all, how much damage could one man cause?

* * * *

About an hour after opening, the pancake house was getting busy. The town was waking up, the residents heading out to brave the weather, some of them ending up at The Flip Side. All of the tables near the cheery, crackling fire had been claimed, the welcoming warmth of the flames drawing in the customers as they escaped the cold and the rain. On my way around the restaurant to offer refills of coffee, I paused to talk with two of The Flip Side's most loyal and reliable customers, Gary and Ed. They were lifelong residents of Wildwood Cove and had been best friends since they were five years old. Now retired, they split most of their time between the pancake house, the local seniors' activity center, and the bowling alley.

"What do you know about this Waffle Kingdom that's opening up next week, Marley?" Ed asked.

"I've heard the self-proclaimed Waffle King grew up here in Wildwood Cove," I said. "But other than that, I really don't know anything more than what's on those flyers he's spread around town."

"A waste of paper, if you ask me," Gary spoke up as he poured maple syrup over his stack of pancakes. "Why would anyone eat there when they could come here? It's not like anyone can compete with Ivan's cooking."

I smiled. "Hopefully you're not the only ones who feel that way."

"We're not," Ed assured me. "And I don't think it'll much matter to people that Wally grew up in Wildwood Cove. He's been away for years, and he wasn't good for much when he was here."

"I've yet to run across a fan of his," I said, topping up the coffee mugs.

Gary chewed on a forkful of pancakes. "Adam Silvester was buddies with Wally back in the day, but I don't know if they stayed in touch. And there's his sister, Vicky, of course. Half-sister, technically. But aside from those two, I'm not sure if anyone's much keen on Wally. People around here have long memories."

I wasn't sure what he meant by that, but I needed to move along and see to other customers.

"I guess we'll have to see what happens when the waffle house opens," I said, happy that I managed to sound unconcerned.

"You'll never find us over there, that's for sure," Ed declared. He lowered his voice. "Unless you want us to go undercover to do some recon."

I couldn't help but smile again. "I doubt that will be necessary, but thank you."

Gary saluted me with his coffee mug. "You can count on us, Marley."

Cheered by their support, I thanked them again and moved on to the next table.

The breakfast rush kept me and Leigh—The Flip Side's full-time waitress—busy for the next hour or so, but I eventually found time to slip into the kitchen and make myself a cup of tea.

"Are you going to the ladies' night at the hardware store tonight, Marley?" Leigh asked as she pushed through the kitchen door, bringing a load of dirty dishes with her.

"I'm planning on it. Are you?"

"No, I'll be looking after the kids. Greg's working at the store tonight."

I took a cautious sip of my hot tea. "I can't help but be amused that ladies' night at the hardware store is an actual thing."

"It's a tradition," Ivan said as he flipped pancakes on the griddle.

"It's true," Leigh confirmed. "The store's been holding this event for more than ten years now. I know it might sound a bit odd at first, but it's really popular. And good fun too. Aside from having things on sale, they have door prizes, demos, samples to give away, and really good food."

"Free food?" Tommy said as he drizzled melted chocolate over a plate of crêpes. "Are you sure your husband can't sneak me in?"

"Sorry, Tommy," Leigh said with a smile. "You'll have to wait for Customer Appreciation Day in the spring." She returned her attention to me. "It's a good chance for you to get some Christmas shopping done. Maybe you'll find something for Brett."

"Maybe," I said, "but he probably already owns at least one of everything the store has for sale." My boyfriend had his own lawn and garden care company, and during the winters he helped out with his dad's home renovation business. He had a whole workshop full of tools behind his house. "I might get something for myself, though. I'll need a few things if I'm going to make a garden in the spring."

"Don't forget to try the mini cupcakes while you're there," Leigh advised. "Greg already knows he's supposed to smuggle one home for me."

She disappeared through the swinging door. I drank down my tea and followed after her a few minutes later. I spent some time in the office between the breakfast and lunch rushes, but then I was back out at the front of the house helping Leigh.

I carried a plate of bacon cheddar waffles over to a man I'd seen in The Flip Side three or four times before. Prior to that morning, I hadn't known anything about him aside from his name—Adam Silvester—but thanks to my chat with Ed and Gary earlier, I now knew he had once been friends with Wally Fowler.

There wasn't anything about Adam that screamed or even whispered lowlife, but maybe I had a distorted view of Wally. Even if I didn't, the fact that Adam had been buddies with Wally back in high school didn't mean he was a bad guy. They weren't necessarily friends any longer, and I couldn't say that I'd always picked the best people for friends when I was a teenager.

As far as I remembered, I'd only ever seen Adam at The Flip Side on his own. While he was always polite, he kept mostly to himself, gazing out the window as he ate or reading the latest issue of the town's local newspaper. That was what he was doing today, perusing the articles as he started in on his waffles.

I cleared up the neighboring table and carried the dirty dishes into the kitchen before delivering mocha mascarpone crêpes and blueberry crumble pancakes to hungry customers. I glanced out the window on my way back to the kitchen, noting that the rain had stopped and the sun was attempting to peek through the clouds. As I was leaving the dining area for the kitchen, the front door opened, admitting three new arrivals—two men and a woman. I didn't alter my path.

Leigh darted through the kitchen door behind me, grabbing my arm.

"That's him!" she said in an urgent whisper.

"Him who?" I asked as I set down two dirty coffee mugs.

"Wally Fowler," Leigh said, keeping her voice low. "The so-called Waffle King."

"He's here?" Ivan's question boomed across the kitchen. "Why?"

"I don't know, but I guess we'll find out." Leigh hurried out of the kitchen.

I followed right on her heels, ready to finally meet Wally the Waffle King.

Chapter 2

I approached Wally Fowler with a mixture of curiosity and trepidation. He wasn't quite six feet tall and was on the hefty side. His head was bald on top, while mousy-brown frizz stuck out from the sides. His watery-blue eyes gave me an uneasy feeling, as did the oily smile that spread across his face when he noticed me heading his way.

"Wally the Waffle King," he said, loud enough for everyone in the pancake house to hear. He stuck out his hand. "Are you the proprietor?"

I shook his offered hand but released it as quickly as I could without being too rude. "That's right. Marley McKinney."

His two companions hovered behind him, looking as though they wished they were anywhere else. The man was tall and burly with a short, dark beard and brown eyes that didn't settle on any particular point. The woman appeared to be about my age. She had the same mousy-brown hair—though much more of it—as Wally, and the same pale blue eyes, making me wonder if the two of them were related.

"Chester and Vicky and I decided to come over and check out your little place," Wally said, his gaze sweeping over the dining area.

Some of the customers continued eating, but most were watching the scene unfolding by the cash counter.

"Quaint, don't you think?" Wally jabbed his elbow into Chester's ribs.

Chester kept his expression neutral and didn't speak.

I forced myself to smile, though I wanted nothing more than for Wally to leave.

"It was nice of you to stop by," I said, doing my best to sound unfazed by Wally's clear attempt to insult me.

"I'm sure you've heard that the Waffle Kingdom will be opening next week."

"Yes."

"You don't mind a bit of friendly competition, hey?" He chuckled, and I had to work hard not to make a face at the grating sound. He addressed the dining room at large. "You're all invited to the grand opening. It's going to be a great event. Fit for a king!"

He laughed at his own joke, but no one else did. Behind him, Vicky's face had flushed with embarrassment.

"You'll get to see our top-of-the-line establishment," Wally continued. "We've got all the modern conveniences. You'll be impressed. This little town hasn't seen the likes of what I've got in store for you."

While a couple of diners appeared mildly interested, most had returned their attention to their meals, one or two with a frown. I caught sight of Adam Silvester across the restaurant and was surprised to see that he was doing more than frowning. He was sending a death glare Wally's way. He must not have considered Wally his buddy anymore.

"We'll have free samples available at the grand opening," Wally went on, oblivious to the fact that few people were still listening to him. "And I'll do a demonstration of how to make ice cream with liquid nitrogen. Sounds amazing, huh? I bet none of you have ever seen that before." His self-satisfied grin stretched across the full width of his face as he gazed around the restaurant.

"That sounds fascinating," I said, though I didn't manage to infuse the words with any enthusiasm.

The kitchen door swung open and Ivan appeared, Tommy behind him.

"Aha!" Wally's watery eyes fixed on Ivan. "You must be the chef of this little establishment."

Ivan's scowl was far stormier than usual, his dark eyes boring into the Waffle King.

"You'll be interested in the demonstration," Wally said to him. "Maybe you'll even learn a thing or two."

I barely managed to keep my jaw from dropping.

"You think I need to learn from you?" Ivan practically bellowed.

Everyone's attention focused on us again.

For the first time, Wally's pompous smile faltered, but he quickly snapped it back in place. "There's nothing wrong with updating your skills." Wally stood taller, but Ivan still towered over him. "When was the last time you cooked with liquid nitrogen?"

"I don't need fancy tricks to make food taste good," Ivan said.

I cringed when Wally chuckled. Ivan's expression had become thunderous, and I worried that the situation might get out of hand.

"Innovation. That's what people want." Wally addressed the diners again. "Right, folks?"

Nobody replied, but he didn't seem to notice. He also didn't notice the daggers shooting toward him from Adam Silvester's eyes.

Wally spoke to me and Ivan again. "I'll tell you what. The two of you should come over to the Waffle Kingdom this evening. I'll give you a tour, maybe even a sneak peek at my ice cream demo. Once you see me in action, I'm sure you'll come to appreciate what the Waffle Kingdom can offer that this place can't."

Ivan's nostrils flared. He reminded me of a bull getting ready to charge.

"You should leave," Ivan said, his deep voice edged with steel.

Wally was about to speak again when Vicky grabbed his arm.

"We've taken up enough of their time, Wally. Let's go." She tugged him toward the door.

He shook his arm free of her grasp, glaring at her for a fraction of a second before smoothing out his expression. "Sure, all right. We'll let you get on with...whatever it is you folks need to do."

I could feel Ivan's wrath radiating off him in fiery waves. I probably wasn't giving off a much better vibe myself.

Vicky and Chester left the restaurant without another word.

As Wally followed, he waved at all the diners. "I hope to see all you folks next week. I think you'll find the Waffle King reigns supreme."

It was a good thing he disappeared out the door at that moment. Ivan had taken a step toward him, and I didn't want to know what would have happened if Wally had hung around any longer.

When the obnoxious man was out of sight, I released a breath I didn't realize I'd been holding.

"Well, that was..." I wasn't sure what to say.

"An experience?" Leigh suggested.

"That's one word for it," Tommy said. With a shake of his head, he returned to the kitchen.

Ivan was still glaring at the front door.

I rested a hand on his arm. "Ivan?"

He finally wrenched his gaze away. "That man is nothing but trouble."

He strode into the kitchen.

Leigh grabbed the coffeepot and set off to refill some mugs. I had to give my head a shake before I could do anything else. The encounter with Wally had left me irritated and uneasy. I couldn't help but believe that

Ivan's words were true. Wally seemed eager to show us up, to prove that the waffle house would be far superior to The Flip Side. That grated at my nerves, and I had to hope he wouldn't succeed.

I pushed the Waffle King from my mind and refocused on waiting on my customers. As I jotted down an order at one table, I caught sight of my friend Lisa Morales sitting across the room, the only occupant at one of the small tables by the window. After I'd relayed the new order to the kitchen, I headed for Lisa's table.

"Hey," I said in greeting. "I didn't see you come in."

Lisa sniffled and blinked away tears.

Alarmed, my smile fell from my face. I put a hand on her shoulder. "Lisa, what's wrong?"

She sniffed again and tried to smile, but she failed miserably. "I don't want to cry in front of everyone. Can I go in the office for a bit?"

"Of course," I said. "I'll join you in a moment."

She grabbed her purse and hurried off down the hall toward the office. I watched her go, concern for my friend erasing the remnants of aggravation Wally's visit had left with me.

Leigh had disappeared into the kitchen seconds ago, so I followed after her.

"I'm going to be in the office for a while," I told her. "Let me know if you need any help out there."

"Everything okay?" she asked, probably sensing some of my concern.

"I don't know. Lisa's upset. I'm going to go talk to her now."

Ivan's gaze snapped up from the crêpe he was folding, but he said nothing.

I hurried to the office, worry for my friend quickening my pace. I shut the door as soon as I was in the room. Lisa sat in one of the two chairs before the desk, so I pulled up the other one.

"What's going on?" I asked as I settled into the chair.

Lisa had gained control of her tears, but the sadness hadn't left her brown eyes.

"It's Wally Fowler." Her expression hardened in a way I'd never seen before. "He's a scumbag."

"I haven't heard anything good about him," I said, "but I also haven't heard any specifics about why he's so unpopular. Did you know him before he left Wildwood Cove?"

She nodded and gazed out the window for a moment before speaking. "His sister, Vicky, was a year ahead of me in school, and Wally was about four years ahead. I'm not sure if he ever graduated, though. He got suspended more than once, I know that. He was dealing drugs by age sixteen, if not earlier."

I thought I knew where this was going. "Does this have something to do with Carlos?"

Her youngest brother had been battling a drug addiction for years.

Lisa nodded again. "Wally's the one who got Carlos into drugs. They're years apart in age, but even after he left school, Wally used to hang around the grounds, dealing to the kids."

"That's awful."

"It gets worse. He was driving drunk one night, with a girl in the car with him. He drove into a tree. The girl died, but he walked away without a scratch."

The brief story left me sickened. "Didn't he get arrested?"

"He did, and he got tossed in jail, but only for a few years. Lizzie Van Amstel is dead, but now he's out walking free. And not only that, he inherited millions from a great-aunt last year. How is that fair?"

"Was Lizzie from Wildwood Cove?"

"Yes. Her sister still lives here."

"And Wally dared to show his face again?" I wouldn't have put much past Wally now that I'd met him, but that seemed even more insensitive than I would have expected from him.

"He's strutting around town, acting like he's better than everyone because he's got money now. He doesn't care about Lizzie's family. He doesn't care about anyone. And if he's still into dealing drugs, if he's going to get more kids messed up like he did with Carlos..."

I squeezed Lisa's hand. "Maybe the waffle house will be a flop and he'll move on before long."

"Maybe." Lisa didn't sound convinced. "But with all that money he's got, he can afford to operate at a loss. He probably would, just to spite those of us who don't want him around. You heard him out there, Marley. He wants to show everyone he's better than you, that his place will be more successful. He could end up hurting your business. You don't deserve that." Her hands had balled into fists.

"I'm going to hold on to the hope that he won't succeed at ruining The Flip Side," I said. "Maybe he won't steal much of our business since he's so unpopular."

Lisa sighed heavily. "If only we could run him out of town."

I squeezed her hand again and decided to shift the conversation. "How is Carlos these days?"

"Better," she said with a hint of a smile. "He's living on the Oregon coast with my aunt and uncle. He finished his in-patient treatment program and he's seeing a counselor regularly. He's even working some shifts at my uncle's store. It's been a while since he had any sort of job."

"I'm glad he's doing better."

"Me too. It's a relief after the last couple of years. Things were getting really bad. I don't think he can ever move back to the peninsula, though. Too many triggers." She drew in a deep breath and let it out slowly. "I'm sorry I got so upset."

"You don't have to apologize. It's totally understandable that you'd react this way."

She picked at the cuff of her sweater. "I guess we'll have to learn to live with that lowlife being in town." She got to her feet. "I should let you get back to work."

"There's nothing pressing I have to attend to," I assured her. "You must have shown up for some lunch. Can I get you something or have you lost your appetite?"

"I did lose my appetite for a while, but I'm getting hungry again. Did Ivan make any of those delicious maple pecan sticky rolls today?"

"He did. And I think there are a few left. How about we go see? Yours is on the house."

This time her smile was a bit brighter. "You're a good friend, Marley."

"So are you," I said, giving her a hug. "Now let's go find those sticky rolls."

Chapter 3

By the time I arrived home late that afternoon, the early morning rain was a distant memory. The last of the clouds had disappeared hours earlier and the sun shone brightly in the perfect blue sky. My orange tabby, Flapjack, was eager to get outdoors when I got home, so I opened the French doors to the back porch. As he wandered out to prowl across the yard, I stayed up on the porch, leaning against the railing and gazing out at the gorgeous view.

I shivered despite the bright sun, the cold wind sweeping up from the ocean and cutting through my clothes. Despite the chilly air, I wasn't ready to retreat indoors, so I stayed put, watching as Flapjack hopped onto a sun-bleached log at the top of the beach, peeking down at the sand now and then as he padded his way along the large piece of driftwood.

If not for the effect Wally's visit had on Lisa, I probably would have all but forgotten it by then. I couldn't erase the memory of my friend's distress, and I wished there was some way I could get things back to the way they were before Wally's return to Wildwood Cove. I didn't see how that was possible, unfortunately. Wally seemed determined to prove that his waffle house would be a success, and I didn't think there was much anyone could do about it except wait and see how things panned out.

I had no intention of taking Wally up on his offer to visit the Waffle Kingdom that evening. I had other plans, but even if that hadn't been the case, I still would have avoided the place like the plague. Business competition aside, I found the man repugnant and had no desire to spend time with him.

Pulling the sleeves of my hoodie over my cold hands, I considered heading indoors until I heard the rumble of a car engine drawing near.

I smiled as a door slammed and footsteps sounded around the corner of the house. I pushed off from the porch railing in time to see Brett jogging up the stairs.

"Hey," he greeted, pulling me close for a kiss. "Isn't it a bit chilly to be out here?"

"It is." I slipped my arms beneath his unzipped jacket and hugged him. "But now I've got you to warm me up."

"One of my favorite pastimes," he said, kissing me again.

We lingered over the kiss this time, until a gust of salty wind blew my curls into both our faces.

"How was your day?" Brett asked as he brushed my hair behind my ear.

"I think I'd rather hear about yours."

"Mine was routine."

"Routine sounds much better than mine."

"It was that bad?"

"Some parts weren't great." I took his hand and led him into the house, too chilly now to stay outside. "Speaking of which, I'd better text Lisa and see how she's doing."

As Brett shrugged out of his jacket, I told him about the visit from Wally the Waffle King and Lisa's reaction. I tapped out a text message as I talked, sending it once I'd wrapped up the story.

"Poor Lisa," Brett said.

"I feel really bad for her." I left my phone on the kitchen table and filled the electric kettle at the sink. "Do you remember Wally from before he left town?"

"Only vaguely. I remember his sister, Vicky, better. I think she was only a year or two ahead of me and Lisa at school."

"A year, I think Lisa said. Vicky came by the pancake house with Wally, but he did most of the talking." I switched on the kettle and leaned against the quartz countertop, recently installed by Brett and his dad's crew as part of my complete kitchen renovation.

Up until a few weeks ago, the kitchen hadn't been updated in at least twenty-five years, and while functional, it had needed sprucing up. I wanted to maintain the character of the old Victorian as much as possible as I renovated the various rooms. But in the kitchen I'd been less strict with that, making sure to have all the modern conveniences incorporated into the design.

I loved the look of the quartz on the counters and island, and the dark wood cabinets warmed up the room. It was a beautiful kitchen, and sometimes I still had to stop and convince myself that it was really mine.

The kettle boiled and I opened a cupboard to take down a mug.

"Hot chocolate?" I offered, holding up a second mug.

"Sure. That sounds good." He came up behind me and wrapped his arms around me as I scooped powder into the mugs. "You're going out tonight, right?"

"Yep. The shindig at the hardware store. I hear it'll be hopping."

"It usually is, so I'm told." He released me so he could accept the mug of hot chocolate I handed him. "Make sure you try the mini cupcakes. They're incredible."

"Leigh mentioned them." I paused with my mug halfway to my lips. "How come you know what the ladies' night food tastes like?"

"I stopped at the hardware store on my way here so I could put in an order for some closet doors. Some of the baked goods had just arrived, and being the loyal customer that I am, I was offered a sample."

I eyed him with suspicion. "Did you purposely time your visit to the store to coincide with the arrival of the food?"

He grinned. "Let's just say I figured it might be a good idea to put in my order at the end of the day."

"That's what I thought."

I picked up my phone on the way over to the couch, where we settled in to enjoy our hot chocolate. Lisa had replied to my text, saying she was feeling better now. I sent her another message, asking if she planned to go to the hardware store that evening.

Yes, she wrote back. *See you there.*

I spent the next hour relaxing on the couch with Brett, talking about our plans for the upcoming holidays. I was looking forward to our first Christmas as a couple. We'd spent Thanksgiving in Seattle with my mom and her fiancé, but we were spending Christmas in Wildwood Cove.

When it was almost time for me to leave for the hardware store, we got up from the couch and headed for the foyer.

"Are you sure you want to go out tonight?" Brett asked, kissing me below my left ear.

"Mmm." I tried my best not to melt into him. "You're tempting me, but so are those cupcakes."

He grinned and pulled me into a hug. "I should have kept quiet about those. How can a guy possibly compete?"

"If any guy could, it would be you." I kissed him and pushed him gently toward the door. "Dinner tomorrow?"

"Definitely."

I stood on the front porch and waved as he drove off along the driveway in his pickup truck. As soon as he was out of sight, I hurried back into the house, shivering. Now that the sun had set, the chilly air had taken on an icy edge.

Flapjack had returned indoors before dark, so I didn't have to worry about tracking him down. I set out some food for him and left him enthusiastically tucking into his dinner. I could have walked to the store, but once again I decided to take my car. With no streetlights on the outskirts of town, the walk would have been dark and cold.

As soon as I turned onto Pacific Street, I could tell that the tales of the event's popularity hadn't been exaggerated. The store's parking lot was already crammed full, and cars lined the curb on both sides of the road. I ended up circling the block and parking well down the street from my destination.

With reluctance, I left the warmth of my car's interior, shivering when the cold air hit me. I hurried along the street, eager to get indoors and hoping I wouldn't return to find my windshield frosted over.

As I passed beneath a streetlamp, I noticed Adam Silvester heading my way, walking quickly with his head down and his hands stuffed into the pockets of his jeans.

"Evening, Adam," I said as he drew within steps of me.

His head snapped up as if I'd startled him. "Oh...hey." He didn't slow down, and by the time his vague greeting was out of his mouth, he'd already passed me.

I stopped and watched him go, wondering what had him so distracted. I shrugged it off after a moment and continued on my way. Light spilled out of the large windows of the hardware store, beckoning me closer. When I pulled open the door, delicious warmth wafted out to envelop me.

As soon as I stepped over the threshold, holiday cheer had me in its grasp. Evergreen boughs, colorful baubles, frosted pinecones, and bunches of holly decorated the store. Upbeat fifties music played in the background, layered beneath the hum of happy conversation and laughter. I'd arrived within fifteen minutes of the event's starting time, but already the party was in full swing. I had to edge my way around clusters of women to get deeper into the store, and I spotted several familiar faces, although not anyone I knew well.

"Good evening!" A brunette wearing a red polo shirt with the store's name stitched on it smiled at me. "Have you entered the giveaways yet?"

"No, I haven't."

She pointed out a small table nearby. A box wrapped in colorful paper sat on it, next to a large gift basket, entry forms and pens lying between the two items. "That's one of many. Feel free to enter all of them if you like. And be sure to check out the food."

"I will. Thank you."

The woman moved on to greet the next newcomers.

I made my way over to the gift basket, waiting my turn as another woman filled out her entry form and pushed it through the slot in the colorfully wrapped box. When I got a good view of the gift basket, I quickly filled out my own entry form. The prize was an assortment of snacks from a local shop.

I wound my way through the crowd, searching for Lisa among the many faces. I paused to enter another draw, the prize a beautiful wreath that would look festive on my front door or at the pancake house.

After squeezing past four women laughing merrily about something, I made my way along an aisle with shelves filled with batteries and flashlights of various sizes. When I exited at the far end of the aisle, I was at the back of the store, an unmanned customer service desk to my right, the food tables visible in the distance to my left. It wasn't hard to choose which way to go.

I'd taken two steps toward the food when a gust of cold air blew my hair into my face. Glancing over my shoulder, I saw a woman slip into the store through the metal door beyond the customer service desk. She patted her blond hair and rubbed at a dark smudge on the back of one hand. She touched her thumb to her tongue and rubbed at the mark again, this time with more luck. Straightening her shoulders, she smoothed out her pink pencil skirt and matching tailored jacket.

She didn't notice me, and soon disappeared down another aisle. I didn't know the woman's name, but she looked vaguely familiar. I must have seen her around town at one time or another. Many faces were familiar now that I'd lived in Wildwood Cove for eight months.

I couldn't see the one face I was actually looking for, however. I hadn't made my way through the entire store yet, though, so there was still a chance I'd run into Lisa.

On my way toward the food tables, I paused to watch a woman giving a demonstration on how to make wreaths out of boughs and other decorations. Out of the corner of my eye, I caught sight of the woman in the pink suit.

"There you are, Glo," another woman said to her. "I've been looking all over for you."

They disappeared into the crowd, and I turned my attention back to the demonstration. When I moved on a few minutes later, I almost bumped into Leigh's husband, Greg. He was busy helping a middle-aged woman pick out drill bits, but she soon headed for the cash counter with a package in hand, leaving Greg free to talk.

"How are you enjoying the event so far, Marley?" he asked.

"I've only been here a few minutes, but it's great. I hear the cupcakes shouldn't be missed."

"You heard right. If I don't take one home for Leigh, I'll be in the doghouse."

"I'm looking forward to trying one. You know Adam Silvester, don't you?"

"Sure. His daughter is in the same class as Kayla," he said, referring to his youngest child. "They play together sometimes."

"Did Leigh mention that Wally Fowler stopped by the pancake house today?"

He grimaced. "She did. He tried to make a show of it, I understand."

"I get the feeling that's his way with everything."

"You wouldn't be wrong about that. I never knew him well, but I never liked him."

"I got the sense Adam doesn't like him either, but I heard they used to be buddies."

"They did. I don't know of anything that might have changed that over the years, unless they just grew apart."

"I think it must be more than that. Adam was at the pancake house when Wally appeared and he didn't look the least bit happy."

Greg scratched his chin. "It could be something to do with Wally, but maybe it's just life in general. Adam's a single dad and he's been struggling financially, so maybe that's why he seemed unhappy."

I wasn't convinced, but didn't say so.

An elderly woman wandered our way and asked for Greg's help with finding the hanging lanterns advertised in the store flyer. I said goodbye to Greg and closed in on the spread of food.

I didn't know the cause of Adam's stormy expression or his distraction when I'd passed him on the street, and I figured I never would. I'd always been curious about people—maybe too curious at times—but I was able to push Adam out of my thoughts because I had a more pressing concern on my mind:

Where was Lisa?

Chapter 4

Before sampling any of the food on offer, I turned in a slow circle, searching for Lisa. I had no more luck finding her than I'd had earlier. I dug my phone out of my bag and sent her a quick text message, asking if she was at the store.

As I made my way closer to the two tables laden with food, my phone buzzed in my hand.

I'm at home, was Lisa's reply. *I don't feel up to socializing after all. Sorry I didn't tell you earlier.*

No worries, I wrote back. *Look after yourself.*

Feeling bad for my friend, I tucked my phone away and took a paper plate from the stack at the end of the closest table. Wally's return to Wildwood Cove had taken a toll on Lisa. I hoped she'd find a way to manage living in the same town as him, because I doubted Wally would pack in his new venture anytime soon, and I didn't want her suffering long-term.

I selected a mini quiche and some crackers and brie cheese before aiming for the desserts on the next table. I spied the famous cupcakes down at the far end, and made my way toward them, adding a piece of shortbread to my plate on the way. The cupcakes were disappearing quickly, I noticed; only half a dozen were left on the large platter. I claimed one for myself before they could all disappear, but then I noticed a store employee heading toward the table, balancing another platter full of the treats.

I tried to save the cupcake for last, but it was too tempting. I only managed to get through the quiche before I gave in and bit into the little cake. Deep, chocolatey flavor spread across my tongue. I savored the heavenly taste. It definitely lived up to all the hype. The only downside was that it was gone in two bites.

The chocolate cupcake was so delicious that I couldn't stop myself from taking another as I passed by the table again. I was halfway through the second one when sixteen-year-old Sienna Murray appeared next to me.

"Hey, Marley. Aren't those cupcakes the best?"

"Mmm," I said, my mouth full of chocolate.

Sienna laughed. "I've already had three."

"Are you doing some Christmas shopping?" I asked once I'd swallowed the last of the cupcake.

"Nah. I came for the food, but my mom's looking for some power tool my dad wants. I'm planning to get her some new wood-carving tools for Christmas, but I'm not going to buy them while she's here. I don't want to spoil the surprise."

"Good thinking."

Sienna's mom, Patricia, was a talented artist. She could transform an ordinary piece of driftwood into a beautiful sculpture. Her specialty was carving animals, anything from eagles to orcas.

A young woman with light brown hair and a camera around her neck approached us. "Sorry to interrupt, but I've got a photo here of the two of you. I was wondering if you'd be okay with it being printed in the next edition of the paper."

"Justine's a reporter," Sienna explained to me.

"And sometimes I have to double as a photographer," Justine said.

She turned the camera so we could look at the photo displayed on the screen. It showed me and Sienna smiling, a cupcake in my hand. Luckily it hadn't caught me in the act of actually eating.

"It's fine by me," I said, and Sienna agreed.

"Great! I'll take down your name then." Justine produced her phone.

"This is Marley McKinney, the owner of The Flip Side," Sienna introduced me.

"Justine Welch. Nice to meet you."

"You too," I said.

"You already know my name," Sienna said with a smile.

"That I do." Justine tapped my information into her phone. "Thanks so much."

She disappeared into the crowd and Sienna and I reloaded our plates with crackers and cheese.

"I can't wait to get back to The Flip Side," Sienna said. "It feels like forever since my last shift."

Sienna had been working at the pancake house since the previous summer, full-time while school was out and now on weekends. She hadn't been in for a couple of weeks because I'd closed the pancake house for the Thanksgiving weekend.

"I know the customers will be glad to see you back." I finished off the last of the cheese and crackers on my plate and eyed the platter of cupcakes at the end of the table.

Sienna followed my gaze and smiled. "Are you going in for another?"

I hesitated. "I probably shouldn't."

"I will if you will."

I looked from the cupcakes to Sienna, considering the idea.

"They've probably got plenty more in the back," Sienna said. "They know how popular they are each year. So it's not like we'd be depriving anyone else of their fair share."

"Twist my arm, why don't you?"

We made a beeline for the cupcakes, taking one each from the dwindling display. Even though I already knew how delicious they were, I still couldn't get over the incredible taste when I took a bite of the latest one.

"I think these are the best cupcakes I've ever tasted," I said, closing my eyes as I savored the rich flavor.

"Right?"

We fell silent as we focused all our attention on eating.

"There you are, Sienna." Patricia made her way around the table toward us, a shopping bag in one hand.

"Did you get Dad's present?" Sienna asked, peeking into the bag.

"I did. That's one item crossed off my Christmas shopping list."

"That's one more than I've got crossed off," I said.

"There's plenty of time yet." Patricia picked up a paper plate from the end of the table. "Time for a snack. Did you try the cupcakes, Marley?"

"Did I ever!"

A teenaged girl with long blond hair passed by us, her sad expression a stark contrast to the cheery ones on all the other faces around us.

"Hey, Bailey," Sienna said to the girl.

She glanced our way and offered a slight smile. "Hey."

Sienna fell into step with her and they wandered off. I joined Patricia at the food table, snacking on more cheese and crackers, not allowing myself to get within arm's length of the cupcakes again. We chatted for a while before we parted ways, Patricia to find Sienna and head home, and me to wander through the section of the store devoted to gardening supplies.

When I'd inherited my beachfront Victorian from my grandmother's cousin, it had come with a workshop full of tools and gardening equipment, but the plastic watering can I'd found in a dusty corner was old and cracked, so I was hoping to replace it before the spring. Since the store had a big sale on for ladies' night, I figured it was a good time to buy.

Despite the crowds of people, I managed to make my way up and down the aisles. When I headed for the cash counter later on, I had a watering can, a pair of gardening gloves, and a wicker basket that would come in handy when I started picking my own produce.

After paying for my items, I stopped to chat with a couple of acquaintances, and then I was out the door, heading down the street toward my car. I shivered as I walked, huddling deeper into my jacket, trying unsuccessfully to escape the bite of the cold winter air. As I passed by the entrance to an alley, I noticed a white van parked outside the back door to the Waffle Kingdom. The waffle house's logo was emblazoned on the sides of the vehicle. I wouldn't have paid much attention to the van as I walked past, except that something struck me as off.

I stopped on the sidewalk and looked more closely at the vehicle, which was illuminated by the light over the back door to the waffle house. The tires had been slashed, I realized a second later. A couple of them had, at any rate. I took a few steps into the alley. Yes, the back two tires had deflated, the rear end of the van sitting lower to the ground than the front.

I wondered if Wally knew about the tires. I wasn't keen on the idea of hanging out in a poorly lit alley at night, but I decided it would be the neighborly thing to do to let Wally know about the vandalism, in case he wasn't already aware of it. Who was responsible, I had no idea. But Wally didn't seem to have too many fans around town, so the list of potential suspects would likely be a lengthy one. I glanced around the alley, but didn't spot any security cameras.

Not wanting to linger any longer than I had to, I knocked on the back door of the restaurant and waited for a response. When I didn't get one, I tried to open the door but found it locked. I left the alley for the sidewalk, hesitating once in sight of my car. While tempted to give up on trying to get in touch with Wally, I ended up in a wrestling match with my conscience. My conscience won within seconds.

After stashing my purchases in the back of my hatchback, I made my way along the street and around the corner. At the front of the waffle house, bright light poured out through the windows. I peered through the glass, but the front of the small restaurant was deserted. I knocked on the door, and tested it to see if it was locked.

It wasn't.

I stepped inside, grateful to escape the cold air, even if it did mean wandering into the Waffle King's territory.

"Wally?" I called out. "Vicky? Anyone here?"

I thought I heard a scuffling sound coming from somewhere in the back, so I headed in that direction. Along the way, I paused and took in the sight of Wally's domain. The dining area was half the size of The Flip Side's and had booths running along one wall with a handful of tables scattered around the rest of the space. The decor was on the gaudy side, with lots of gold, including light fixtures made to look like crowns. The wall above the row of booths featured a painted mural with a cartoonish Wally standing outside a castle, wearing a crown and fur-lined purple cape. He was surrounded by what I guessed were supposed to be his adoring subjects—waffles with faces, arms, and legs.

One thing was for sure: Wally certainly hadn't held back on the kingdom theme.

I shook my head and made my way around the counter so I could get to the door leading to the back of the building. The door stood open, and I'd almost reached it when a shadow shifted and a large figure stepped into the doorway.

I stifled a yelp of surprise and clapped a hand over my heart as it thumped away in my chest.

"Ivan?" I said, shocked to see my chef standing before me. "I didn't think you'd show up for the tour."

"I didn't," he said in his gruff way. "I came by to tell Wally that someone slashed his tires."

"That's why I'm here too." I glanced past him but couldn't see anything other than the bright lights of the kitchen. "Does he know who might have done it?"

"He doesn't know anything now." Ivan put his hands on my shoulders, turning me around and guiding me toward the counter.

"What do you mean?"

"I need to call the police."

"Wally's not going to do that?"

"He can't." Ivan glanced at my tote bag. "Do you have a phone? I left mine at home."

I retrieved the device from my bag and woke it up before handing it to him. "Why can't Wally call the police?" I asked, a strange feeling settling over me.

Aside from the sound of our conversation, the waffle house was completely silent.

"Because," Ivan said as he tapped at my phone, "he's dead."

Chapter 5

My first reaction was to stare at Ivan, speechless. My second reaction was to step toward the open door.

"Don't go back there," Ivan said, bringing me to a halt.

He turned away as he spoke to the emergency dispatcher. I stood there with a heightened awareness of the thudding beat of my heart.

Wally was dead? How?

I knew I should heed Ivan's advice, but almost without conscious thought I stepped into the back hallway so I could see into the kitchen.

At first I didn't notice anything amiss. The stainless steel counter in the middle of the room was spotlessly clean and clear of equipment. When I leaned forward so I could see farther, however, the scene changed. A large stainless steel bowl lay upside down on the floor, a white substance that looked like cream or milk splattered across the cupboard doors and forming a puddle near the overturned bowl. A canister of some sort lay on its side in the middle of the mess, but what really caught my eye was the foot sticking out from behind the central counter.

Part of me wanted to turn and run the opposite way, to wait with Ivan while he spoke with the emergency dispatcher, but somehow I found myself taking two more steps so I stood in the kitchen doorway.

I gasped at the sight before me.

Wally lay on his back, a thick rubber glove covering his left hand and forearm. A matching glove was on the floor nearby. Up until that moment, I'd assumed Wally had died of natural causes. A heart attack, maybe, despite the fact that he was no older than forty. But now that I'd had a glimpse of his body, I knew that wasn't the case.

His face was yellow and waxy, nothing natural about it. As I stared at him, I could feel myself growing queasy.

"Marley!" Ivan's voice boomed from behind me.

I hurried away from the kitchen, eager to escape now. Ivan still had my phone in his hand, but he held it away from his ear.

"You need to stay out of the kitchen. And don't touch anything."

Unable to speak, I nodded and wrapped my arms around myself, wishing I could erase the hideous sight of Wally's grotesque face from my memory. His wasn't the first dead body I'd seen, but it was the most ghastly. What had happened to him?

Ivan spoke into the phone again and then ended the call. We stood there, silent and hardly moving, until a siren sounded in the distance, growing louder before cutting off. Seconds later, a sheriff's department cruiser pulled up to the curb outside the restaurant, its lights flashing.

Deputies Kyle Rutowski and Eva Mendoza entered the waffle house, their faces serious. I'd met both deputies before, thanks to my unfortunate habit of finding dead bodies.

"We received a report of a death," Mendoza said, her gaze pausing on me before shifting to Ivan.

"In the kitchen," Ivan said, indicating the door behind him.

I stepped aside to make room for the deputies to pass.

"Are you okay?" Ivan asked me, his voice as gruff as ever but a hint of concern in his dark eyes.

"Yes." I rubbed my arms. "What happened to him? His face..." I shuddered at the memory.

Ivan rested a large hand on my shoulder. "Liquid nitrogen."

I absorbed those words. "Cryogenic burns?"

Ivan nodded. "It's dangerous if not handled properly." He returned my phone to me.

"But doesn't it evaporate quickly?" I asked, tucking the phone into my bag.

He nodded again but said nothing more.

I recalled the large bowl upended on the floor. Had Wally poured the liquid nitrogen into it and accidentally flipped the bowl in a way that sent the contents splashing up into his face?

No matter how it had happened, it must have been a terrible way to die.

"Vicky," I said, suddenly thinking of Wally's sister. "Someone should tell her."

"The deputies will take care of that."

"Right. Of course." My thoughts were a jumbled mess, darting from one thing to another. I stared at the mural on the wall without really seeing it, the bright colors blurring together.

"Did you see anyone in the area before you came in here?" Ivan asked.

"No. I was walking from the hardware store to my car and didn't see another soul." I turned away from the mural to face him. "Why?"

The chef's frown deepened, but he didn't respond. His silence was as telling as a hundred words.

"You don't think Wally's death was an accident?" I asked with surprise.

It took a second for Ivan to speak. "Maybe he stumbled as he poured out the liquid nitrogen, and the bowl spilled onto his face."

"But?" I prompted, knowing he didn't put much stock in that theory.

"If someone shoved his face down in the bowl of liquid nitrogen as he was pouring it, that would explain the burns."

A chill tingled its way over my body. "That's terrible."

My gaze wandered to the door leading to the back of the restaurant. The deputies had yet to reappear, although I could hear their low voices and the occasional crackle of a radio.

"Do you think he died from the burns or from asphyxiation?" I asked, knowing the latter was a possibility with liquid nitrogen involved.

"Either one, or both."

"I guess it doesn't really matter which way it happened," I said. I thought back to what he'd asked me minutes earlier. "Did *you* see anyone in the area before you came in here?"

Ivan turned his head away from me, but not before I saw a flicker of worry in his eyes.

"Ivan?" I pressed when he didn't answer the question.

Deputy Mendoza appeared in the doorway. "I'll need to speak with both of you," she said to us.

The front door opened and Sheriff Ray Georgeson stepped in out of the cold.

"Excuse me a moment," Mendoza said to me and Ivan. She approached the sheriff and spoke to him in a low voice before leading him toward the kitchen.

Ray nodded at me as he went by, his face grim, but he didn't offer any other greeting. If Wally was murdered, the sheriff wouldn't be thrilled about finding me at the scene of the crime. He was Brett's uncle, and a good man, but he wasn't keen on my habit of poking my nose into murder investigations.

Thinking of Brett made me long for his company. I was tempted to text him but left my phone in my bag. I could wait until I'd spoken to Deputy Mendoza. I wanted to get that over with as soon as possible so I could go home. The waffle house was warm enough, but I couldn't rid myself of the chill that had worked its way into my bones. Knowing that Wally was lying dead in the next room, possibly murdered, was creepy and unsettling.

Mendoza reappeared a moment later and asked Ivan to join her in the far corner. They remained standing as Mendoza asked him some questions and Ivan provided succinct responses. I wanted to listen in on what they were saying, but they spoke quietly and I couldn't pick out more than one or two words.

It didn't take long for Mendoza to wrap up her questioning of the chef, and then it was my turn. She asked me how I'd ended up at the waffle house, and I explained about seeing Wally's slashed tires in the back alley. She also asked if I'd seen anyone before I'd entered the restaurant. I gave her the same response I'd given Ivan earlier. There wasn't much else I could tell her, other than stating that I'd gone as far as the entrance to the kitchen but hadn't touched anything in the waffle house aside from the front door.

When the deputy had finished asking questions, Ivan and I each filled out a witness statement form before she told us we could leave the scene. I was relieved to get out of the waffle house, even though it meant stepping out into the cold, damp air.

"I'll walk you to your car," Ivan said as he zipped up his jacket.

We set off along the sidewalk, both of us remaining silent until we reached my car.

"Who did you see before you went inside the waffle house?" I asked, knowing from his earlier reaction that he'd definitely seen someone.

Ivan glowered at the lamppost a few feet down the street. "No one involved in Wally's death."

"Can you really be sure about that?"

"Yes."

"Did you tell Deputy Mendoza you saw someone?"

He focused his scowl on me. "It's cold out here. You should get home."

I didn't press the matter. There was no point. Ivan wasn't one to be coerced into answering questions he didn't want to. As curious as I was about who he'd seen and why he was unwilling to share the information, I climbed into my car and drove off, gladly leaving the scene of Wally's terrible death well behind me.

* * * *

I texted Brett about the evening's events when I arrived home and went to bed soon after. My mind refused to shut down, and I tossed and turned for a couple of hours before finally slipping into a deep sleep. I expected Wally's death to be the talk of the town in the morning, so I wasn't the least bit surprised when it was the hot topic of the day at The Flip Side. I also wasn't surprised to hear from various sources that the sheriff's department had initiated a murder investigation.

It seemed everyone had a theory about who the culprit might be. As I waited tables during the breakfast rush, I heard Vicky's name pop up and Chester's too.

"Why would Vicky kill her own brother?" I asked, joining the conversation at one table as I filled mugs with coffee.

"Money," Marjorie Wells said. "Wally was rich. He inherited several million dollars a while back, and Vicky is his closest relative. He probably left everything to her."

"But killing her own brother," Marjorie's friend Eleanor said from across the table, "that's a bit extreme. Can you really picture Vicky doing that?"

I left the two ladies to debate the matter. I was inclined to agree with Eleanor. It was hard to picture Vicky killing her brother, even though I really didn't know her at all. As for Chester, I had no idea if he had a reason for wanting Wally dead.

I half-listened to the rest of the gossip buzzing around the pancake house, not paying too much attention, until I heard Ivan's name.

"What are people saying about Ivan?" I asked, stopping at Ed and Gary's table.

"That he's the one who found the body," Gary said.

"And maybe he's a suspect," Ed added.

"An official suspect?" I didn't like that thought.

Gary cut into his stack of pancakes. "I don't know about that, but there are some folks who think he should be."

"That's crazy! Ivan wouldn't hurt anyone."

"We don't believe it, Marley," Ed assured me. "But he's an intimidating guy, he found the body, and Wally was opening the waffle house in direct competition with this place."

"Plus, Ivan nearly kicked him out of here the other day," Gary chipped in. "He definitely wasn't a fan of the Waffle King."

"Was anyone?" I asked.

Both men shrugged.

"We've heard your name come up a couple of times too," Ed said, clearly not happy to be sharing the news. "You were there when the police showed up, weren't you?"

It shouldn't have surprised me that so many details were already common knowledge. It never took long for news to spread through the town.

"I didn't kill Wally, and neither did Ivan," I said, unable to prevent myself from getting annoyed.

"We know that, and we've set a few people straight already." Gary chomped down on a piece of crispy bacon. "But not everyone around town knows you and Ivan like we do."

I assured them that my annoyance wasn't directed at them and thanked them for the information. As much as I tried to focus on nothing but taking orders and delivering meals to waiting customers, I couldn't stop worrying about what Ed and Gary had told me.

I wasn't too concerned about myself. Ivan could attest to the fact that I'd arrived at the waffle house after he did, and several people had seen me at the hardware store before that, so I doubted the sheriff's department would consider me a suspect. The same might not be true for Ivan, though. Maybe it would be determined that Wally was dead for quite some time before Ivan found him. If Ivan had an alibi for the time of death, then he'd be in the clear.

But what if that didn't turn out to be the case?

I tried to push my concerns aside but was unsuccessful. I had no doubt at all about Ivan's innocence, but I knew full well that Ray and his deputies might feel differently.

Chapter 6

After The Flip Side had closed for the day and I'd taken care of all pressing administrative matters, I stayed in town to run a few errands. When I returned to my car and stashed two bags of groceries in the back, I set off for home but didn't make it far before pulling over to the curb again. I'd stopped in front of the waffle house and could see lights on inside the building, although I couldn't see anyone from my vantage point.

I sat in my car with the engine still running, trying to decide what to do. I wanted to offer my condolences to Vicky, but I didn't know if I'd find her at the waffle house. It was entirely possible that the place was still a crime scene and I wasn't sure if she'd be there even if the sheriff's department had finished processing the kitchen. I had no clue where Vicky lived, though, so I decided to find out if she was at the restaurant.

Out in the frosty air, I hurried over to the door and knocked on the glass. Vicky peeked cautiously through the doorway leading to the back of the building. When she saw me, she hesitated, but then she emerged from the back and came over to unlock the door.

"Yes?" she said, only opening the door a crack.

"Vicky, I'm Marley McKinney from The Flip Side."

"I remember." She watched me warily through the glass; her eyes bloodshot, dark rings beneath them.

"I came to say how sorry I am for the loss of your brother."

She swallowed and averted her gaze as she pressed her lips together in a thin line.

I wasn't sure if she was displeased with my presence or trying not to cry. I was about to apologize for bothering her when she opened the door wider.

"Come in."

I stepped past her into the warmth of the waffle house and she let the door fall shut behind me.

"I'd offer you tea or coffee, but the kitchen…" She fingered the collar of her shirt.

"Is it still off-limits?" I asked.

"No, the police are finished with it, but I can't stand the thought of going in there."

"I understand, and don't worry. I don't need anything. I just came to see how you're holding up."

Vicky sat down at the nearest booth and I took the seat across from her. She stared past me, out the front window, for a second or two before speaking.

"People have been peering in the window all day long. I was afraid you might be a reporter. I was getting ready to go home. I'm not sure why I even came here today. I felt like I should be here doing something, but I don't know what. Mostly I sat in the office staring at the wall."

My heart ached for her. "Do you have any other family in Wildwood Cove?"

"No, none."

"Where's Chester?"

"I sent him home earlier. He's torn up about Wally. He practically idolized my brother."

I bit down on my tongue before a surprised comment could slip out of my mouth. Idolizing a guy like Wally Fowler was something I had a hard time wrapping my mind around.

Vicky's hand went back to her collar as she stared at the tabletop. I knew I should probably leave her in peace.

"Is there anything I can get you?" I asked. "Anything I can do for you?"

"Unless you can tell me why this happened…" She trailed off. "Thank you, but no. All I need right now is answers."

"Has the sheriff given you any?"

"No. He only had questions for me, not answers." She glanced around until her gaze fell on the clock on the wall. "That reminds me, I should get home. I need to find some receipts for the sheriff."

"Receipts?"

"From my trip to Seattle. Have you heard that Wally was murdered?"

"I did, yes," I said.

"I guess everyone knows by now. The sheriff called me in the middle of the night to tell me what happened. I got back here as fast as I could. It was bad enough to hear that my brother had been murdered, but then the sheriff wanted to know where I'd been. I told him I was driving to Seattle last night, but he asked for proof." A strangled sound escaped her throat, something between a sob and a laugh. She took a moment to compose herself again. "I'm a suspect in my brother's murder."

"They probably just want to rule you out," I said. "If you can prove you were out of town that will likely be the end of it."

"I can prove it if I can find the receipts. I seem to have misplaced them. But Chester can vouch for me."

"Chester was with you?"

She nodded, her gaze drifting around the room as if she were hoping to spot her missing receipts lying out in the open.

"I also need to tell the police that the money's still missing," she said, so vaguely that I wondered if she was talking to herself rather than me.

"What money?"

"Wally had cash in the safe in the office. About thirty grand."

My eyes widened. "And it's gone?"

"Yes. Wally must have removed it before he died, but I don't know what he would have done with it."

"Did anyone else have access to the safe?" I wondered if Wally's murder could be tied in with a robbery somehow.

"Just me." For the first time since I'd entered the waffle house, Vicky looked right at me. "You were here last night, right? With your chef. The police told me that, but everything's a bit of a blur."

"I was here," I confirmed.

"Did you…" She stopped herself and frowned. "No, don't tell me if you saw Wally. I don't think I really want to know." Her gaze drifted back to the window, going out of focus.

I got up from my seat. "If there's anything I can do for you, all you have to do is let me know."

She tried to smile. "Thank you. And I'm sorry about yesterday, the way my brother acted at the pancake house."

"You don't need to apologize for that," I assured her.

"Wally always wanted everyone's admiration, but he didn't know the right way to go about getting it." She pushed herself up from the booth and walked me to the door.

"Will you still be opening the waffle house next week?" I asked.

"No. The waffle house was Wally's dream, not mine. He picked Wildwood Cove for his latest venture because he'd heard about the popularity of your pancake house, and popularity was always what he wanted." A cloud seemed to pass across her face, and her attention drifted away from me.

"Again, I'm sorry about Wally."

She acknowledged the statement with a vague nod, and I pushed out the door, leaving her alone with her grief.

* * * *

I drove home after leaving the waffle house, but I didn't stay long. After putting my groceries away and spending a few minutes with Flapjack, I decided to check in on Lisa. It was nearly five o'clock by then, so she'd soon be finished work for the day. Brett was working with his dad on a renovation project across town and wouldn't be free before six, so I had time to kill before we met up for dinner. I could have texted Lisa to see how she was doing, but I wanted to see her in person instead.

I put out some food for Flapjack—receiving a grateful purr in response—and returned to town in my car. As I pulled up to the curb outside of Lisa's cute white-and-green house, I spotted her walking along the street with Justine Welch. I climbed out of my car and met them on the sidewalk.

"Hi, Marley." Lisa smiled, but she seemed tired and her eyes weren't as bright as usual. "Do you know Justine?"

"We met recently," I said. "How are you, Justine?"

"Great, thanks."

"Do you want to come inside?" Lisa asked both of us.

"Actually, I have to get going," Justine said. "I need to pick up my daughter. It was nice to see you both."

She waved and continued along the street.

"How about you, Marley?"

"If it's not a bad time."

Lisa's tired smile made a brief reappearance. "Of course not."

"How do you know Justine?" I asked as we headed for the front door. "Did she grow up here in Wildwood Cove?"

"She did. I didn't know her well back then because she's several years younger than me, but she was in my yoga class last summer. She's working for the newspaper now."

"That's how we met." I told Lisa about the photo Justine had taken at the hardware store.

"I really admire her." She fished her keys from her purse. "She had a disastrous marriage and a messy divorce, but she's really bounced back." Inside the house, Lisa dropped her purse and keys on the small table in the foyer. "What brings you by?"

"I wanted to see how you're doing."

"I'm all right." She hung her coat in the closet and did the same with mine.

"Are you sure? You don't seem quite yourself."

She kept her eyes on the closet doors as she shut them. "It's been a rough couple of days."

"I'm guessing you heard about Wally."

"I don't even know how to feel about him being dead," she admitted. "I'm horrified that someone killed him, of course, but I'm also relieved he won't be around town anymore. Is that awful of me?" Her brown eyes shimmered with tears.

"It's perfectly understandable." I hugged her. "All your feelings toward him are perfectly legitimate."

She tucked her wavy dark hair behind one ear and gave me a glimpse of a tremulous smile. "Thanks, Marley. Give me a minute to change out of my work clothes." As she headed up the stairs to the second floor, she called out, "Help yourself if you want something to drink."

I was about to wander toward the kitchen at the back of the house when I heard footsteps on the front porch. I peeked through the sidelight and saw someone familiar.

"Ivan?" I said, opening the door before he had a chance to knock.

If the chef was surprised I'd opened the door instead of Lisa, he didn't show it.

"Is Lisa here?" he asked.

I stepped back and opened the door wider. "She's upstairs, but she'll be down soon."

As if on cue, Lisa's footsteps sounded on the stairway. She appeared a second later, wearing jeans and a sweater instead of her suit.

She wasn't as surprised as I thought she might be to find the chef standing in her foyer, and her face brightened at the sight of him. "Hi, Ivan."

Subtle suspicions that had lurked at the back of my mind in recent weeks began to creep forward, growing stronger.

"How are you?" Ivan asked her.

Whatever light had returned to Lisa's expression faded away. "All right." She attempted a smile. "Come back to the kitchen, you guys. I could use a hot drink. Do either of you want tea or coffee?"

"Nothing for me, thanks," I said. "I'm meeting Brett for dinner so I won't stay long."

Ivan requested tea, so Lisa put the kettle on and took two mugs down from a cupboard.

"Marley, you usually know what's going on with the sheriff's investigations," she said. "Does he know who killed Wally?"

"If he does, he hasn't told his sister. I stopped by to see her earlier and she didn't seem to know much about the investigation."

"Have you heard if there are any suspects?"

I thought I detected a slight tremor to Lisa's voice when she asked the question. I glanced Ivan's way and saw him watching Lisa, a deep frown on his face. The downturn of his mouth wasn't unusual, but his eyebrows had drawn together and there was a worried light in his eyes, one I'd rarely seen.

"Lisa's the one you saw outside the waffle house last night, isn't she?" I asked Ivan, the dots connecting in my head.

He didn't reply, but I read the answer in his eyes. I turned my attention to Lisa. Her hand shook as she removed two tea bags from a box and dropped them into a stout green teapot.

"The sheriff will suspect me." Her eyes filled with tears, but she blinked them back before they could escape. "What am I going to do, Marley?"

"Hey." I took her hand and gave it a squeeze. "Why would Ray suspect you?"

"Everyone who lived here when Wally was around before knows I blame him for getting Carlos into drugs. And then last night I decided to go to the waffle house."

"Why?" I glanced at Ivan and suspected he already knew.

"To give him a piece of my mind." Lisa poured hot water into the teapot.

"And he was still alive?" I asked.

"I don't know. I never went inside. I ran into Ivan and he convinced me to go home."

"He wouldn't have cared about anything you had to say," Ivan said. "He only would have upset you more."

Lisa nodded.

"Did you tell Deputy Mendoza that you saw Lisa last night?" I asked Ivan. His only reply was a curt shake of his head.

"You didn't have to lie to the police for me," Lisa told him.

"I didn't lie. The deputy asked if I'd seen anyone outside the waffle house. We were well down the street when I saw you."

My growing suspicions solidified. Ivan was trying to protect Lisa, and I knew he didn't go to such efforts for just anyone. He really cared for her. And from the way she looked at him in that moment, I knew she reciprocated his feelings.

"So no one knows you were nearby on the night Wally died," I said to Lisa. "That's good. That means you aren't on the suspect list."

"I hope that's true." She poured the tea and handed one mug to Ivan, keeping the other for herself.

I wanted to give them some time alone together, but I had another concern to address first.

"What about you, Ivan?" I said. "Do you think you're on the suspect list?"

Alarm registered on Lisa's face. "Why would he be?"

"I found the body," Ivan said. "And I didn't like the man. He wanted to run Marley out of business, and to put me, Leigh, and Tommy out of jobs."

"But you wouldn't have killed him," Lisa protested.

"We know that," I said, "but that's not enough to keep his name off the suspect list. Have you been questioned again?" I asked Ivan.

"Not yet, but I won't be surprised if it happens."

"I'll tell the sheriff I stopped to talk to you that night," Lisa said. "I'll be your alibi."

"No." Ivan's tone was resolute.

"I can't stay quiet knowing you might be wrongly accused."

"*You* might be accused if you say anything."

Lisa opened her mouth to protest again, but I cut in.

"He's right, Lisa. And I'm not so sure it would do any good if you told the sheriff. Unless there's some way for him to know exactly when Wally died, down to the minute, and that you were talking to Ivan right at that moment, he doesn't have an alibi." I turned to the chef. "Am I right?"

He nodded and scowled into his tea as he took a drink.

Lisa's shoulders sagged, but then her face lit up with hope. "Maybe we won't have to worry. If the sheriff finds the killer quickly, everything will be fine."

Someone knocked on the front door before Ivan or I could comment on Lisa's statement. She set her mug on the counter and headed for the foyer, with me and Ivan following. I intended to set off for home, but when I saw who stood on the front porch I stopped short.

"Ms. Morales," Sheriff Ray Georgeson said to Lisa, "I'd like to ask you a few questions."

Chapter 7

"Come in," Lisa said, stepping back to let the sheriff in.

I was impressed by her composure. She appeared calm and at ease, unlike the way she had been in the kitchen only minutes earlier.

"Does this have something to do with Wally Fowler's death?" I asked, knowing that was most likely the case.

"It does." Ray ran his gaze over all three of us before addressing Lisa again. "Could we speak privately for a few minutes?"

She hesitated.

"Do you want us to leave or should we wait in the kitchen?" I asked her.

"The kitchen," she said, sending me a flash of a grateful smile.

I wanted to offer some words of support before I left the room, but I didn't want to give Ray the impression that she needed any. Ivan didn't move at first, but after a couple of seconds he followed me to the kitchen.

"She'll be fine," I whispered, as much for my own benefit as Ivan's.

Judging by the unhappy, concerned energy radiating off him, I expected him to pace back and forth along the length of the kitchen. Instead he planted himself in the middle of the room, crossed his arms over his chest, and glowered at the open doorway that led to the dining room, which was connected to the living room.

Unable to help myself, I crept closer to the doorway and tried to listen in on the conversation going on in the other room.

"You were seen heading in that direction last night," I heard Ray say.

"Yes, I was out walking, but I didn't go as far as the waffle house."

"Did you see anyone else while you were walking?"

"I saw Ivan." Lisa's voice sounded strained. "We stopped and talked for a minute or two. After that I headed home. I saw my neighbor Joan

Crenshaw out walking her dog, but that was much closer to home than to the waffle house."

"And you didn't see anyone else?"

"A couple of cars went by when I was on Pacific Street, but otherwise no."

"I understand you knew Mr. Fowler when he lived in Wildwood Cove before."

"I knew *of* him, that's for sure. His sister was a year ahead of me in school. I never had anything to do with Wally, but I knew who he was. Most people did."

"I've heard it said that you blame him for getting your brother Carlos hooked on drugs."

There was a beat of silence before Lisa spoke again. "I do. Wally wasn't good for this town, and I'd be surprised if anyone disagreed with me."

I couldn't see how Ray reacted to that statement, but a moment later Lisa continued.

"He didn't deserve to be murdered, though."

"Do you have any idea who might have killed him?"

"None. If you want a list of people who didn't like him, I could give you one, and it would be a long one, but I can't imagine any of them killing Wally or anyone else."

"Is there anyone in particular who had a recent grievance with Wally, or a particularly strong one that might have survived all the years he was out of town?"

"Aside from me, you mean?"

I itched to peek around the corner to see Ray's reaction, but I stayed put.

"I can think of one person," Lisa continued, "but I'm sure you already know about her. Glo Hansfield."

"I'm aware of Mrs. Hansfield's connection to Fowler."

Hearing movement in the other room, I took a few hurried, silent steps away from the door so I wouldn't be caught eavesdropping. Voices murmured farther away, and then the front door opened and closed.

Ivan and I left the kitchen to meet Lisa in the living room. She stood by the couch with a hand pressed to her forehead.

"Are you okay?" I asked.

She lowered her hand. "I think so. He didn't grill me like he considered me a suspect. That's a good thing, right?"

"It is," I said, although I knew that didn't necessarily mean she wasn't under suspicion.

"I know we decided I shouldn't mention it, but I told him that I saw you, Ivan." She closed her eyes briefly. "I'm sorry. He asked if I'd seen anyone and it just came out."

"Don't worry," he said.

"But I realize now that it contradicts your statement. What if he thinks you lied?"

"I'll sort it out."

Before Lisa had a chance to say anything more, he was out the door. We moved to the front window and watched as he approached Ray by the cruiser parked at the curb.

"I've messed things up, haven't I?" Lisa said.

"I don't know about that. Ivan will explain, and hopefully that will be the end of it."

Outside, Ivan exchanged a few more words with Ray before heading back toward the house. We hurried to meet him in the foyer.

"What did he say?" Lisa asked as soon as he'd stepped inside.

"Not much."

"But he accepted your explanation?"

"I think so."

Lisa's shoulders lowered by an inch or two. "Maybe everything will be okay."

"Everything will be fine," I assured her, hoping that was the truth.

I wanted to question her about her conversation with Ray, and the people she knew of who had a grudge against Wally, but I sensed it would be best to give her some time alone with Ivan.

"I need to get going, but call me any time, okay?" I said to Lisa.

"Thanks, Marley."

"Bye, Ivan," I said as Lisa walked me to the door. "And we definitely need to talk later," I added in a whisper once I'd stepped out onto the front porch. "About you and Ivan."

Her cheeks took on a pink tinge and she smiled. "We will."

I mirrored her smile and headed down the steps as she shut the door.

Ray hadn't left yet. He stood outside his cruiser, speaking into his radio. When he saw me, he waved me over. My smile faded and my concern for Lisa made a comeback. I was afraid he was about to question me about my friend, that despite the impression he'd given Lisa, he really did consider her a suspect.

"Marley, you know both Lisa and Ivan well."

"Yes," I said slowly, wary of where the conversation might be heading.

He glanced over my shoulder at Lisa's house. "What's the nature of their relationship?"

"Their relationship?" I echoed, not knowing what else to say.

"Ivan's still in the house with her. I'm guessing they have a relationship of some sort."

"I'm assuming you mean a romantic one. And I'm not sure, but they're at least heading in that direction. Why?"

"How far do you think one would go to protect the other?"

The frosty air seeped deep into my bones when he asked that question. "You think one of them is covering for the other?" I shook my head. "They're not. Neither of them killed Wally."

Ray removed his hat and ran his hand through his hair. "I hope that's the case." He replaced his hat on his head and walked around the front of the cruiser to reach the driver's door. "Marley, your interest in past investigations has put you in danger," he said over the roof of the vehicle.

I knew what was coming next.

"Leave this one to me and my deputies, all right?"

"I'm planning on it," I said, and that was the truth.

He climbed into the cruiser and I headed in the direction of my own car. Before I reached it, I noticed Lisa's neighbor Joan Crenshaw walking along the street with her West Highland terrier, Angel. Instead of getting into my car, I remained on the sidewalk as she approached.

"Hi, Marley," Joan said as I crouched down to give Angel a pat. "Everything okay?"

I followed her gaze to the sheriff's cruiser. Ray sat in the driver's seat now, but he hadn't yet pulled away from the curb.

"Lisa was out walking on Pacific Street last night, so the sheriff wanted to ask if she'd seen anyone hanging around the waffle house."

"Oh my, yes, isn't it terrible what happened? I'm guessing that means no one's been arrested for the murder yet."

"Not yet."

The engine of Ray's cruiser rumbled to life and he pulled out into the street. He activated the lights and siren and sped off.

"Looks like there might be another emergency," Joan remarked as we watched the cruiser disappear around the corner.

"Hopefully nothing serious," I said.

I spent another minute or so chatting with Joan about the weather and her dog, and then I set off for home.

Flapjack was pleased to see me, rubbing against my legs as I kicked off my sneakers in the foyer. I picked him up and he purred happily as I carried him to the family room at the back of the house.

Brett was likely finished or nearly finished work for the day, so I sent him a quick text message once I'd set Flapjack down on the couch.

Do you want to go out for dinner or stay in?

While I waited for a response, I poured myself a glass of sweet tea and drank it while standing by the French doors, gazing out into the darkness. I would have loved to sit out on the back porch, listening to the waves crashing ashore, but I knew I'd freeze in short order so I remained inside and contented myself with enjoying my drink.

I checked my phone for a response from Brett every few minutes, but none appeared. After a while, I decided to send him another message.

Are you still at work?

When I still hadn't heard back from him after several minutes, I tried phoning him. The call went to voicemail. I hung up without leaving a message; a current of unease humming through my bones.

"He's probably just working late," I said to Flapjack, although it was myself I was trying to reassure. "He'll get back to me when he's free."

Flapjack tucked his front paws beneath him and closed his eyes, unconcerned.

It was past six thirty now, and my stomach complained that I hadn't consumed anything other than iced tea for hours.

I'll put something together for us here, I wrote to Brett in another text message.

Opening the fridge, I assessed my supplies and decided to make my favorite lentil curry. I gathered ingredients and set them out on the island, not for the first time appreciating how much prep space I had in my new kitchen.

Another twinge of concern tried to get my attention when I glanced at the clock, but I did my best to ignore it. Maybe Brett's phone had died and he'd show up on my back porch once he'd had a chance to have an after-work shower. He'd be hungry when he arrived, so I focused on chopping vegetables and measuring out spices.

I was about to turn on the stove when my phone finally rang. I snatched it up off the kitchen table, a quick glance at the screen confirming that Brett was the caller.

"Hey, I'm about to start cooking some curry," I said by way of greeting.

"Marley…"

My stomach dropped at the sound of his voice. I tightened my grip on my phone. "What's wrong?"

"It's my dad. He collapsed at the jobsite."

I sank into a kitchen chair. "Oh, my God. Is he okay?"

"He's alive."

I held on to the edge of the kitchen table. It was as if the world was spinning wildly around me. "Where are you?"

"The hospital in Port Angeles."

"Your mom? Chloe?"

"My mom's here. Ray drove her. Chloe was already in Port Angeles. I got in touch with her and she's on her way here now."

There was no doubt in my mind what I'd do next. "I'll be there as soon as I can, okay?"

"Okay."

That single word sounded so fractured that my heart almost shattered. I didn't want to break the connection, but I had to if I wanted to get to him quickly. I spared only a few seconds to shove all the food from the island back into the fridge so Flapjack wouldn't get into anything that might make him sick. Then I was out the door, hating every mile that stood between me and Brett.

Chapter 8

When I reached the hospital waiting room, the first person I spotted was Brett's younger sister, Chloe. Her hair was the same shade of blond as her brother's, although hers wasn't curly like his. She also had the same blue eyes, usually bright with happiness. At the moment, however, her eyes were wide with shock as she sat in a chair, staring at the opposite wall. Her mom sat next to her, gripping Chloe's hand as if her life depended on it.

I had to take two steps farther into the room before I saw Brett seated on the far side of his mom. He was leaning forward, forearms resting on his legs as he stared at the floor. But when he raised his gaze and saw me, he got to his feet.

I rushed across the room and put my arms around him. He pulled me in close, holding me tightly, burying his face in my hair.

"Is there any news?" I whispered without letting go of him.

"Not yet."

For a moment we remained there, holding on to each other without saying a word. As much as it pained me to do so, I stepped back eventually, knowing I needed to say something to his family.

"I'm so sorry, Elaine," I said to Brett's mom, taking her hand and giving it a squeeze.

Elaine gave me a shaky ghost of a smile. "Thank you for coming, Marley."

Chloe got to her feet and hugged me. When she sat down again, she wiped tears from her cheeks with the back of her hand. I returned to Brett, hugging him again.

"Was it a heart attack?" I asked quietly.

"I think so," Brett said.

I rested my cheek against his chest, wishing I could absorb all the pain and fear he was feeling at that moment, wishing I could somehow make everything better.

"Marley," Brett said after a moment, his voice little more than a whisper.

I pulled back so I could see his face. The fear and suffering in his blue eyes sent a deep ache through my chest.

When he spoke again, his voice sounded even more broken than it had on the phone. "When he collapsed, he had no pulse. I had to do CPR."

It was as if my heart broke into a thousand pieces. I could hardly breathe knowing he'd gone through that, but I wouldn't let myself crack, not when he needed me to be strong.

"The paramedics arrived with a defibrillator and got his heart beating again."

"You helped save him," I said.

Doubt flickered in his eyes. "Maybe."

I put my hands to his face. "You gave him a chance." I needed him to believe those words, to hold on to that shard of hope. I knew the desolation of losing all hope and I never wanted him to feel that.

I could see in his eyes that he was struggling, wondering if he'd done enough, if there was anything more he could have done.

"I know you, Brett Collins," I said, placing a hand on his chest, over his heart. "You did everything you could for him. You've given him the best chance you could have."

Brett closed his eyes and rested his forehead against mine. I held on to his hands, running my thumbs over his knuckles, hoping to give him some measure of comfort.

"I'm glad you're here," he said quietly.

I squeezed his hands. "I wouldn't be anywhere else."

* * * *

After a time, we claimed two empty seats next to Brett's mom. I kept hold of Brett's hand and rested my head on his shoulder as we waited for news about his dad. Three other people sat at the far end of the waiting room, but no one spoke above a whisper, and all the noises of the hospital blurred together in the background.

The minutes crept by, each one filled with worry and dread. Finally, a doctor arrived to speak with the Collins family. I hung back, not wanting to intrude. I'd left my seat when the doctor arrived, but I returned to it, clasping my hands in my lap to keep them from shaking. My heart raced and I had to focus on breathing to keep the oxygen flowing into my lungs.

I'd been where Brett was now, standing on the brink, not knowing if the news he was about to receive would be positive or utterly devastating.

I could remember the crushing blow of hearing the worst news possible, and I knew what it was like to have the world ripped out from beneath your feet so fast that you couldn't regain your balance, couldn't imagine anything ever being right again.

I wouldn't have wished for anyone to go through that, least of all Brett, but I couldn't stop it from happening. And that helplessness, mixed in with my too-vivid memories of my own experiences, left me teetering on the verge of panic.

Closing my eyes, I tried to push everything away—memories, worries, what-ifs. I didn't want to do anything but breathe in and out, but I couldn't keep any of those things at bay.

A familiar hand rested on my shoulder and my eyes flew open. I jumped to my feet, grasping one of Brett's hands in both of my own.

"He's stable." Relief slipped out with his words.

The vise that had tightened around my chest loosened.

"The doctor confirmed that it was a heart attack," Brett said. "He needs bypass surgery."

That information sank in slowly.

"But he's stable now," I said, clinging to those words. "And they can make him better."

Brett nodded. "My dad's strong. He'll make it through."

"He will," I agreed, desperate for that to be the truth. "Will they do the surgery now?"

"They're going to transfer him to Seattle first. My mom is staying with him. Chloe and I are going home to pack a few things and then we'll drive to Seattle."

"Okay," I said, trying to take in all the information.

"Chloe's not up to driving, so I'll drive her home in her car. I came in the ambulance with Dad, so my truck's still in Wildwood Cove."

"Are you okay to drive?" I asked.

"Yes, I'll be fine."

I searched his face, wanting to be sure that was true. "I can drive you both if you need me to."

He gently brushed my hair back from my face. "It's okay. I can drive."

"You'll be in Seattle for a few days at least," I said, my mind sluggishly processing everything. "I'll call my mom. If you or your mom or Chloe need some sleep or a shower or whatever, you can go to her place. She won't mind at all."

He kissed the top my head. "Thank you."

"Did you see your dad?"

"For a minute. He's weak, but conscious. Considering what he's been through, I'd call that a blessing."

"It is," I agreed. "It most definitely is."

* * * *

The drive home seemed to take longer than it actually did. I followed behind Chloe's car, wanting to be sure that Brett would really be all right driving, that they'd make it back to Wildwood Cove safely. Only once we were off the highway did I relax my grip on the steering wheel. A minute or so later, I turned off into my driveway while Brett and Chloe continued on into town.

Before leaving the hospital, we'd decided that Brett would drop his dog, Bentley, off at my place before continuing on to Seattle. I sat on the couch in the family room to wait for him, holding Flapjack. In the stillness of my home, with my cat purring on my lap, tears finally welled in my eyes and spilled out onto my cheeks.

I could have broken down into full-out sobs, but I didn't let myself. I didn't want to be a mess when Brett arrived with Bentley. Mixed in with my tears was the relief that came with knowing Brett's dad was stable and in good care, but he wasn't out of the woods yet, and I felt terrible for Brett's whole family. It didn't help that the worst memories of my life had clawed their way up closer to the surface than they had in a long time.

My world had changed forever the day my stepdad and stepsiblings had been caught in a rockslide while driving on a mountain highway. My stepdad and stepbrother, Dylan, had died at the scene, but my stepsister, Charlotte, had clung to life in the hospital for three days before she slipped away.

I knew too well the hell that Brett had gone through that day—was still going through—and I hoped with every ounce of my being that everything would turn out okay in the end.

I managed to cry out my tears, clean myself up, and phone my mom before Brett's silver pickup pulled into the driveway and trundled to a stop out front of my house. Chloe remained in the passenger seat while Brett got out into the cold night air and let his goldendoodle out from the backseat.

Bentley, unaware of the troubles plaguing his favorite humans, bounded up the porch steps to greet me with enthusiastic licks while I patted him on the head. When he finally settled down, he left the porch to go sniff at a tree at the edge of the illumination cast from the porch light. Brett removed a bucket, food and water dishes, and Bentley's leash from the back of the truck and carried them over my way.

"I think that's everything he'll need," Brett said as he set Bentley's things on the porch.

"Do you want me to go with you?" I asked in a rush. "I don't want to be in the way, but I could stay at my mom's place so I'd be closer to you."

Brett folded me into his arms. "You could never be in the way, but I don't want to take you away from the pancake house."

"I could make it work," I said into his chest.

"I'm tempted," he said after a moment. "But there'll be a lot of waiting at that end, and I'll feel better knowing Bentley's being well taken care of in a familiar place."

I sighed against him, not wanting to let go. "Okay. But if you change your mind, all you have to do is say the word. And please keep me updated."

"I will. I promise."

He kissed me before stepping back with reluctance matching my own.

"I love you, Marley."

"I love you too."

Bentley trotted up to the porch and I held on to him as Brett returned to the truck. I ruffled Bentley's fur as he whined at the sight of Brett and Chloe driving off without him.

"It'll be okay, buddy," I said, trying to comfort him.

He settled down once the truck disappeared from sight and I carried his dishes and bucket of kibble inside while he tore down the hall to the back of the house, going in search of Flapjack. He found the tabby on the couch, but didn't do anything more than wag his tail in greeting, not getting too close. He'd learned his lesson many months ago when Flapjack had put him in his place with a swat to the nose.

Now that I was home and had calmed down, my hunger returned full force. I wasn't interested in cooking at that hour, so I ate a peanut butter and banana sandwich to tide me over until morning. Bentley had a dog bed at my place and I carried it upstairs to my room, where he settled down with only a brief whine when he saw Flapjack join me on my bed.

The emotions of the evening had left me wiped out, but sleep kept dancing out of my reach no matter how much I chased it. Concern for Frank and Brett and the rest of the Collins family filled my thoughts, and even though I'd seen Brett off only an hour or so earlier, I already missed him.

Eventually, I drifted off into an uneasy sleep, but instead of granting me some respite, my worries stayed with me, haunting me and invading my dreams.

Chapter 9

By midmorning the following day, the news of Frank's heart attack had spread to most of the customers at the pancake house. Those who knew Frank personally were upset and concerned, and I provided them with what little information I could. Wally's murder was also a hot topic of conversation.

Although I was tired and distracted, I picked up tidbits of conversation here and there around the restaurant. From what I heard, it didn't seem as though there had been any new developments in the sheriff's investigation. Not any that the general public was aware of, at least. I heard one or two whispers about Ivan's potential status as a suspect, but whenever I drew near, the conversations broke off.

It irked me that people were gossiping about Ivan, speculating that he could be involved in Wally's murder. I knew it wasn't easy to see past Ivan's gruff exterior, but I wished people would understand what a good man he was, and how ridiculous it was for anyone to believe he could be the killer. I tried not to let the gossip get to me, but I wasn't having much success.

At least once every hour, I ducked into the office to check my phone. Brett's dad had arrived at the hospital in Seattle and was awaiting surgery. Brett had been in touch with my mom and had picked up a key to her house, but he wasn't yet ready to spend enough time away from the hospital to attempt to get some sleep. The same was true of his mom and Chloe.

Around midmorning I received a text saying Frank's surgery was scheduled for later in the day. Once I knew that, I had more trouble than ever focusing on work. After accidentally delivering plates of gingerbread crêpes to the wrong table, I decided to leave Leigh to deal with the orders and restricted myself to clearing tables.

When I carried a load of dirty dishes into the kitchen, I could feel Ivan's eyes on me. I glanced his way, but he didn't say anything until the dishes were in the dishwasher.

"Sit down," he said, pointing at one of the stools that stood against the far wall.

"I'm all right," I assured him, heading for the door. I halted when he glared at me. "Then again, maybe I could use a bit of a rest."

He nodded with approval as I pulled the stool over to the counter and sat down.

"Any news about Brett's dad?" Tommy asked as he plated a serving of pumpkin pie crêpes. The dish had been added to the menu as a special item for October, but it had proven so popular that I'd decided to keep it on offer up until Christmas.

I told Tommy and Ivan about the scheduled surgery. "I won't be able to stop worrying until it's done. About Frank *and* Brett."

"Did you eat breakfast?" Ivan asked, eyeing me closely.

"I had a banana." I'd skipped my usual smoothie. My most restful spell of sleep occurred in the last couple of hours before my alarm went off, so I'd been sluggish about getting out of bed and ended up running late.

Ivan slid two slices of eggnog French toast onto a plate. The dish was one of The Flip Side's holiday menu items, along with candy cane pancakes and gingerbread crêpes. I'd had the enviable job of taste-testing and approving the holiday dishes back in November, and I'd taken several opportunities since then to indulge in the scrumptious breakfast foods.

Ivan pushed the plate across the counter to me. "Eat this. You need to remember to take care of yourself."

"I know, and thank you. Between Brett's dad and Wally's murder, it's hard to focus on ordinary things. And hard to sleep."

I bit into a piece of bread that had been soaked in a mixture of eggs, eggnog, vanilla, and cinnamon before it was cooked. It was only as I swallowed my first bite that I realized how hungry I was, my stomach growling and clamoring for more. I tried to eat slowly so I could savor the delicious flavors so reminiscent of the holidays, but I was too hungry to hold back and had cleaned the plate in no time.

As I was chewing my last bite, Leigh stopped by the kitchen and saw me sitting at the counter. "Why don't you go home, Marley? I can handle things out there."

"Thanks, Leigh, but I'll be okay." I glanced at the clock on the wall. "Although, I should go and let Bentley out of the house for a few minutes."

"Go on then," Leigh encouraged me. "And you don't have to come back if you don't feel up to it."

"Call me if you need me in the meantime," I said.

She assured me that she would and practically ushered me out the door. When I arrived home, Bentley was ecstatic. He was even happier when I let him out in the yard and threw a tennis ball for him to chase. I considered trying to take a nap, but I knew there was no way I could settle my mind enough to rest, so I returned to The Flip Side until closing time.

I texted back and forth with Brett whenever I could, trying to keep him company from afar while he waited for his dad to get out of surgery. Later, when I took Bentley down to the beach so he could run and play, I kept my phone in my pocket, checking it every so often even though I knew it would vibrate if any new messages came in.

As darkness crept over Wildwood Cove, I returned home with Bentley and picked up where I'd left off with the lentil curry the day before. It was a perfect meal for a chilly winter evening, and I was glad for the company of Flapjack and Bentley, though I missed Brett terribly. The frequency of his text messages had slowed as the day wore on, and I hoped that was because he was dozing while he waited for news of his dad.

I found it hard to sit still, even while eating. I wanted to be in Seattle, looking after Brett, but aside from keeping him company, I knew there wasn't much I could have done. It would be best to stay busy so I wouldn't worry so much, I knew, but after eating dinner I wasn't sure what to do with myself. I considered watching TV, but in the end I decided to head up to the attic. I wanted to start decorating the house for the holidays, and I knew I'd seen some boxes labeled as Christmas decorations on the few occasions I'd ventured up among the rafters.

In the second-floor hallway, I pulled down the attic stairs and climbed my way up the creaking steps, a flashlight in hand. Bentley sat at the bottom of the steep stairs, whining as I disappeared from sight.

"It's all right, buddy," I called down to reassure him. "I won't be long."

With the aid of the flashlight, I found the string dangling from the attic's single lightbulb. Between the two light sources I could see well enough to get around. First, I took down the box of my own decorations I'd stashed in the attic when I moved in. Then I returned to look at the other boxes I'd seen. One held an assortment of tree ornaments while the other was filled with lights, snow globes, figurines, and other holiday knickknacks.

I gathered several strings of lights in my arms, deciding to start by testing them. I accidentally bumped another box and caught sight of an antique trunk behind it. Setting the lights back in the box, I cleared a path to the trunk and aimed the beam of my flashlight at it. A thick layer of dust covered the dome top and cobwebs clung to the sides, but I could still see the wrought-iron hardware and copper-toned tin.

In those first few seconds I'd already fallen in love with the trunk. All it needed was a bit of cleaning and then it would look great in the family room or maybe at the foot of my bed. I lifted the lid and took a look inside. Beneath a beautiful but dusty quilt was a photo album. I opened it and scanned some of the pictures. I spotted my cousin Jimmy and his wife, Grace, no older than age forty, along with some unfamiliar faces.

Setting the album aside to study more closely another time, I checked out the rest of the trunk's contents. Half a dozen leather journals were stacked in one corner and another album sat beneath them. I opened the top journal and read the rounded handwriting on the first page:

Diary of Camelia Winslow.

Grace had an older sister named Camelia. And Winslow was Grace's maiden name, so the journals must have belonged to her sister. That intrigued me, not because I'd ever met Camelia—I hadn't—but because I'd heard her mysterious story on more than one occasion while I was growing up.

When she was seventeen, Camelia had disappeared, never to be seen or heard from ever again. The incident had haunted Grace throughout her life, so I'd been told by my mom and Cousin Jimmy. I'd never heard Grace speak of her sister, and I'd never dared to raise the subject with her.

I checked the first page of each journal, noting that Camelia had started a new one for each year. I wasn't entirely sure of the year of her birth, but I guessed the first journal dated back to when she was somewhere between ten and twelve years old, and the last to when she was in her mid to late teens.

A tingle of excitement and fascination scurried up my spine. Mysteries always captivated me, and this one had to do with my own family. I didn't expect the diaries to reveal what had happened to Camelia, but I hoped they'd give me a chance to get to know her. She'd always seemed unreal to me, a mythical figure on a branch of the family tree. I wasn't going to pass up a chance to learn more about her, and maybe the reading material would keep me occupied and distracted while Brett was away.

I tried shifting the trunk toward the rickety stairs, but I knew right away that it would be too cumbersome for me to get it down on my own. It would have to wait in the attic until Brett returned and could help me. For the time being, I'd take the journals and leave the rest.

Before heading back downstairs, I took a moment to examine the album at the very bottom of the trunk. I expected to find more photographs, but instead the pages held newspaper clippings, glued down and yellowed with age. As I flipped through the album I noticed that all of the articles related to Camelia's disappearance as well as the disappearance of another local girl. More intrigued than ever, I was tempted to sit down on the dusty attic floor and read my way through the clippings and the diaries. My eyes were already protesting, though, the light not bright enough to allow me to read comfortably.

I added the album to the stack of journals and carried them down to the second-floor hallway. I returned to the attic to haul down the lights and other decorations, sneezing as I set the last box on the floor. After shoving the decorations up against the wall so they wouldn't block the hallway, I left them there and headed downstairs with only the journals and albums.

With a cup of hot chocolate to keep me warm, I snuggled up on the couch with the last album I'd found, Flapjack and Bentley close by. Although the pages held numerous clippings, most were fairly short so I skimmed through them. Each one filled in one or two of the many gaps in the vague story I'd heard about Grace's sister while growing up.

In the weeks before Camelia went missing, nineteen-year-old Tassy James—also a resident of Wildwood Cove—had disappeared. I gathered from reading between the lines that Tassy had come from a poor family. She'd worked as a maid for the mayor and his wife. One night she never arrived home, and no one ever heard from her again. Compared to the coverage of Camelia's disappearance, relatively little had been said about Tassy. Only one short article covered the maid's case until Camelia had gone missing. Then speculation had run rampant, with many of the locals quoted in the articles expressing certainty that the two cases were linked.

Although never described as Camelia's boyfriend, the mayor's eldest son, Harry, had been seen in her company on several occasions before she vanished. None of the writers of the articles came right out and accused Harry of being involved in the two incidents, but it wasn't hard to tell that the journalists and townsfolk believed he was tangled up in both cases.

The last article in the album stated that the mayor had denied his son's involvement and was standing by him, but whether or not the police had investigated Harry wasn't clear. I shut the album with a prickle of frustration. I wanted to know what had happened to Camelia and Tassy, but if no one had solved the mysteries back then, the likelihood of me ever finding out the truth was slim at best.

I was reaching for Camelia's first diary when my phone chimed on the coffee table. I grabbed it and saw a text message from Brett bearing the news I'd hoped for all afternoon: *The surgery went well.*

With a surge of relief I hugged Bentley, then Flapjack, momentarily forgetting about the mysteries from the past. I knew Frank still had a long road ahead of him, but I hoped he was through the worst, and the news that he'd made it through his surgery allowed me to sleep better than I had the night before.

Chapter 10

Before leaving for The Flip Side the next morning, I tucked the last of Camelia's diaries into my tote bag. I'd skimmed through the earlier ones the night before, getting glimpses into the teenager's mind as I read. On the pages, Camelia had written about classmates and crushes, adventures and spats with her sister, and other ups and downs of daily life. I was eager to know what she'd written in the final pages of her last diary.

I knew her disappearance wouldn't have remained a mystery for so many years if she'd explained it in her diary before she'd vanished. Grace had clearly kept the journals, and I figured it was far more likely than not that she'd read through them, searching for any clues that might lead her to her sister or to the truth of what had happened to her. Still, I'd become invested in Camelia's story, and Tassy's too, though I still knew very little about the maid. The diary seemed to call to me from my tote bag, and between that and my occasional texting back and forth with Brett, I was no better at focusing on work than I had been the previous day.

As soon as the breakfast rush was over, I shut myself in the office and grabbed my phone. I knew from our exchange of texts that Brett was still at the hospital and hadn't left since he'd picked up a key from my mom. He'd dozed in a chair for a few minutes here and there, but he hadn't had any real sleep since the night before his dad's heart attack. I wanted to hear his voice so I could better gauge how he was holding up. All I could get him to say via text was that he missed me but he was doing fine. I needed to know if the latter was really true.

Can we talk today? I asked in a text message. *I miss hearing your voice.*

While I waited for a response, I opened Camelia's diary. I read each entry this time, instead of flipping through the pages. Camelia had written less as the years passed, the entries in this last diary often shorter than a page long. At first, they covered only mundane topics, but several pages in I spotted a name that grabbed my attention.

Harry Sayers.

He was the mayor's son, the one many suspected of killing Tassy James, or at least so I'd gathered from reading the old newspaper clippings.

Eagerly, I read the entry.

Harry Sayers is so sweet and handsome. I wish he'd ask me to the spring formal, but he's already graduated and Mom and Dad don't want me to date until I'm eighteen. That's nine whole months away! Other girls in my class have been dating for ages.

I skimmed through three more entries until I came across Harry's name again.

Harry likes me! We met up by chance at the soda shop and he walked me home. He's even sweeter than I thought and such a gentleman. He wants to date me. I had to tell him about Mom and Dad's rule, but he said he'd wait for me to turn eighteen! In the meantime he's going to walk me home every chance he gets. I'm so happy I could float away!

I found myself smiling at Camelia's exhilaration, but the smile faded when I remembered that Harry might have been responsible for her disappearance and Tassy's too. I continued reading, following Camelia's life through her first kiss to falling in love with Harry. Despite Harry's willingness to wait until Camelia turned eighteen before taking her on a date, she'd soon started spending time with him in secret.

The tone of the diary entries changed slightly as the weeks progressed, Camelia sounding more mature by the time I reached the pages written in the early summer of that year.

By then I was fully engrossed in her life and when I turned the page to find a blank one, I stared at it for a moment before I came to terms with the fact that there were no more entries. I flipped through the remaining pages, just to be sure I wasn't missing anything, but there was nothing to find. I checked the date of the last entry and thought back to the newspaper clippings in the album I'd left at home.

If I was remembering the date of Camelia's disappearance correctly, she'd stopped writing in her diary several days before she vanished.

Why?

For years she'd penned entries on an almost daily basis. Maybe it didn't mean anything that she'd stopped writing in her diary shortly before going missing, but I had a hard time believing that. A long-standing habit of hers had changed during that timeframe. What else might have changed?

The mystery had intrigued me the moment I'd found the journals and albums in the old trunk, but now it had its claws in my skin, sinking ever deeper. I wanted to know what had happened to Camelia and Tassy to satisfy my own curiosity and because it seemed so wrong for the two young women to have no real ending to their stories, to have no justice, if any was called for.

If I'd brought the album of newspaper clippings with me to the pancake house, I would have buried my nose in it right then and there to check for any information I might have missed when I'd skimmed through the articles. I'd left the album on the coffee table along with Camelia's earlier diaries, though, and maybe that was for the best. The lunch rush would be underway soon. Leigh and Sienna could probably handle all of the customers, but I still wanted to check in and see how things were going.

As I got up from my seat, my phone buzzed and I snatched it up off the desk. Brett had replied to my message.

I miss your voice too. I'm sitting with my dad while my mom and Chloe get some sleep. I'll call when they get back to the hospital.

I sent a quick reply before heading down the hall to check on things out front. I wished time would go by faster so I could talk to Brett sooner, but the minutes ticked by sluggishly.

Lisa showed up shortly after closing time, distracting me from my thoughts of Brett and Camelia. I waved goodbye to Leigh and Sienna as they left, locking the door behind them.

"How are you doing today?" I asked Lisa.

She rubbed her arms and shivered. "I'm worried about Ivan."

"Ivan?" I led her over to the large stone fireplace. I'd let the flames die down to glowing embers, but it was still warmer over there than by the door. "Because of Wally's murder?"

Lisa pulled a chair out from beneath the nearest table and sank into it. "Deputy Mendoza came by my house this morning."

"You were questioned again?" I pulled out a chair for myself.

She nodded and twisted the silver ring she wore on her right hand. "This time mostly about Ivan. How close we are, whether he knew about me blaming Wally for getting Carlos hooked on drugs, how protective he is, how insulted he was by the things Wally said here at the pancake house."

That didn't sound good. "So he's on the suspect list," I said as my stomach sank.

"He must be." She hesitated before she said anything more. "I shouldn't even be asking you this, but can you think of some way to clear his name? You're good at finding out the truth."

"Why shouldn't you be asking me? I care about Ivan too."

"I know, but you've got so much else going on lately. How are Brett and his dad doing?"

"His dad made it through surgery, so that's a major relief. As for Brett… I'm going to talk to him later."

"I should have asked as soon as I got here. I'm sorry."

"Don't be. You've got a lot on your mind too." I stared at the dying embers in the fireplace for a moment. "Let me think about what we can do for Ivan. There must be something."

I'd told Sheriff Georgeson that I had no plans to launch my own investigation, but with Ivan on the suspect list—maybe even at the top of it—I couldn't help but change those plans. Lisa could be in trouble, too, considering the questions Ray had asked us both the other day.

"Thanks, Marley." Lisa glanced toward the kitchen. "Is it all right if I go say hi to Ivan and Tommy?"

"Of course." I put a hand on her arm to stop her from getting up. "But you can't keep me in the dark. What exactly is going on with you and Ivan?"

The worry lines across Lisa's forehead smoothed out and she smiled. "I'm not entirely sure myself, but we've been spending more and more time together."

"Have you kissed?"

"Not yet." Her eyes sparkled. "But I won't let much more time pass without that happening."

I jumped up and hugged her as she got to her feet. "I'm excited for both of you."

"Thanks." She returned my hug, still smiling. "I'm heading over to the craft fair at the elementary school in a bit. Do you want to come with me?"

"I'd forgotten about that," I said. I'd seen a notice about the fair in the last issue of the local newspaper, but I hadn't given it a single thought since then.

"It's a great chance to get some early Christmas shopping done."

"That sounds good. I just need a few minutes to finish up around here."

"I'll go say hi to the guys and then I'll give you a hand."

Lisa was true to her word, spending only a minute or two in the kitchen before helping me tidy up the dining area. Once that was done, we headed to the bank, where I needed to make a quick stop before we moved on to the craft fair. When we reached the school, handmade signs directed us to the gymnasium. Tables filled the large room, laden with all sorts of goods for sale.

I spotted Patricia Murray seated at a table at the far end of the room, her driftwood carvings on display. Her wares had several people interested at the moment, so I decided to work my way over to her slowly instead of heading over to say hi right away. As Lisa and I moved from table to table,

I kept my phone in one hand, not wanting to miss any call that might come from Brett. We'd stopped in front of a display of handmade soaps when my phone buzzed and Brett's picture popped up on the screen.

"I'll be back soon," I said to Lisa, holding up my phone so she'd know why I was leaving. I made my way through the crowd, tapping the screen of my phone as I went.

"Hey, I'm glad you called," I said, pushing my way out the door.

"It's good to hear your voice."

My heart ached at the exhaustion underscoring his words. "Same here. How are you holding up?"

Brett let out a huff of air and I could picture him scrubbing a hand down his face. "I'm all right."

"Really?" I rounded a corner and leaned against the side of the building, stuffing my free hand deep into the pocket of my jeans, trying to keep it warm.

"Tired, of course, and worried. But a weight has lifted off my chest now that Dad's made it through surgery."

"That's a huge relief," I agreed. "How's he doing today?"

"The doctors are happy with his progress, but he's mostly been sleeping. I guess that's for the best."

"Probably. Chloe and your mom are back at the hospital now?"

"They got back a few minutes ago. Your mom's been great, by the way. They got some sleep and she cooked them a hot meal."

"What about you?" I asked. "Have you eaten today?"

"I had a muffin from the cafeteria this morning. I haven't been all that hungry."

I huddled deeper into my jacket, wishing I could magically transport myself to his side. "You're going to my mom's place now, right? You need to get some sleep and eat some real food."

He didn't respond.

"Brett?"

He sighed on the other end of the line. "I miss you, Marley."

The emotion and fatigue in his voice brought tears to my eyes. "I miss you too. So much. Please take care of yourself, Brett. You need to sleep."

"All right. I'll go to your mom's place for a few hours."

Some of the pressure that had been building in my chest fizzled away. "But don't drive. Take a cab or ask my mom if she can pick you up."

"That's okay, Marley. I can drive."

"You're so exhausted I'm guessing you can't even see straight. Please, don't drive."

I've lost too many people to car accidents, I wanted to say, but I couldn't get the words out.

"Okay," he said gently, and I suspected he knew what I'd left unsaid. "I'll take a cab."

A siren blared to life on his end of the line, fading seconds later.

"Sorry. I'm standing outside the hospital."

"Then you must be cold."

"It's not too bad. The fresh air's actually nice after being inside the hospital for so long." He fell silent for a second or two before speaking again. "I wish you were here."

"So do I." My heart was on the verge of bursting beneath the renewed pressure constricting my chest. "And I could be. The Flip Side's closed for the next two days. I could be there tonight. I'm sure Lisa or Patricia would look after Bentley and Flapjack."

"Don't leave yet. I don't know if Chloe's planning on going back to work tomorrow or if she's taking time off. We've only got one car here, so I might need to drive her back."

"Not until you've had some sleep," I reminded him.

"No. I'll go get some sleep now. How about I call you tonight?"

"That sounds good. Let your dad know that I send my love?"

"I will. I really love you, Marley. And I miss you like crazy."

"Right back at you," I whispered, my throat tight.

When I disconnected the call, I had to take a moment to breathe deeply and allow the threat of tears to subside. Once I'd regained control of my emotions, I pushed off from the building, ready to go back inside and meet up with Lisa.

"I told you *I'd* take care of it," I heard a woman say in a low, angry voice.

"Like you did with Fowler?" a man's voiced snapped.

Instead of turning the corner, I paused.

"What were you thinking?" the man asked. "What if someone finds out…" His voice faded, as if he were moving farther away.

I peered around the corner. Glo Hansfield—the woman I'd seen slipping into the hardware store through the back entrance—was entering the gymnasium, a tall man in a dark overcoat at her side.

They were inside the building now, so I headed for the door myself and sought out the warmth of the school gymnasium. But as I left the cold air behind me, a frosty shiver danced its way along my spine.

Chapter 11

I wound my way around clusters of shoppers to reach Lisa's side. She'd mentioned Glo Hansfield's name to Ray Georgeson the other day, as someone who might have held a grudge against Wally Fowler. Although eager to ask Lisa about the connection between the two, I forced myself to wait. With so many people around, someone was bound to overhear us and I didn't want to start any wild rumors.

By the time we reached Patricia's table, I'd bought some handmade soap and candles, two bags full of holiday decorations for The Flip Side, and a paper plate of chocolate fudge brownies that had made my mouth water as soon as I spotted them. When Lisa and I greeted Patricia, a sculpture of a majestic eagle in flight caught my eye. I'd admired a similar one on display at Patricia's home and I loved this one even more. On a whim, I decided to buy it. The fireplace mantel at The Flip Side would be the perfect place for it.

While Patricia carefully wrapped up the driftwood sculpture for me, I asked her and Lisa about the possibility of pet sitting for me and Brett if I went to Seattle. They both assured me they'd be happy to help, and that put my mind at ease. Now I just had to wait to hear back from Brett.

As I handed Patricia the money for the sculpture, Sienna appeared out of the crowd and plopped down in the empty chair next to her mom.

"Is that Bailey Hansfield you were talking to?" Patricia asked her once Sienna had said hello to me and Lisa.

I glanced over my shoulder to follow Patricia's gaze and noticed the blond girl Sienna had spoken to at the hardware store.

When Sienna answered in the affirmative, Patricia commented, "She doesn't look very happy."

It only took a quick glimpse of the girl to see that Patricia was right. Bailey stood on her own, leaning her back against the wall, her head down as she picked at the polish on her fingernails.

"She's been like that for the last few days," Sienna said. "I asked her what's wrong, but she wouldn't tell me."

"Did you say Hansfield?" I said to Patricia. "Is Glo Hansfield her mother?"

"That's right," Patricia replied. "Do you know Glo?"

"No, but I've seen her around."

"I wouldn't be surprised if things haven't been too happy at the Hansfield home lately." Patricia lowered her voice before adding, "I'm sure it wasn't easy for Glo when Wally Fowler returned to town."

More than ever, I wanted to ask about the woman's connection to Wally, but several other shoppers approached the table then and Lisa and I moved on after saying goodbye to Patricia and Sienna.

"Do you want to look at anything else?" Lisa asked as we surveyed the last few tables we hadn't yet visited.

"I'm ready to go if you are," I said.

The other vendors were selling handmade baby clothes, knitted scarves and hats, and hair accessories—nothing I needed.

Lisa zipped up her jacket as we stepped outside. "Want to grab a bite to eat?"

I did up my own coat. "Sure, but I might get a call from Brett at some point."

"No worries. What do you feel like?"

I thought for a second. "Seafood?"

"Yum. Good idea. How about CJ's?"

"Sounds good."

We drove to CJ's Seafood House in my car and were soon settled on opposite sides of a table in a corner of the restaurant. Darkness had fallen by then, obscuring what otherwise would have been a gorgeous view of the water. After the waiter had brought us drinks and had taken our orders, I couldn't keep my curiosity at bay any longer.

I leaned forward and kept my voice low. "What's the story about Glo Hansfield and Wally Fowler?"

"Ah." Lisa took a sip of her daiquiri. "That's a sad one. Remember how I told you about Lizzie Van Amstel?"

"The girl who died when Wally crashed his car?"

She nodded. "Lizzie was Glo's younger sister."

"That's terrible. Poor Glo."

Lisa was about to take another sip of her drink, but she set down her glass, a spark of anger flashing in her eyes. "Ruining lives was Wally's specialty."

"It must have been awful for Glo when Wally came back to town."

Lisa frowned into her daiquiri. "It was bad enough for me, and Carlos is still alive. It wouldn't surprise me if Glo's happy that Wally's dead. I'd never wish for anyone to be murdered, but I'm not exactly torn up about him being gone."

"Do you think—" I cut off the thought before I voiced it.

Lisa's eyes met mine. "That Glo might have killed him?"

Speaking barely above a whisper, I told her about the conversation I'd overheard between Glo and the man I was assuming was her husband. Lisa's eyes grew wider as I spoke.

"I wonder if she has an alibi," she said when I'd finished.

"Maybe we can find out."

"It would be the first step toward clearing me and Ivan of any suspicion."

"You know," I said, thinking back, "Glo was at the hardware store for the ladies' night event."

The hope that had appeared on Lisa's face faded away. "So she does have an alibi."

"Maybe not. Right after I arrived, I saw her sneaking in through the back door, like she didn't want anyone to notice her. She wasn't wearing a coat, so maybe she'd already been at the event and slipped away for a while."

"Long enough to kill Wally?"

"Possibly. Do you know if she smokes?" I asked, wondering if that could explain why she'd gone outside that night.

"She doesn't, unless she does it in secret."

"Hmm. I wonder if the hardware store has security cameras outside the building."

"Even if it does, how would we get to see the footage? I doubt Sheriff Georgeson would look into it just because we suspect Glo of possibly being involved in Wally's death."

"Let me work on that," I said as the waiter arrived with our meals.

I breathed in the aroma of the marinated jumbo shrimp and rice pilaf the waiter had placed in front of me. My stomach grumbled, urging me to get eating, so I dug in while Lisa sampled her braised trout.

As we ate, I told Lisa about the trunk and diaries I'd found in the attic.

"That's so sad," she said once I'd related the story of the unsolved disappearances of Camelia Winslow and Tassy James. "But also fascinating."

"Right? I can't stop thinking about it. I'm going to have a closer look at all the newspaper clippings in the album, as soon as I get a chance."

"If you want to find more information about the Winslow and James families, or what was happening in town at the time, you should ask Nancy Welch at the Wildwood Cove Museum and Archives."

"Welch? Is she related to Justine?"

"She's Justine's stepmother." Lisa swallowed a bite of trout. "No one knows this town's history better than Nancy."

"Talking to her is a good idea. I might do that after I've read over everything I've already got."

"Keep me posted? I'd love to hear more about both girls."

I promised I'd let her know about any information I came across.

When the waiter brought our check later that evening, Lisa snatched it up off the table before I had a chance to look at it.

"My treat tonight," she said as she dug around in her purse for her wallet.

"You don't have to do that," I protested.

"Consider it an early birthday dinner. If you go to Seattle I might not see you again until after your birthday."

"True. Thanks, Lisa."

"Do you have any special birthday plans?" she asked after she'd paid the bill and we were getting into our coats.

"To be honest, I haven't given it any thought."

"I guess you're not in a very celebratory mood this year."

"No. But if Frank continues to get better and I get to see Brett soon, I'll be plenty happy."

"The two of you are so sweet together," she said with a grin as we walked to my car.

I couldn't help but smile. "So are you and Ivan."

"We aren't even a couple. Yet."

"Doesn't matter."

We were still smiling as I drove her home. Once I'd dropped her off and was on my own, my thoughts kept bouncing from Brett to Wally's murder to Camelia's long-ago disappearance. I had an idea of how I could check into Glo's movements outside the hardware store on the night of Wally's murder, but I'd need Leigh's help. When I got home, I sent her a text message and then busied myself with feeding Flapjack and Bentley.

I hadn't heard back from Leigh yet, so I phoned my mom, wanting to check in with her about a couple of things.

"Hi, sweetie," my mom said when she answered the call. "How are you doing?"

"I'm all right. I miss Brett, though. Is he there at the house?"

"He is. He showed up this afternoon. I made him a sandwich and thought he was going to fall asleep while eating it. He went to lie down in the guest room and I haven't heard anything since."

"Hopefully he's sound asleep."

"I think that's a pretty safe bet."

"Did he mention I might come to Seattle?"

"He did, but it sounded like he was planning to talk to Chloe again before anything was decided for certain."

"Yes, that's what he told me too."

"I know I just saw you for Thanksgiving, but I'd love to have you here on your birthday."

"I'd like that too. We'll see how things go." I wandered over to the large family room window and pulled the curtains. "Mom, do you remember the story about Grace's older sister, Camelia?"

"Of course. But I haven't heard that name in years. What made you think of her?"

"I found her diaries in the attic when I was looking for Christmas decorations. And there's an album full of newspaper clippings about her disappearance. I'm assuming Grace put that together."

"Most likely. Although I suppose it could have been one or both of her parents."

"Do you know anything beyond the fact that Camelia disappeared and was never found?"

"Goodness. I don't think so. I heard about her from Cousin Jimmy decades ago. Grace never talked about her in my presence and I got the sense from Jimmy that it wasn't a topic she talked about with anyone. All I know is that Camelia vanished without a trace when she was about seventeen or so. I think Grace was twelve or thirteen at the time. From the sounds of things, it put an early end to her childhood. Never knowing what happened must have been terribly hard on the whole family."

"Yes, it must have."

"Did you read the diaries?"

"I skimmed through them. I'll read them more closely at some point. I was hoping to find out more about her disappearance. I'll see what the newspaper clippings have to say. So far I've only flipped through those as well."

"If you're looking for answers about what happened to her, I don't think you'll find them, sweetie. I gather the police had their suspicions back then, but they weren't able to solve the case."

"I know, but I'm still going to take a look."

We talked for a while longer and then I headed upstairs to my bedroom. I pulled a gym bag out of my closet, deciding to pack a few things in case I did end up going to Seattle. After I'd set the packed bag by my bedroom door, I changed into my pajamas and grabbed a mystery novel from my bedside table, curling up on the window seat. Flapjack jumped up to settle at my feet and Bentley curled up on the floor close by.

I read through two chapters before my phone rang, showing Brett's picture on the screen. I nearly dropped my book in my rush to answer the call.

"Hey, did you have a good sleep?" I asked.

"I did. I was out like a light the moment my head hit the pillow and I slept like a log up until a few minutes ago."

"That's good." I was relieved not only by the fact that he'd slept, but also by his voice. He sounded so much more like himself than he had earlier in the day.

"I talked to Chloe. She's taking at least a couple of days off work, so she won't be heading home yet."

"I can leave for Seattle first thing in the morning."

"Actually, I'm thinking it would be best for you to stay put."

I couldn't stop the barb of disappointment that poked me in my gut.

"It looks like I might be heading your way."

The sharp sting of disappointment ebbed away. "You're coming home?"

"I think so. Before I left the hospital earlier, my dad was awake and worrying about his business. I reminded him that Pedro's been foreman for years and can handle everything, but he wouldn't stop worrying. Chloe says he's still getting worked up about it. I'm going back to the hospital now. I'll tell him I can check in on things for him if that'll make him feel better."

"Okay. I can't say I wouldn't be happy with that plan. I'd really love to see you."

"I want to see you too. I'm not sure when my dad will be awake next, but I'll text you as soon as I know for sure if I'm coming home."

"All right. I'll be awake for a while yet."

"What are you up to?"

"Reading."

I considered telling him about the two mysteries weighing on my mind but decided to hold back on that for the time being. I didn't want to trouble him with talk of murder when he had so much else on his mind. Instead we chatted for another minute or two about his dad and then said our goodnights.

When we ended the call, loneliness settled over me like a heavy blanket. In recent weeks Brett had been spending more nights at my house than at his place. I'd grown accustomed to having him beside me as I slept. I knew from years of being single that I could manage fine on my own, but now that I had Brett in my life, I didn't want to be without him.

It's only temporary, I reminded myself. *You might see him as soon as tomorrow.*

That helped to ease the weight of my loneliness, but not by much.

When my phoned chimed, I was glad for the distraction. My mood got a boost when I read Leigh's text message.

Greg might be able to help you. Can you drop by the hardware store tomorrow morning?

Yes, I replied right away. *Thank you!*

Maybe I wouldn't be able to figure out what happened to Camelia and Tassy all those years ago, but if I had even the slightest chance to clear Ivan and Lisa of suspicion, I intended to pounce on it.

Chapter 12

Before falling asleep, I received a text from Brett saying he'd be heading back to Wildwood Cove the next day. I woke up in the morning with a smile on my face and channeled some of my excited energy into a run with Bentley along quiet residential streets, followed by a walk along the water's edge. After showering and getting dressed for the day, I set off for the hardware store. Brett wouldn't arrive for another couple of hours, so I figured the best way to kill some time was to try to make some progress with clearing my friends of suspicion.

When I reached the store, Leigh's husband, Greg, was helping a middle-aged woman at the customer service counter. As soon as the woman left, Greg smiled and waved me over.

"Hey, Marley," he greeted. "Leigh says you're interested to know if anyone was hanging around in the back alley the night Wally Fowler was killed."

"That's right. She thought you might be able to help?"

"Sure. I talked to Drew—the store's manager—and he said to bring you up to his office so we can have a look at the surveillance footage."

"Perfect," I said, eager to get to it.

Greg led me through a door with a Staff Only sign on it, and then up a staircase to a hallway with gray walls and gray carpeting. A door stood open to our right. Greg tapped on it before stepping into the room. As I followed him inside, a fifty-something man with dark hair and broad shoulders stood up from behind a nondescript desk, extending a hand to me.

"Ms. McKinney? I'm Drew Garner. I understand you'd like to see our security footage."

I shook his offered hand. "Marley, please. And yes, that would be great. I know it's a bit of an odd request…"

He waved off my concern. "Greg tells me you're an amateur sleuth."

"I guess you could say that."

"You can definitely say that," Greg said. "She's had a hand in solving several murders."

"Then I'm glad to help," Drew said, making a few clicks with his computer mouse. "We don't want Fowler's killer running loose around town." He motioned for me and Greg to join him behind the desk. "I've brought up the footage for the night of the murder. It was our ladies' night event that evening."

"I was there," I said. "It was a great event."

"I'm glad you enjoyed it." He turned his attention to the computer screen. "As you can see, this is the view of the back alley. It's paused at 5:00 p.m. I'll fast forward through the evening. Let me know if you want me to stop it at any time." He clicked a button on the screen and the footage zoomed forward, time-wise at least. The dark image of the alley, illuminated only by a security light behind the store, remained static.

We watched in silence for several seconds before something moved on the screen.

"Hold on a second." Drew rewound the footage and then let it play at real-time speed.

On the screen, the store's back door opened and a man emerged into the alley, a load of what looked like cardboard tucked under his arm. He shoved the cardboard into a large recycling bin, and then went straight back into the store.

"That's one of our guys," Drew said. "Dave Orton."

I checked the time code on the screen. "I'm not sure exactly when Wally was killed, but I doubt Dave's a witness. He didn't even look around while he was out there."

"I can ask him if he saw anything," Greg volunteered. "Just in case."

"That would be great," I said.

"He's downstairs right now. I'll go see if I can find him."

Greg left the office and Drew hit the fast-forward button again. This time we had to wait longer before something new appeared on the screen. When Drew had stopped and rewound the video, I checked the time code again. The footage was from right around the time I arrived at the hardware store. With luck, this would be Glo's appearance in the alley.

Sure enough, a few seconds later, the back door opened and a woman exited the building, keeping hold of the door until it had shut gently behind her. She glanced left and right, and then set off briskly along the alley, wearing no coat despite how chilly it was that night.

That fit with what I'd seen when she returned to the store.

"I'm not sure who that is," Drew said, squinting at the screen as he re-watched the segment.

"Glo Hansfield," I supplied.

Recognition dawned on his face. "Right. I wonder why she went out the back way, and with no coat."

"Maybe she forgot something in her car," I suggested, although I suspected otherwise. "Can you fast-forward to see if she reappears?"

I knew she would, but I didn't want to explain that.

Drew got the footage moving quickly again, and when a dark shape moved along the alley, he stopped the video and rewound. "That's her."

Glo walked along the alley, still moving briskly. She glanced over her shoulder and slipped through the back door to the store, disappearing from the screen.

I checked the time code again and did some math in my head. In total, Glo was gone from the hardware store for about seventeen minutes.

Was that long enough for her to get to the waffle house and kill Wally?

It was entirely possible.

"Should I keep going?" Drew asked.

"Sure."

Since we were already looking at the footage, it wouldn't hurt to see if there were any other people in the alley that night. Aside from several employees who left through the back door after the ladies' night event was over, there was no other movement in the alley. By the time those individuals exited the building, I'd already found Ivan at the Waffle Kingdom and Wally was already dead.

"Thank you," I said as Drew exited the program displaying the footage. "That was very helpful."

I now knew for sure that Glo hadn't stepped outside to smoke or make a phone call. She'd gone in the direction of the waffle house, and that solidified her status as a suspect in my mind.

"Glo Hansfield is a great woman," Drew said. "She's always involved in charity work. She couldn't have had anything to do with Fowler's death."

"She could be a potential witness," I said, not bothering to dispute his opinion.

"She's probably talked to the sheriff if she is."

"Maybe. But if she saw something without realizing its significance—like someone else out at that time of night—it might not have occurred to her to tell anyone."

"Good point," Drew conceded. "Should one of us talk to her?"

"Talking to the sheriff would be better," I said, not wanting Glo to get tipped off that she was under suspicion in case she was indeed guilty.

"I can give him a call," Drew said.

"That would be great." That way Ray was less likely to get annoyed with me for sticking my nose into the investigation.

I thanked the store manager for his help and made my way downstairs. I met up with Greg in the stairwell.

"Dave didn't see anything that night," he said.

"Thanks for checking. We found a potential witness on the footage from later in the evening."

"So it was helpful in the end?"

"Definitely."

Once I'd thanked Greg again, I left the store. Out on the sidewalk, I paused and raised my face to the sun that was shining brightly down from the clear blue sky. I could feel only the barest hint of warmth from the sunlight, but the weather was still bright and cheery, matching my mood. It wouldn't be much longer before I'd see Brett, and I'd managed to move my investigation forward. I still had a ways to go before Ivan's and Lisa's names were cleared, but at least I now knew that my top suspect had the opportunity to commit the crime.

At the speed Glo had been walking on the surveillance video, it wouldn't have taken her long to reach the waffle house. All she had to do was reach the end of the alley, cross the street, and then head around to the front door of the Waffle Kingdom.

As I set off along the street, a tiny speck of doubt worked its way into my thoughts. Glo wasn't a tall woman. Even in high heels, she would have been shorter than Wally. While I hadn't heard any official announcement on the way Wally had died, the state of the scene of the crime supported Ivan's theory that Wally had died from exposure to liquid nitrogen. Whether the burns had killed him or he'd died of asphyxiation, it seemed likely that the murderer had forced Wally's head into the bowl.

Now that I thought it over, I wasn't so sure Glo could have done that. Then again, if she'd been mad enough, maybe she could have managed. Or perhaps she threw the bowl, causing the liquid nitrogen to splash into Wally's face.

She still belonged on the suspect list, I decided. I wasn't sure what my next step should be in terms of investigating Glo, but I decided to put that problem aside temporarily.

I'd reached Marielle's Bakery and wanted to pop inside to pick up something sweet. I still had some of the chocolate fudge brownies I'd bought the day before, but I wanted to have Brett's favorite treat on hand when he got home. Fortunately, Marielle's display of butter pecan tarts was still full.

I purchased half a dozen of the tarts and then, on a whim, asked for another half-dozen in a separate box. Although not part of my original plans for the morning, I decided I'd pay Vicky a visit—if I could find her—to see how she was holding up, and I wanted something to give her. I didn't know if she had many friends in Wildwood Cove, and as much as I didn't like her brother, I felt sorry for her and what she was going through.

As I left the bakery, I was tempted to make a detour on my way to the waffle house so I could stop in at my favorite store—an antiques shop on Main Street. I'd been in there countless times since I'd moved to Wildwood Cove and I'd made several purchases, rarely leaving the store empty-handed. I hadn't let myself go into the store for a couple of weeks. I'd spent a lot of money on the kitchen renovations and didn't want to go overboard with buying antiques, especially since I already had plenty of furniture. Cousin Jimmy had left me a generous nest egg along with his house, but I wanted to be prudent with my money.

Still, it wouldn't hurt to go and have a look for holiday gifts.

Mr. Gorski, the store's proprietor, had some gorgeous vintage jewelry in stock that I'd practically drooled over on my last visit. Somehow, I'd managed to leave the store without buying any of it, but I hadn't been able to forget two pieces in particular—a gorgeous seahorse pendant and a gold butterfly brooch. I loved seahorses, and I had the brooch in mind for a Christmas gift for my mom.

I decided I should buy the brooch if it was still there. I didn't want to leave it until the last minute and end up finding that someone else had bought it in the meantime. If the seahorse pendant was still available... maybe I'd consider buying it for myself. It was expensive, though, so I wasn't sure I could justify the purchase in my mind.

When I entered the antiques shop, the bell above the door announcing my presence, I breathed in the familiar, comforting smell of wood and leather. Mr. Gorski was in the middle of ringing up purchases for a burly, dark-haired man, so I simply said hello and moved on to the jewelry cabinet at the far end of the sales counter. When I glanced back toward the two men, I realized the customer was Wally's buddy Chester Burns. Mr. Gorski was wrapping up an antique necklace and a set of dangly pearl earrings for him.

I paid him no more attention and focused on the jewelry in the display case in front of me. I'd known that I'd taken a liking to the seahorse pendant, but I was surprised by how disappointed I was when I saw that it was no longer in the case. The butterfly brooch was still there, however, so as soon as Mr. Gorski was available, I pointed it out to him and he removed it from the case. As much as I loved to spend time browsing the aisles, I decided to keep my visit short. I wanted to be home when Brett arrived, and I still planned to stop by the waffle house to see if Vicky was there.

When I'd paid for the brooch and had it tucked away safely in my tote bag, I set a course for the Waffle Kingdom, determined not to let myself get distracted again. I didn't know if Vicky had any reason to be at the waffle house that day, but I didn't know where she lived, so that was the only place I knew to look for her.

When I arrived at the restaurant and peered in through the large front window, I saw that I was in luck. I could see Vicky near the counter at the back, but she wasn't alone. Chester was with her, and the two of them were locked in a passionate embrace.

Chapter 13

I almost turned away, deciding it wasn't the best time to interrupt, but then the two lovebirds broke apart and Vicky spotted me through the window. She waved and came toward the door, so I stayed in place.

"Hi," Vicky said, sounding breathless when she opened the door. "What can I do for you?"

I held up one of the bakery boxes. "I brought something for you. I thought I'd stop by and see how you're doing."

"Oh. That's kind of you." She patted a hand over her hair, as if afraid it might be messy. She glanced back at Chester, but then opened the door and stood back. "Come on in."

As I stepped inside, I passed her the bakery box.

She peeked inside. "Those look delicious. Thank you."

My gaze shifted to Chester. He still stood near the back of the restaurant, his eyes on Vicky as he shifted his weight, clearly uncomfortable.

When Vicky noticed him watching her, she forced a smile for my benefit. "Just give me a moment."

I waited near the door as she set the bakery box down on the nearest table and hurried over to Chester.

"I'll see you later," she whispered, though not quietly enough to prevent me from hearing.

"But the lawyer's supposed to call," Chester said.

"And I'll let you know once I've heard from him." Vicky leaned in closer to him and whispered something further, this time too quietly for her words to reach my ears. Then she gave him a quick kiss and tipped her head in the direction of the front door.

With obvious reluctance, Chester took his cue and headed out, barely acknowledging me with a slight nod as he passed by. Once we were alone, Vicky smoothed down the dark blue T-shirt she wore with her jeans.

"Sorry about that."

"No need to apologize," I assured her. "I'm sorry I interrupted you two."

"Oh." Her cheeks flushed. "That's all right."

"I didn't realize the two of you were an item," I said.

"We weren't until recently. He's been so supportive and sweet since Wally died. He told me he's had feelings for me for a long time but didn't say anything because Wally was his best friend and he wasn't sure what he'd think about the two of us dating." Her hand went to the silver-encircled pearl hanging from a chain around her neck. "Anyway, who knows where things will go, but at the moment it's nice to have him around."

"Was that a gift from him?" I asked, indicating the pendant. "I saw him at the antiques store earlier buying a necklace like that one."

Vicki beamed as she fingered the piece of jewelry. "Yes, he just gave it to me. Isn't it beautiful?"

"It's gorgeous."

I looked at her ears but they weren't pierced. Maybe Chester hadn't realized that when he'd bought the necklace and earrings.

"I couldn't help but overhear Chester mention a lawyer," I said, my mind tracing its way back to their whispered conversation. "I hope you're not in trouble. Did the sheriff accept your alibi?"

"Oh, it's nothing like that. Wally's lawyer is supposed to call me. He's got Wally's will, you see. I'm hoping he can tell me what's going to happen to this place and with Wally's money."

"Wally never told you what he had planned for his estate?"

"He told me a lot of things, but I don't know what was the truth and what wasn't. He liked to use his money as a way to get people to do what he wanted. Like with this place." She gestured around at the restaurant. "He told me if I came back to Wildwood Cove and helped him run the waffle house, he'd make me a partner in the business and give me a big bonus check."

"But he didn't?" I guessed.

"No." A note of bitterness had crept into her voice, but when she spoke again, it was gone, her voice neutral. "He kept promising, but I don't know if he ever would have delivered."

I wanted to ask about her alibi again, but she didn't give me a chance.

"I'm afraid I can't chat long. The lawyer could phone at any moment. I really appreciate you coming by, though. It's not like people have been tripping over each other wanting to express their condolences." Again, the note of bitterness had slipped back into her voice.

I wasn't sure what to say to that, but the ringing of a phone somewhere in the back of the restaurant saved me from responding.

"That must be the lawyer now." Vicky yanked open the door and ushered me out onto the sidewalk. "Thanks again for stopping by!"

She raced toward the back of the waffle house, disappearing through the door that led to the kitchen and office. I stood there on the sidewalk for a moment before accepting the fact that I wouldn't be getting any further information out of her. I'd hoped to broach the subject of Glo, to see if Vicky thought she could have killed her brother, but that wouldn't happen now, and I still didn't know if her alibi had withstood Ray's scrutiny. I'd have to come back another time or find a different way to get the information I wanted.

I didn't know how to find out about the state of Vicky's alibi—Ray certainly wouldn't want me asking him about it—but I could probably find out more about Glo without too much trouble. I decided to start by asking Patricia about her. Sienna's mother not only ran a bed-and-breakfast and created stunning pieces of art, she was also involved in the community and knew almost everyone in Wildwood Cove.

Before talking to Patricia, however, I was heading home. Brett would be there soon and I didn't want to miss his arrival.

Flapjack and Bentley greeted me when I returned home, and I let them out into the yard after doling out pats and hugs. Once I got them back into the house, only a minute or two passed before I heard a familiar rumble coming along the driveway. Bentley and I nearly tripped over each other in our excited rush to reach the front door.

We spilled out onto the porch as Brett brought his silver truck to a stop. Bentley bounded down the steps and jumped up at Brett as soon as he opened the truck door.

"Hey, buddy." Brett gave Bentley a hug and a pat.

The dog dashed over to a tree and rushed back to Brett, a tennis ball in his mouth. Brett laughed as Bentley dropped the ball at his feet. He grabbed it and threw it across the yard, the goldendoodle enthusiastically giving chase.

With his dog occupied for a few seconds at least, Brett turned my way. A smile stretched across my face as I hurried down the steps and threw my arms around him. I felt him let out a long sigh as he hugged me back, and for some reason that nearly brought tears to my eyes. I kissed him before I had a chance to start bawling, and by the time I stepped back, I was beaming, no tears in sight.

"I'm so glad you're here." I kept hold of his hands, not wanting to break contact with him.

Dark rings beneath his eyes told of his exhaustion, but there was nothing weary about his smile. "It's so good to see you." He pulled me in for another kiss, and then kept an arm around my shoulders as we watched Bentley bounce around us, thrilled to have his favorite human back home.

I leaned into Brett, soaking up his presence. "How's your dad today?"

"A little bit better than yesterday."

"That's good. Little by little, right?"

He kissed the top of my head. "Exactly."

Bentley dropped the tennis ball at Brett's feet, so he picked it up and threw it across the yard again.

"Are you hungry?" I asked.

"Starving. For food and for your company."

"You've got me, so how about we get you something to eat?"

"Sounds like a plan."

Bentley followed us inside and Flapjack appeared from the back of the house to wind around Brett's legs. I put together a couple of sandwiches, ready for lunch myself, and we sat on the couch to eat, sitting close enough that our arms and legs touched. I brought out the butter pecan tarts and fudge brownies for dessert. We munched on both until we were too full to eat any more and Brett's eyes were threatening to close on him.

"Are you meeting up with Pedro today?" I asked as I brushed some crumbs off my shirt, onto my empty plate.

"I am, but not until four."

I kissed him on the cheek and brushed a blond curl off his forehead. "That gives you time for a nap."

"Good thing. I'm already half asleep."

"I noticed," I said with a smile.

I got up and took his hand, pulling him to his feet. "You go get some rest."

"Not quite yet." He tugged me in close for a long hug and an even longer kiss.

I put a hand to his chest as he rested his forehead against mine. "I know you were only gone a couple of days, but I missed you so much."

"Same here."

"Are we crazy?"

"Crazy in love."

A smile took over my face. "That's definitely true."

My smile faded and I sighed, not wanting to be apart from him but knowing he needed to rest. With reluctance, I pulled back and gave him a gentle shove toward the hallway. "Sleep."

He squeezed my hand before letting go. Bentley followed him upstairs and quiet fell over the house. Flapjack was snoozing on the back of the couch, and all I could hear was the ticking of the clock in the kitchen. I eyed the stack of Camelia's diaries I'd left on an end table, tempted to curl up with them and the album of newspaper clippings, but there was a more current mystery that needed my attention. As long as a cloud of suspicion hovered over Ivan and Lisa, I needed to keep digging, to do my best to find the truth and clear their names.

After pulling my jacket on, I slipped quietly out the back door and headed along the beach, frothy waves crashing against the shore on my left, whitecaps dancing on the blue-green water. I pulled up my hood and buried my hands deep in my pockets, trying to protect myself from the wind's icy bite.

When I reached the yellow-and-white Driftwood Bed-and-Breakfast, I hurried up the steps to the back porch and knocked on the French doors. Sienna jumped up from the dining table to let me in the house.

"Hi, Marley," she said as she shut the door behind me. "Are you here to see my mom?"

"I am. Is she home?"

"She's out getting some groceries. I can text her and tell her you're here."

"That's all right. I can talk to her later. How come you're not at school?"

"I don't have classes this afternoon."

I took in the sight of the textbooks and papers strewn across the dining table. "It looks like you have homework, though."

Sienna made a face. "Unfortunately. Will you stay for a bit?"

"I should probably let you get back to work."

"Please don't. I could use a break. Do you want something to drink?" She was already heading for the fridge.

I accepted a glass of root beer and joined Sienna at the table. "I was wondering if your mom knows Glo Hansfield, but you're friends with her daughter, right?"

"Bailey? Sort of, I guess." She took a sip of her drink before elaborating. "We were friends when we were little, but once we got to middle school we sort of drifted apart."

"She hasn't looked very happy lately."

Sienna frowned, the piercing in her bottom lip catching the light. "No. I asked her what's wrong, but she wouldn't tell me. Her parents have been looking seriously stressed lately too. Probably because of that guy who got murdered. He killed Bailey's aunt in a car accident a long time ago, before Bailey and I were born."

"I heard about that."

"How come you want to know if my mom knows Mrs. Hansfield?"

I hesitated, not sure if I should voice my suspicions.

As it turned out, I didn't have to.

Sienna's heavily lined eyes widened. "Do you think she killed the waffle guy?"

"I'm not sure."

"But she's on your suspect list?" She leaned forward, surprising me with her eagerness. "Please tell me."

"Okay, yes. She's on my suspect list." I told her about Glo's disappearance from the event at the hardware store on the night of the murder.

"And she totally has a motive," Sienna said once I'd finished. "Revenge." She tapped a pencil against one of her textbooks. "So now what we need is evidence."

"We?" I sputtered, almost choking on the sip of root beer I'd just taken.

Sienna grinned at me. "Yes, we. I'm officially your sidekick."

Chapter 14

"Since when?" I asked once I'd managed to finish swallowing my root beer.

"Since five seconds ago."

"I don't think your mom would appreciate me dragging you into a murder investigation, even if it's an unofficial one."

"You're not dragging me anywhere, and it's not like she has to know." I raised my eyebrows.

"Come on," Sienna beseeched, giving me the teenage girl equivalent of sad puppy-dog eyes. "I can help you. I've got connections."

"Connections?"

"We need to know what the police know, or don't know. Right?"

"And how are you going to find that out?"

Sienna's smile reminded me of the Cheshire cat. "Connections." She jumped up and grabbed her jacket from the coatrack by the back door. "I'll explain on the way."

"Don't you need to finish your homework?"

She waved off the question. "I'll finish it later."

I followed her out to the driveway where her red secondhand Toyota was parked, a present from her parents when she turned sixteen.

"So where is it we're going?" I asked as soon as I was in the passenger seat.

"To see Justine Welch."

"The reporter?"

"I babysit for her sometimes." Sienna turned out of the driveway onto Wildwood Road, heading toward the center of town. "My mom knows her stepmom. When Justine moved back to town, she needed a sitter, and Nancy—that's her stepmom—suggested me."

"Nancy's the one who works at the museum," I said, remembering what Lisa had told me.

"Yep. Justine knows people, and she knows how to get information. She'd rather be a big-city reporter, but she stopped working when she got married and since she got divorced she's had to start over. Anyway, if anyone can tell us what's going on with the official investigation, it'll be her."

"And she'll just tell us everything she knows?"

Sienna shrugged. "Maybe we should introduce the subject casually and see what she's willing to share. Is there anything in particular you want to know?"

I mentioned Vicky's alibi. "It would be nice to know if the sheriff's department was able to confirm it." I thought for a moment. "And maybe she can tell us if the police have found any physical evidence."

"Like what? Wasn't the guy killed with liquid nitrogen or something freaky like that?"

"Yes, liquid nitrogen." I chewed on my lower lip as Sienna turned onto Main Street and pulled into a free parking spot by the curb. "Come to think of it, the killer probably would have ended up with cryogenic burns if they weren't wearing any protection on their hands. But the only gloves I saw at the crime scene were Wally's."

"There haven't been any rumors about someone walking around with cryogenic burns, so maybe the killer disposed of their gloves somewhere away from the scene of the crime."

"It's definitely a possibility," I agreed.

"Hmmm." Sienna tapped the steering wheel.

"What are you thinking?" I asked, suspicious.

"That we should see what we can find out."

Before I could question her about the truthfulness of her response, she was out of the car and gesturing for me to follow. She led the way to a small stationary store nestled between a café and a hair salon. A sign in the window indicated that the office of the *Wildwood Cove Weekly* was located in the back of the store.

Charlene McGinnis—the owner of the store and the newspaper—stood behind the checkout desk, focused on her computer screen, but she looked up and greeted us when we entered the shop. She'd eaten at The Flip Side on a few occasions since I'd taken over the restaurant, so we were already acquainted.

"They've got some really nice notebooks over here, Marley," Sienna said, waving me over to a shelf at the back of the shop. She managed to make it sound like we were there on a hunt for notebooks rather than information.

When I joined her by the display, she lowered her voice. "I'll see if Justine's in."

Even though I wasn't really looking for a notebook, a white one decorated with colorful sea creatures caught my eye. I picked it up off the shelf as Sienna poked her head through the open door at the back of the store.

"Hey, Justine," I heard her say. "Working on a story?"

A phone rang over by the checkout counter, and Charlene answered it. Still holding the notebook, I wandered over in Sienna's direction and joined her in the open doorway.

"I'm writing a piece about the ladies' night at the hardware store," Justine was saying.

Since the newspaper only had one issue per week—on Wednesdays—an edition hadn't been published since the event, or since the murder, for that matter.

"And Charlene's approved the use of the photo I took of you and Marley," she added, once she and I had exchanged greetings.

"Cool," Sienna said. "Have you written an article about the murder?"

I had to admit, Sienna was doing a good job of casually steering the conversation in the direction we wanted it to go.

"Yes." Justine craned her neck to peer around us and out the door. When she spoke again, her voice was barely above a whisper. "It's not quite what I wanted to write, but Charlene's the boss, so..." She shrugged.

"What was it she didn't want you writing about?" I asked.

"The many reasons why Wally Fowler might have been killed. More than one person in town had an ax to grind with him, but Charlene thinks detailing those grudges comes too close to accusing specific individuals, and she doesn't want to upset people. So instead I've got this bland article that doesn't say much more than the official statement we got from the sheriff's department."

"What does that statement say?"

"Not much. Just that Fowler's death has been ruled a murder and they're pursuing their inquiries. I can add in a bit of harmless background information, but it's not the juicy story I was hoping to write."

"Do you think his sister is a suspect?" Sienna asked.

I would have given her a thumbs up if I could have done so without Justine seeing.

The reporter picked up a pen and tapped it against her leg. "She stood the most to gain since she's inheriting Wally's money."

I made a mental note of that information.

"How come Wally inherited money and Vicky didn't?" Sienna asked.

"Maybe because they were half siblings," I guessed.

"Yes," Justine said. "They had the same mother but different fathers. Wally's inheritance came from his father's aunt."

"What if Vicky hated that he got so much money and she got nothing?" Sienna said. "That would give her even more reason to want him dead."

"But she's got an ironclad alibi," Justine said.

"Really?" I said. "I heard she was out of town, but I didn't know if that had been confirmed."

"Apparently there's security footage from a convenience store in Seattle to show she was in the city when her brother was killed. Besides, she's not very tall."

I latched on to that statement. "And the killer was?"

"According to my source at the sheriff's office. The killer had to be tall enough and strong enough to shove Fowler's head into a bowl while he was in the middle of pouring liquid nitrogen into it. And then the murderer held his head there until he died."

So Ivan's theory about the method of killing was correct.

"Did the sheriff and his deputies find any physical clues at the scene?" I asked.

"They may have, but I don't really know."

"Wasn't there someone else working with Wally and Vicky at the waffle house?" Sienna asked.

"Chester Burns," I supplied.

"He's tall and strong," Sienna said. "I've seen him around. He looks like a bouncer or something."

Justine dropped the pen back on the desk. "Chester has an alibi. He was with Vicky." She slid her chair closer to her computer. "Sorry, guys. I need to get back to work. It might not be the story of my dreams, but I still need to finish it."

"Sure," Sienna said, backing out of the room. "See you around."

Charlene was finishing up her phone call, so I took the notebook over to the counter and purchased it.

"So, what do you think?" Sienna asked once we were back in her car. "Was that helpful at all?"

"Somewhat. At least we now know Vicky and Chester's alibi was confirmed."

"So we can strike them off our suspect list."

"Sienna—"

She cut me off before I could get any further. "I know, I know. You don't want me getting involved in the murder investigation. But I helped out, didn't I?"

"You did," I conceded. "But I don't want you doing anything risky."

"You're not going to tell my mom, are you?"

"I don't think there's any reason to. You didn't do anything dangerous. Let's keep it that way."

Sienna smiled with relief as she pulled into my driveway. "No problem. Let me know if you make more progress?"

"Maybe," I said, not wanting to commit. I didn't think Patricia would appreciate me fueling her daughter's newfound enthusiasm for amateur sleuthing.

Sienna rolled her eyes, but she was smiling. "Don't worry so much, Marley. You're not corrupting me or anything. I'm just curious about what you might find out."

"I know." I got out of the car without making any promises. "See you this weekend, if not sooner."

She turned the car around and drove back along the driveway. I'd already noted that Brett's truck was gone. Judging by the time, he was probably on his way to meet up with Pedro. I was sorry I'd missed seeing him before he left, but hopefully he wouldn't be gone too long and we could spend the evening together.

To pass the time until his return, I curled up on the couch with Flapjack and the album of newspaper clippings I'd found in the attic, deciding to read them again, more closely this time. A few of the articles printed shortly after the disappearances of Tassy and Camelia were several paragraphs long, but most of the pieces were short and didn't take more than a minute or two to read. As more time passed after the disappearances with apparently no real leads, the news items became shorter and less frequent until they stopped altogether, at least in the album.

I hadn't learned anything new during the second pass of the articles and I was hungry for more information. Maybe tomorrow I could stop by the museum and talk to Nancy Welch. Even if the album contained all the news stories available about Camelia and Tassy, there could be other information of interest to me. I wanted to know more about Harry Sayers, what kind of guy he was. It didn't seem like there had been any other potential suspects, but maybe Nancy would know otherwise. It was worth asking, at least.

Setting the album aside, I took Bentley outside and let him run around on the beach until my face felt numb from the cold. When we headed back up toward the house, Brett's truck was coming along the driveway. Bentley raced over to greet him, and I followed at a slower pace, but not with any less enthusiasm.

"How did things go with Pedro?" I asked once I'd given Brett a kiss.

"Good. Things are a bit behind schedule with me and Dad both off work, but otherwise things are going as smoothly as could be expected in the circumstances." He put his hands to my cheeks. "You're freezing."

"Bentley and I were down on the beach, but I think I've had my fill of fresh air."

"How about we go out and grab a bite to eat?"

"That sounds like a good idea. Where do you want to go?"

"The pub?"

"Sure."

We took Bentley back inside and I set out food for him and Flapjack while Brett texted his mom with an update on the job sites. Hopefully getting the information to Frank would put his mind at ease and let him focus on recovering.

At the Windward Pub, we settled into a booth and ordered our meals without needing to check the menu. Brett asked for a cheeseburger and I requested a veggie burger, both with fries. It was open mic night and a young woman was up on the small stage by the bar, strumming an acoustic guitar and singing a lilting melody.

With the mellow music relaxing me, I looked across the table at Brett, unable to keep myself from smiling.

"What?" he asked, a smile of his own appearing.

"I'm just happy you're here with me."

He reached across the table and took my hand, running his thumb over my knuckles. "So am I." His smile faded. "I'll probably need to go back to Seattle, though, for a few days at least."

"I know. But for now I'm going to enjoy every minute that you're here."

"That's my plan too."

"Does Chloe know when she's going back to work?"

"Probably by Thursday. So I might head back on Wednesday. Gwen's there with Mom and Chloe right now," he said, referring to his aunt and Ray's wife. "But I don't know how long she can stay and I don't want my mom to be there on her own. She'd probably try to stay at the hospital twenty-four-seven."

"Remember, my offer still stands. If you need me in Seattle, I can make it happen."

A man's voice pulled our attention away from each other. The singer had left the stage and Chester had replaced her.

"Who knows what it's like to be used?" he said into the microphone, his speech slightly slurred.

More heads turned his way.

"That's all that ever happens to me," Chester continued. "I get used and used and used."

"That's Chester Burns," I whispered to Brett.

"Who?"

I remembered that Brett was out of the loop. He knew Wally had been killed, but he hadn't followed the story at all and we hadn't talked about it in any detail.

"But you know what?" Chester swayed to one side before regaining his equilibrium. "I'm done with getting used. I could take people down, you know that? I could. If the truth gets out, I'm not going down alone. You can count on that."

He dropped his chin to his chest. His shoulders shook and I realized he was crying.

The bartender hopped up onto the stage and took his arm. "I'll call you a cab, Chester. It's time you went home."

Chester mumbled to the bartender as they left the stage. I strained to hear his words but it was no use. The bartender patted Chester's shoulder and led him away.

A tall woman with short hair and an athletic build sat at a table a few feet away from me and Brett, her head turned to follow Chester's progress across the room. I'd seen her at The Flip Side before, but I couldn't recall her name. I gave up trying to remember it when I caught sight of two more familiar faces across the pub.

I raised a hand to wave, but Lisa and Ivan hadn't noticed me. I dropped my hand when I realized that Lisa looked upset. She grabbed her purse and jumped up from her seat. Ivan followed quickly after her, putting a hand to her back as they hurried for the door.

They left without catching sight of me or Brett.

"Lisa and Ivan were having dinner together? Have I missed something?" Brett asked.

"Yes." I was too distracted to elaborate.

"What's wrong?"

"I've got a lot to fill you in on." I spotted the waiter heading our way with our food. "After we've eaten?"

Brett agreed to wait and we chatted about other things as we ate our burgers, but Chester's slurred words and Lisa's unhappy face were never far from the forefront of my mind.

Chapter 15

On the way home from the Windward Pub later that evening, I brought Brett up to speed on everything—Lisa and Ivan's growing romance and Wally's murder. Once we were back at my place, I also showed him the diaries and newspaper clippings I'd found in the attic and told him about Camelia.

Seated on the couch beside me, he shook his head as he flipped carefully through the album of old newspaper articles. "I was only gone for a couple of days, but it seems like I've missed out on a lot."

"It's been an eventful week, that's for sure."

He shut the album and set it on the coffee table. "Have you been investigating?"

"The murder or Camelia's disappearance?"

"The murder."

"A little bit." When I saw a crease of concern appear between his eyebrows, I hurried to add, "Nothing dangerous. I talked to a reporter and Wally's sister. That's about it so far."

"Does Ray know?"

I hesitated. "I don't think he knows I've been asking questions, but it probably wouldn't surprise him."

"He probably wouldn't be impressed either."

"I know. To be honest, I'm trying to avoid him."

"He's got your best interest at heart, Marley."

"I know that too. But I think I test his patient nature and I don't want him getting annoyed with me."

"Hopefully there won't be any reason for that." Brett tugged me closer to him. "I'm sorry you saw Wally's body. It must have been gruesome."

I leaned against his chest. "It wasn't nice."

"I know there's no point in asking you to let the matter drop, especially when people you care about are in trouble, but I really don't want anything bad happening to you. Please keep me in the loop?"

"Of course."

"Even when I'm not here. I don't want you holding back with anything because you think I have enough on my mind."

"You do, though."

"I want to know what's going on with you, Marley. Always. No matter what."

My heart gave a happy squeeze. "Okay. No holding back." I sat up. "Before we go to bed, I want to show you what else I found in the attic."

"Dead rodents?"

"No, thank goodness. At least, not yet, and I hope it stays that way."

I led the way up to the attic to show Brett the old steamer trunk. He carried it down the rickety steps to the second floor for me and pushed it off to one side of the hallway, where it would stay for the time being. It needed a good dusting before it could go in my bedroom. That's where I wanted it, I'd decided. It would look great at the foot of my bed, and I could use it to store extra bedding or out-of-season clothing.

A short time later, we went to bed, Flapjack curled up near our feet and Bentley on his dog bed across the room. Comforted by Brett's presence, I drifted off to sleep soon after shutting my eyes. I slept soundly for an hour or so before waking up, chilled. I'd managed to kick the blankets off me in my sleep, leaving myself exposed to the cool air in the dark room. I was about to reach for the blankets when Brett tugged them up over me.

I rolled over onto my side so I could face him. "You're awake?" I said quietly. "I thought you'd be so tired that you'd sleep right through the night."

"I am tired, but my mind doesn't want to shut down."

I raised myself up on my elbow. "Are you thinking about your dad?"

He nodded as he fingered a lock of my hair.

"Wishing you were in Seattle with him?" I guessed.

"And here with you at the same time."

I shifted closer to him so I could snuggle up against him. He put an arm around me, his fingers tracing lazy circles over my back.

"He survived the worst part," I said. "He's going to be okay."

His fingers continue to skim over my back, but he didn't say anything. The room was silent around us, but I could almost hear the gears turning in his head.

"Brett?"

He let out a sigh that I felt more than heard, his chest falling beneath my cheek. "Was it hard for you? Being at the hospital the day my dad had his heart attack?"

It took me a moment to respond, my mind shifting back through difficult memories. "It would have been harder to *not* be there for you."

His hand stilled on my back. "I've always known that you're strong. You must be to have made it through what you did. I still don't know exactly what it must have been like for you after your family's accident, but I feel like I caught a glimpse. When I didn't know if my dad was going to make it or not, I caught a glimpse."

I breathed through the growing tightness in my chest, my eyes damp. "I wish you'd never had to."

"And I wish you'd never had to experience even half of what you did. That day with my dad... It's the worst thing I've ever been through." He moved his hand from my back to settle it on my hip. "I hope I haven't upset you by bringing this up. I know it's not something you talk about much."

I swallowed, trying to get rid of the lump that had formed in my throat. I rested my hand over his heart, the steady beat against my palm grounding me. "I've never talked about that part of it, learning about the accident, waiting in the hospital, the moment I knew Charlotte wouldn't pull through. Not in any detail, anyway. I just...can't." The word died away on my tongue, barely making it out as a whisper.

"And you don't have to." Brett kissed the top of my head. "Not unless you want to."

I closed my eyes, his heartbeat thrumming steadily against my palm, up through my arm, and into my own heart. My chest was still tight, but the pressure wasn't threatening to suffocate me, not like it had done so many times in the past.

"Maybe someday," I said quietly.

Brett placed a hand over mine where it rested on his chest. "I'll be here."

* * * *

I woke up first in the morning and was in the midst of scrambling eggs when Brett made his way into the kitchen, dressed in jeans and a gray Henley with the sleeves pushed up to his elbows. He came up behind me and put his arms around my waist as I dropped slices of bread into the toaster.

"Happy birthday," he said quietly into my ear.

I leaned back against his chest and smiled up at him. "Thank you."

"Shouldn't I be the one making breakfast for you this morning?" he asked before kissing the side of my head.

"I wanted to let you sleep." I turned off the heat beneath the pan of scrambled eggs. "Besides, you're the one going to work today, not me."

He was planning to work a few hours with Pedro and the rest of the crew at the house they were renovating.

"True." He released me. "But I can't go anywhere until I give you your birthday present."

"Present?" I turned away from the stove to face him.

"You sound surprised."

"I am. With all you've had going on, I'm amazed you even remembered my birthday."

"That's not something I'm going to forget." He picked up a small square box from the kitchen table. "And I've had this for more than a week already."

I eyed the box with curiosity. "What is it?"

"See for yourself."

He handed over the box and I lifted the lid. My jaw nearly dropped when I saw the seahorse pendant and its silver chain resting on the gray satin lining. The seahorse was outlined in silver, stones of different sizes and varying shades of blue making up the body, and a small but beautiful sapphire for the eye. It was the same vintage pendant I'd fallen in love with at the antiques shop two weeks earlier, the one I'd been so disappointed to see missing from the display case on my last visit to the store.

"But…" I was still too stunned to speak.

Brett grinned. "Surprised again?"

"I'll say. How did you know I wanted it?"

"I saw you admiring it that day we went into the antiques store together."

"I really wanted to buy it."

"Now you don't have to."

"No." I picked up the pendant, running my thumb over the smooth stones. "Thank you, Brett. I love it."

He took the necklace out of my hand and stepped behind me. I lifted my hair as he fastened the silver chain around my neck.

"It's perfect for you," he said, his fingers brushing against the back of my neck, sending a pleasant shiver down my spine. "And not just because you love seahorses. All the shades of blue go with your eyes."

I fingered the pendant again. "My eyes are more dull gray than blue."

His arms snaked around my waist from behind and he kissed the side of my neck. "There's nothing dull about them. They're like the ocean. Sometimes stormy gray, sometimes blue, and always full of depth."

I smiled as I turned to face him, his arms still around me. "I don't know about that, but you definitely know how to charm me."

He grinned, sending my stomach into a happy back flip. I loved that he still had that effect on me.

"I mean every word," he assured me.

"I know you do. Thank you."

I kissed him, but not for as long as I would have liked. The toast popped out of the toaster and I realized the eggs would get cold if we didn't eat them soon.

We enjoyed a leisurely breakfast before Brett left for the day. I planned to head into town to run some errands, but I had some time to kill first. Most of the shops wouldn't be open for a while yet. I was thinking about going for a long run and leaving my errands until later in the morning when I heard footsteps on the back porch.

Sienna waved at me through the French doors and I hurried to unlock them so she could come inside. The sun was still low in the sky and when I opened the door the wintry air that wafted into the house had a sharp bite to it.

"Brrr." Sienna shivered as she stepped inside. "Morning."

"Morning," I returned as I shut the door to keep out any more of the icy draft. "What brings you by so early? Shouldn't you be on your way to school?"

Sienna crouched down to greet Bentley and Flapjack as they approached, one with tail wagging and the other purring. "Not quite yet, and I didn't want to have to wait all day to tell you about my investigating."

"Investigating?" I echoed the word with apprehension. "What have you been up to, Sienna?"

Her eyes lit up as she spied the pendant hanging around my neck. "Wow. That's a gorgeous necklace. Is it new?"

I couldn't help but smile. "Brett gave it to me this morning. It's a birthday present."

"Happy birthday! I didn't know it was today."

I forced my thoughts back on track. "Sienna…"

"Oh, right. Don't freak out, okay?" She shrugged out of her black down jacket and hung it over the back of a kitchen chair.

"Now I'm scared," I said, my apprehension growing.

"Seriously, don't be. All I did was go through the Hansfields' garbage."

I stared at her. "What? When?"

"Last night." She grinned, practically bubbling with excitement. "Remember how we decided the killer might have discarded their gloves somewhere away from the crime scene?"

"I remember."

"So even though Mrs. Hansfield might be too short to have killed Wally, I thought it would be a good idea to check her garbage anyway, just in case."

I put my hands to my face. "Please tell me you didn't break into her house."

"Of course I didn't. It's garbage day today, so I figured they'd probably put the garbage out yesterday, and they did. It was in the alley, so I went after dark and poked around." She wrinkled her nose. "It was kind of disgusting, but I guess investigating crime is dirty work sometimes."

I groaned as I let my hands fall from my face. "You were alone in a dark alley, poking through the garbage of a possible murderer?"

"I wasn't alone. I took Logan with me."

Logan was her former boyfriend, now relegated to the friend zone.

"Your mom's going to kill me," I said with another groan.

"Not if she doesn't find out."

"She's my friend," I reminded her.

"I am too, aren't I?" Again, she whipped out her version of sad puppy-dog eyes.

"Of course, which is exactly why I don't want anything bad happening to you."

"Nothing bad *will* happen. Don't you want to know what I found?"

"Gloves?"

"No. Something else." She retrieved a rumpled, folded piece of paper from the pocket of her jacket.

As she unfolded it, I saw that it was stained with something that looked like coffee, and something else I couldn't—and didn't particularly want to—identify.

"Sorry. It smells a bit." Sienna handed over the paper. "It should have been in the recycling, not the garbage." She shook her head.

I took the paper between my fingertips, trying to avoid the stains. It was a typewritten letter with the occasional word crossed out and replaced with a new one in red ink. I skimmed through the letter, realizing it was a draft that Glo had written to the residents of Wildwood Cove. In the letter, she requested that everyone boycott the Waffle Kingdom because Wally Fowler was a scourge on the community. She went on to say that he'd already caused too much devastation in the lives of locals and shouldn't be permitted to create any further problems.

When I'd finished reading the letter, my gaze traveled to the top of the page. It was dated the day of Wally's death.

"Interesting, right?" Sienna said.

"It is," I conceded, my thoughts swirling. "It's proof that Mrs. Hansfield really didn't want Wally in Wildwood Cove."

"And maybe she thought a letter wasn't enough," Sienna theorized. "So she decided to get rid of him herself."

"A definite possibility. Although there's still the fact that she's much shorter than Wally."

Sienna squished her lips to one side. "That's true. So my search was pointless?"

"Not necessarily." I held up the letter. "This tells us that Mrs. Hansfield should still stay on the suspect list, at least for the time being. Maybe she had a taller accomplice."

Sienna's eyes widened. "Mr. Hansfield!"

I considered that idea. The only time I could remember seeing Glo's husband was outside the elementary school during the craft fair. But that brief look was enough to know that he was at least six feet tall and broad shouldered. Plenty tall enough and strong enough to overpower Wally, especially if Wally was taken by surprise.

"You could be on to something there," I said.

Sienna's eyes brightened. "So what do we do next? Maybe I could ask Bailey some subtle questions about her dad."

"Sienna, no. We don't want anyone knowing we're looking at him as a suspect. And it's best not to involve Bailey."

It didn't escape me that I'd started to use "we" when talking about the investigation. I wanted to keep Sienna out of it for her own safety, but judging by her actions the night before, I'd be fighting a losing battle.

She frowned. "We have to do something. What if the police don't have any suspects? They could be working on this case forever without getting anywhere."

"They have suspects," I said. "That's kind of the problem."

"What do you mean?"

"Ivan and Lisa are under suspicion."

"But that's crazy!"

"To you and me it is. Not so much to the sheriff and his deputies."

"All the more reason to get this case solved," she said with more determination than ever.

I realized I'd probably made a mistake by letting her in on Ivan and Lisa's peril. She barely knew Lisa, but she'd worked at The Flip Side for several months now and had a good deal of affection for Ivan. There was no way she'd give up on sleuthing now. Not that she would have before.

Sighing, I realized that I really did have a sidekick now. There was no way around it, so I'd have to do my best to keep her safe.

Chapter 16

After Sienna left for school—with a promise that she wouldn't question Bailey about anything to do with Wally's murder—I set off on my run, taking Bentley with me. I didn't go as far as I'd originally planned, too eager to get to town now that I had a new angle to investigate. Before leaving, Sienna had told me where the Hansfields lived, and it was only a few houses away from Leigh's place. I was hoping Leigh might know something about her neighbors that would be helpful. It was a long shot, maybe, but worth asking about.

Once I'd showered and dressed after my run, my seahorse necklace back on, I wasted no time heading into town. My first stop was at a business on Glover Street. The talk I'd had with Brett in the night had left me more in love with him than ever. It had also led me to a decision, one I had no doubts about.

After leaving Glover Street, I headed for Swallow Drive, where I parked in front of the two-story blue-gray house where Leigh lived with her husband and their three daughters. When I knocked on the door, I was relieved to find that Leigh was home, although she was wearing a white robe and slippers, her bleached-blond hair slightly frizzy.

"Oh, hey, Marley. What brings you by?"

"I was hoping to talk to you about something. I didn't wake you, did I?"

She laughed and ushered me into the house. "No, I've been up for ages, but Greg took the girls to school today so I thought I'd make the most of my day off by lazing about with a cup of coffee and a good book."

"Sorry to disturb you."

"Don't be silly. I'm glad to have company. Let me make you a cup of tea."

I joined her in the kitchen, where she filled an electric kettle with water. "So what is it you wanted to talk about? Is anything wrong?"

"I guess you could say so." I told her about the fact that Ivan and Lisa were on the sheriff's radar in connection with Wally's murder.

A frown appeared on her face as I talked, and her hazel eyes took on a hard glint. "But Lisa's a sweetheart and Ivan… People don't understand what a good man he is."

I agreed with her statement.

"You must be trying to help them," Leigh said as steam poured out of the kettle. "So what can I do?"

"I was hoping you could tell me a bit about the Hansfields."

"Glo and Forrest?"

"Is that her husband's name?"

Leigh nodded and handed me a mug of orange pekoe tea. "I wouldn't say we're friends with the family, but we're neighborly enough, and we've lived up the street from them since we moved into this place twelve years ago."

She refilled her coffee mug and led me over to the kitchen table, where a paperback thriller with a creased spine lay next to a stack of what looked like children's drawings, a scattering of pencil crayons, a green binder stuffed with papers, and an assortment of paperclips and hair elastics.

"Sorry about the mess," she said, sweeping everything over to one side of the table. "What do you want to know about the Hansfields? Are they involved in Wally's murder somehow?"

"Would it surprise you if they were?" I asked.

"Yes. For sure. They've always seemed nice enough. A little bit stuffy, perhaps, but not too bad. Glo's always volunteering for some committee or charity project and she always says hello when we see each other. That said, I wouldn't be the first person to be completely shocked to find out that their neighbor's a murderer."

"I don't *know* that they're involved," I said. "But Glo certainly didn't want Wally Fowler back in Wildwood Cove."

"Understandable," Leigh said after taking a sip of coffee. "You know the story there?"

"Lisa filled me in about Lizzie. And there's this." I pulled the crumpled paper out of my pocket and passed it to Leigh.

She wrinkled her nose as she took it from me. "Did you fish this out of a dumpster or something?"

"You're not too far off," I said.

Leigh looked at the paper for only a second or two before saying, "Ah, this."

"You've seen it before?"

"No, but I knew Glo planned to appeal to the community to boycott the waffle house. I was on board, of course. I wasn't about to set foot in the place. Wally was hoping to run you out of business and leave the rest of us without jobs."

"I'd like to think he wouldn't have succeeded."

"He wouldn't have," Leigh said with conviction. "But I still wouldn't have gone near his Waffle Kingdom." She shook her head. "What a ridiculous name. And calling himself the Waffle King! I bet he didn't even know how to make a waffle." She sobered. "I guess I shouldn't be speaking ill of the dead, but that man…"

"I know," I said, understanding and sharing her feelings. "How did you find out about Glo's plan to get everyone to boycott the waffle house?"

"Her cousin Jill told me about it. She's been to The Flip Side a few times. She's tall and muscular with short, dark hair. She's a bodybuilder, I think."

"I know who you mean," I said, dots connecting in my mind. "I saw her at the Windward Pub last night."

"Anyway, I ran into Jill at the grocery store last week. She told me about Glo's plans. She was ready to throw her full support behind the boycott, and I assured her she could count on me to steer clear of the waffle house too." She clasped her hands around her coffee mug. "Do you really think Glo could be involved in the murder? That would be another sad layer to an already tragic story."

"It would, and at the moment I'm just trying to leave no stone unturned. There's actually a problem with the theory of her being the killer." I explained how the murderer was likely taller than Glo. "So I was wondering about her husband. Does he strike you as the vengeful type? Maybe the type to do anything to protect his wife?"

Leigh opened her mouth to speak, and then closed it again, a line forming across her forehead.

"What is it?" I pressed.

"There was an incident right after Wally moved back to town."

"What kind of incident?"

"Apparently Forrest was at the Windward Pub with some friends when Wally came strutting in. Forrest had had a couple of drinks and ended up shoving Wally up against the wall and getting in his face. His friends pulled him off Wally and managed to calm him down without too much trouble, but from what I heard, Forrest was spitting mad that Wally was back and dredging up terrible memories for his wife."

"So he's tall enough and angry enough to be a killer. The question is did he have the opportunity?"

"I really hope he and Glo aren't involved. That would be terrible for their daughter."

"It would," I agreed, my heart squeezing as I remembered Bailey's sad eyes.

I didn't want her to have a killer as a parent, but I needed to find out the truth, no matter what it was.

"How much do you know about Adam Silvester?" I asked. "Greg mentioned that Kayla's in the same class as his daughter."

"That's right, but why do you want to know about Adam? He's not involved in the murder, is he?"

"I don't know, but he sure didn't seem happy with Wally the other day."

Leigh shook her head. "I can't believe he'd hurt anyone. He seems like such a nice man."

"Maybe he is. Greg mentioned that Adam has had some financial problems, so it's possible that's what had him looking unhappy." I still didn't believe that explanation, but I couldn't disprove it.

"That's more likely it." Leigh seemed relieved by that idea. "His daughter has a problem with her leg or hip and needs surgery to fix it, but Adam's a single dad and doesn't have a lot of money. I heard the bank turned him down when he tried to get a loan."

"That does sound like a stressful situation. Maybe the town could help out somehow?"

"A couple of the mothers at school have been tossing around ideas for a fundraiser, so it looks like that might happen. I'm not sure we could raise anything close to the amount Adam needs, but every bit will probably help."

Leigh didn't have any further information about Adam and I left her place soon after finishing my tea. I returned to Glover Street for a quick stop before parking my car across the street from the grocery store on Main Street. Instead of getting out into the cold right away, I checked my phone and found happy birthday text messages from my mom and Brett's sister, Chloe. I responded to the messages and immediately received a new one from Chloe.

Maybe Brett's already told you this, but our dad will be released from the hospital tomorrow!

I was surprised but pleased to read that news.

Already? That's great! I wrote back.

I exchanged a few more texts with Chloe before sending one to Brett.

I heard the good news about your dad! Miss you!

The warmth inside my car was slowly seeping away, the cold creeping in to replace it, so I tucked my phone into my tote bag and decided to get on with my grocery shopping. I'd made my way through half the store before I paused by the dairy products and checked my phone again. Brett had replied to my text message, clearly excited that his dad would be home soon.

I made some arrangements with my mom. I'll fill you in later, he added.

It was getting close to noon and I knew the house he was working on was just around the corner, so I asked him if he wanted me to bring him some lunch.

An extra chance to see you? Definitely, he replied.

Smiling from the message and the news about Frank, I made a stop at the deli counter to get two sandwiches before paying for my groceries. I left all my purchases except for the sandwiches in the back of my car and made the short trip to Brett's job site on foot. I texted him to let him know I'd arrived, and he appeared from around the back of the house a moment later.

"It's such good news about your dad," I said, giving him a hug and a kiss. "I thought he might be in the hospital for ages."

"So did I, but apparently he's doing well enough to come home. He's still got a lot of rehabilitation ahead of him, but at least he'll be here."

We sat in Brett's truck while we ate our sandwiches, bundled up in our jackets to keep warm.

"I'm going to drive to Seattle first thing in the morning," Brett said after he'd eaten a big bite of his sandwich. "Once Dad's released from the hospital, I'll drive everyone back home."

I squeezed his hand. "It'll be good to see your dad again, as soon as he's up to having a visitor."

When we'd finished eating, Brett grinned at me, and I realized that I'd pulled the seahorse pendant out from beneath my jacket and was fingering it again.

"I'm glad you like it," he said.

"I love it. Even more so because it's a reminder of you that I can keep close to me."

He kissed me then and afterward I rested my head on his shoulder. "I guess you have to get back to work."

"I should. And you should get somewhere warm so you don't freeze."

"Mmm," I said without moving.

"Any plans for the afternoon?"

"I'm going to take my groceries home and then I think I'll head over to the museum to see Nancy Welch."

"To ask about Camelia?"

"And Tassy James."

"I hope she has some information for you."

"Me too."

I let him head back into the house to rejoin his crew. I walked briskly back to my car but slowed to a near stop when I was a few strides away from it. Glo was walking along the sidewalk in my direction, her steps hurried, her features pulled down by a frown that bordered on a scowl. Justine was following her, half a step behind, talking nonstop, although I couldn't hear her words at first. As they drew closer, I was able to catch what she was saying.

"But your story is such a compelling one," she told Glo, who didn't slow her steps in the least. "I bet if I pitch it to Charlene, she'd give me the green light."

Glo stopped abruptly and Justine had to skirt to the side to avoid a collision with her.

"I don't want to talk about that man." Her voice trembled with emotion.

"But he's considered a victim now, and yet we both know that the real victims are you, your sister, and maybe even Wally's sister and Chester."

"Vicky and Chester?" Rage clouded Glo's face. "They *chose* to follow him here, to help him set up that restaurant so he could insinuate his way back into this community where he didn't belong. They aren't victims; they're accomplices!"

"I'm not sure I'd go that far," Justine said.

"Well, I would! And now they're covering for each other!"

Justine stayed glued to her side. "What do you mean?"

"You're the reporter. You figure it out."

I edged around the front of my car, heading for the driver's side door as Glo stormed away from Justine, stepping off the curb behind my hatchback to cross the street. Justine hurried after her, apparently undeterred by Glo's ire.

I heard the roar of an engine and saw a dark SUV hurtling down the street. I glanced at the two women, but Glo was so caught up in her emotions that she wasn't paying attention to her surroundings, and Justine was fixated on Glo. As they stepped out from between the parked cars, the SUV gained speed. It barreled along the middle of the street, and then swerved our way. Fueled by a burst of adrenaline, I yelled in warning and threw myself toward the two women as the SUV rushed at us, a menacing, dark shape on a mission to kill.

Chapter 17

Glo screamed in my ear as I crashed into her, sending us both slamming into the hood of a parked van. My elbow hit metal and my head knocked against Glo's shoulder. Tires squealed and the SUV thundered past, mere inches away from me. My feet were tangled up with Glo's, so it took me a second to find my balance and push myself away from the hood of the van. I peered up the street, but by then the SUV had disappeared around the corner.

Glo was still slumped against the van, a hand to her throat, her eyes wide with shock. She'd taken the worst of my tackle. Justine had been knocked backward and had ended up sitting on the curb, where she remained.

"Are you okay?" I asked them as I rubbed the side of my head where it had hit Glo's shoulder.

Glo focused her stunned eyes on me. "Yes…yes, I'm all right."

"Justine?" I asked.

She blinked, and then nodded. I extended a hand to her and helped her to her feet.

A woman hurried out of a nearby shoe store at the same time as a man jogged across the street toward us.

"What on earth happened?" the woman asked.

"Is everyone okay?" The man directed the question at all of us.

"We're okay," I answered. "Did anyone see the driver or get the license number?"

"I didn't see anything," Glo said, a faint tremble in her voice.

"All I saw was a dark SUV." The man pulled a cellphone out of his pocket. "I'm going to call 9-1-1. This should be reported."

"I didn't see much of anything," the woman from the shop told me. "I just heard a scream and squealing tires." She put a hand on Glo's arm. "You're looking pale, dear. Why don't you come in my shop and sit down for a few minutes."

"I…think that would be a good idea, thank you." Glo followed the woman into the shoe store.

Justine stood on the sidewalk now, and I went over to join her.

"No one got a look at the driver?" she said, all the shock gone from her expression.

"No, not really. I only caught a brief glimpse."

"So you can't identify them?" It sounded like her reporter instincts were kicking in. Like she was already putting a news story together in her head.

"No. I got the impression it was a man behind the wheel, but I can't be sure." I rubbed my arms, only then realizing that I was chilled and a little on the shaky side. At least my head wasn't quite so sore now.

Three more witnesses had converged on the scene, but none of them could add to what little we knew about what had happened. I thought about sitting in my car until someone from the sheriff's department arrived, but I wanted to go somewhere warmer so I could hopefully stop shivering. I asked Justine if she wanted to join me down the street at Johnny's Juice Hut, and she agreed. It was only a few doors down, and the large front window would allow us to watch for the arrival of the authorities.

I ordered a hot bubble tea to help warm me up and Justine got herself a coffee with cream and sugar. At first I attempted to make conversation with Justine, but she was busy tapping away at her phone between sips of coffee. After a few monosyllabic responses to my questions, I gave up and watched the street through the window as I sipped at my bubble tea.

When Ray or one of his deputies arrived, I wouldn't be able to tell them much, but I was already sorting through possible theories in my mind. I didn't doubt for a single second that the SUV's run at us was intentional. The driver had gunned the engine as soon as Glo stepped out from between the parked cars, and it had changed its course to come straight for her.

Or me.

That thought started me shivering again. I took a long drink of my bubble tea and chewed on one of the tapioca pearls. The SUV could have been aiming for me, but why? I'd asked a few questions since Wally's murder, but not all that many, and the driver couldn't have been Justine, and it definitely wasn't Leigh.

No, it seemed more likely that Glo was the intended victim. But again, *why?*

Did somebody know or strongly suspect that she was involved in Wally's death and was seeking revenge? The only people I could think of who might want to do that were Vicky and Chester, and I wasn't all that sure about Vicky. She was upset by her brother's murder, but she didn't strike me as devastated or consumed by a need for vengeance. As for Chester, I didn't know enough about him to come to any conclusions.

If the driver didn't suspect Glo of being involved in Wally's death, then why try to run her down?

I couldn't think of a reason. That didn't mean there wasn't one, but I was clueless.

By the time a sheriff's department cruiser crawled along the street, I'd finished my bubble tea and was on my way out the door of Johnny's Juice Hut, Justine still sitting inside, texting from her smartphone.

I waved to Deputy Devereaux, and he pulled into a free space by the curb. I talked to him for a few minutes, outlining what had happened and providing him with what little information I could. The man who'd rushed over to see if we were all right got out of a truck parked halfway down the street and came over to talk with Devereaux. The deputy told me I was welcome to leave, but instead of getting into my car, I entered the shoe store, looking for Glo. She was sitting on one of the many chairs set out for customers to use while trying on shoes. The shopkeeper was helping another woman near the back of the store, so I took the opportunity to approach Glo.

"How are you feeling now?" I asked.

"Much better. And thank you for pushing me out of the way. I'm afraid I was too shaken up earlier to acknowledge what you did."

"You're welcome. I'm glad you weren't hurt." I glanced out the shop window and was relieved to see that Deputy Devereaux was still occupied, now speaking with Justine. "There's a deputy here who will probably want to talk to you."

Glo stood and smoothed a hand over her pencil skirt. "I don't think there's much I can tell him, but I'll do my best."

I was far too curious to hold back my next question. "What did you mean when you told Justine that Vicky and Chester are covering for each other?"

She frowned and her eyes narrowed. "Vicky claimed Chester was with her in Seattle when Wally was killed, but I saw the light on in his apartment that night and a short time later it was off."

"So you don't think he was with Vicky," I concluded.

"No, I don't." She strode toward the shop door.

I hurried to catch up with her. "Do you have any idea who might have wanted to run you down?"

"Surely the driver wasn't trying to run me down. Whoever it was, they were probably on their phone or something. Distracted drivers are all over the roads these days."

"I'm not so sure," I said, opening the door and holding it for her. "It looked to me like the driver was aiming for you."

Glo's face paled. "Nonsense. Why would anyone do that?"

"Maybe someone has a grudge against you?"

"Like I said, nonsense."

"Could it have something to do with Wally Fowler? Maybe someone close to him is upset with you."

Fear flashed in her eyes and her face flushed, but she quickly schooled her features. "I have no idea what you're talking about." Without another word, she turned her back on me and approached Deputy Devereaux.

I watched her for a moment, but then set off for home, certain that she'd lied to me.

* * * *

Bentley and Flapjack were happy to see me when I got home, but I didn't stay there for long. I let them out in the yard while I put my groceries away, and then I called them inside and returned to my car. I still wanted to pay a visit to the museum, and a quick check of its website told me that it would only remain open until four o'clock.

The museum was housed in what was once a private residence. The cute bungalow had white siding, bright blue shutters, and a covered porch. When I stepped inside, a bell tinkled above the door and the hardwood floors creaked beneath my feet. To my right was a counter with an unoccupied chair behind it. To my left an open door led to a room filled with display cases. Straight ahead of me another door was shut all but a crack.

Before I could ring the bell sitting on the counter, the door ahead of me opened and a woman emerged into the foyer. She had straight gray hair cut to chin-length and wore a dark blue cable-knit sweater with her gray pants. She smiled warmly when she saw me, and hurried forward to greet me.

"Hello. Welcome to the museum. What can I do for you?"

"Are you Nancy Welch?" I asked.

"I am," she confirmed.

"I'm Marley McKinney. I'm looking for some historical information and my friend Lisa suggested I come see you."

"If it relates to the town's history, then she definitely sent you to the right place. What is it you're interested in?"

"Several decades ago, two teenage girls went missing from Wildwood Cove."

"Ah, yes." Nancy nodded. "Tassy James and Camelia Winslow. Both cases unsolved."

"Camelia Winslow was my grandmother's cousin's wife's older sister." I thought back on what I'd said. "Does that sound complicated?"

"Not to someone like me who spends a lot of time on genealogy." She smiled. "You're the owner of the pancake house, right?"

"That's right."

"And you inherited Jimmy Coulson's house by the beach."

"Right again. Did you know Jimmy?"

"Oh, yes. He was a good man, and always lots of fun."

I smiled. "He was."

"I knew his wife, Grace, too, although not well. You're looking for information on the two disappearances?"

I confirmed that I was and explained what had sparked my interest.

"Why don't we get you set up at one of our computers?" she suggested. "We've digitized the archives of the local paper, so you can search through those, if you'd like."

"That sounds great. I'm hoping to find some articles that aren't in Grace's album."

Nancy led me to a small back room with two computer stations along one wall and a table and chairs taking up the rest of the space. Within a couple of minutes, she had me sitting at one of the computers with access to the digitized newspaper archives at my fingertips. When a phone rang elsewhere in the museum, she excused herself and left me to my research, telling me to let her know if I had any questions or needed assistance.

I sat there and searched through the archives for nearly an hour before sitting back and rubbing a hand across my eyes. Grace had been thorough about collecting clippings for her scrapbook, so I didn't turn up much that I hadn't seen before. I only came across two short articles that I hadn't already read. One stated that the sheriff had spoken to Harry Sayers about the two disappearances, but the authorities didn't believe he was involved. The second item was more of an anniversary piece published five years after the girls had disappeared. It simply reiterated the facts I already knew and stated that the cases remained unsolved at the time. Unfortunately, that hadn't changed over the ensuing decades.

A hint of disappointment wriggled its way into my mind. I tried to push it aside. I'd known before ever arriving at the museum that I wasn't likely to find out more than I already knew. If the sheriff's department couldn't solve the cases when they occurred, there was no reason to think I could uncover some vital clue all these years later simply by spending an hour at a computer.

Gathering up my tote bag, I wandered out to the front of the museum and found Nancy sitting behind the counter in the foyer, removing stacks of glossy brochures from a cardboard box.

She looked up as I approached. "Did you find what you were looking for?"

"Not much more than I already knew, unfortunately."

She gave me a sympathetic smile. "The sheriff never had much to go on. At least, that's what he wanted people to think."

"What do you mean?" I asked, my interest piqued.

"It was all before my time," Nancy said. "Not by too much, though, so I heard the stories from my parents and others around town while growing up. Most people believed a young man named Harry Sayers had something to do with the disappearances."

"I read a bit about him. He was the mayor's son. Camelia mentioned him in her diaries too. She was in love with him."

Nancy nodded. "I understand they were seen together a fair bit in the weeks before she disappeared. And the other girl worked as a maid for his family, so he was connected to both girls."

"But the sheriff didn't think he was involved."

"No." She hesitated. "Understand, these are rumors, rather than historical facts, but the sheriff and the mayor were buddies. A lot of people believed that even if Harry was involved, nothing would have come of it. The mayor wouldn't have wanted his family's reputation tarnished, and that could have influenced the sheriff's investigation, or lack thereof."

"So it really could have been Harry who was responsible."

"It's possible, and a lot of people sure seem to believe it."

"So what happened to Harry? He went on living his life like nothing had happened?"

"That's the thing. Nobody quite knows what happened to him. A week or so after Camelia's disappearance, he took off. Nobody knows where he went and he wasn't heard from again. For most of the townsfolk, that solidified his guilt in their minds."

I thought about that for a second. "There was never any speculation that he might have been a victim too?"

She shook her head. "He packed up his clothes and other belongings before he took off. There was never much doubt that he left voluntarily. Nobody was really surprised. Most people had him pegged as a murderer. Guilty or innocent, life wouldn't have been easy for him here."

It sounded as though the popular opinion was probably accurate and Harry was behind both disappearances, but it bugged me that I couldn't be absolutely positive about that.

"Is there anyone in town who was alive back then, who might remember something?" I asked.

"There is," Nancy replied. "Harry Sayers had four younger siblings. The youngest is still living here in Wildwood Cove. Her name's Crenshaw now. Joan Crenshaw."

Chapter 18

"Joan Crenshaw?" I echoed. "She's my friend's neighbor!"

"Then you know where to find her," Nancy said with a smile. The expression faded from her face a second later. "Of course, I don't know how she'll feel about digging up the past. I've never known her to talk about Harry or the missing girls. Mind you, I don't know her terribly well, so that might be why."

"I don't want to upset her, but I can at least ask if she's willing to talk about it," I decided.

I thanked Nancy for her help and left her to close up the museum for the day. The light was fading from the sky by the time I pulled away in my car. The temperature was supposed to dip down close to the freezing point that night, even on the coast, and from the feel of the air, it was well on its way there. I cranked up the heat in my car and drove to Lisa's neighborhood. I parked in front of Joan Crenshaw's house and knocked on the door, but only received excited barking in response. Joan's terrier, Angel, jumped up on the back of the couch to look out the living room window at me, still yapping.

After calling out a hello to the terrier, I gave up and returned to my car. There was no point in paying a visit to Lisa's house—she wouldn't be off work quite yet—so I headed for home, deciding to stop by Joan's house again in a day or two.

Once I'd greeted the animals and had played a short game of fetch with Bentley in the darkening yard, I shed my outerwear and rubbed my chilled hands to warm them up. I put on the kettle, planning to make hot chocolate, before fishing my phone out of my tote bag. I hadn't looked at it for hours and was surprised that I'd received several texts from Brett and had missed three calls from him. I'd left my phone on vibrate and hadn't heard it while it sat deep in my bag.

All of the texts were similar, asking if I was okay and requesting that I call him. The string of messages grew increasingly frantic. I was puzzled for only a second or two before I realized that he must have heard about the incident in town with the SUV. I was about to select his number when his picture flashed on the screen of my buzzing phone.

"I was about to call you," I said when I answered.

"Marley. Thank God. I've been trying to get hold of you for an hour." He sounded rattled. "I heard a car tried to run people down in town. I couldn't get any details, other than the fact that you were there and maybe someone was hurt. Then you weren't answering my texts or my calls."

"I'm okay, Brett."

"I drove to your place but you weren't there, so I went to the museum, but it's closed." He wasn't any less agitated.

"Brett, relax."

"I can't relax. I thought you might have been hurt!"

Just in time, I managed to stop myself from raising my voice to match his. "Okay, but I'm fine," I said calmly. "I promise. I'm sorry I didn't call you after it happened. Sometimes I forget how fast news travels in this town. But I wasn't hurt. No one was, other than maybe a bump or two. I saw the SUV coming and pushed Glo Hansfield and Justine Welch out of the way. Nobody was hit."

I heard him let out a breath and could picture him running a hand through his hair.

"I'm sorry you were scared," I said, knowing his reaction stemmed from the still-fresh fear for his dad. "I should have called."

"I didn't mean to freak out like that." Now he sounded more weary than upset.

"It's okay. Where are you?"

"Parked outside the museum. Can I come over to your place?"

"Of course. I was hoping you would."

He told me he'd see me in a few minutes, and then we ended the call. I busied myself with feeding Bentley and Flapjack, anxious for Brett to arrive. I hated that he'd been so worried and wished I'd thought to call him, or at least check my phone sometime in the past couple of hours.

"What's done is done, right?" I said to Flapjack as I set down his food dish in the laundry room, safely away from Bentley.

The tabby ignored me, digging into his dinner with a contented swish of his tail.

When I heard footsteps on the back porch, I hurried to meet Brett at the door. I barely had it shut behind him when he pulled me into a hug. He was cold to the touch, bringing in a blast of frosty air with him, but I didn't care.

"I'm sorry," he said.

"Don't be."

"I overreacted."

I stepped back, and Bentley took the opportunity to nose his way between us.

"And I should have called or checked my phone," I said as Brett gave his dog a one-armed hug and a scratch on the head. "So why don't we say we're even and move on?"

He managed a smile, although not with its usual brightness. "All right." He ran a hand down his face. "I meant to buy you flowers. And I should be taking you out for dinner."

"You already bought me a present and we were out for dinner last night."

"But it's your birthday."

"And all I really want is a quiet evening in with you."

"Are you sure?"

"Positive." I brushed white powder from his cheek. "Plaster dust?"

"Most likely," he said, and I noticed that his shoulders were finally relaxing. "I should take a shower."

I took his jacket as he shrugged out of it. "Go ahead. I'm about to make myself some hot chocolate. Do you want any?"

He declined and disappeared upstairs with Bentley at his heels.

I took some homemade soup out of the freezer to thaw and made myself a mug of hot chocolate. Then I curled up on the couch with Flapjack on my lap. While stroking the tabby's orange fur and sipping my drink, I tried to get my thoughts in order. Although I was eager to see if Joan would talk to me about her brother and the long-ago disappearances, I couldn't forget that Ivan and Lisa still had a cloud of suspicion hanging over their heads.

As frustrating as it was to admit to myself, I hadn't managed to do much—if anything—to help them. I was certain that Glo was guilty of something involving Wally, but she didn't fit the physical profile of his killer, and I didn't have any evidence to tie her husband or anyone else to the crime. It was tempting to do as Sienna had suggested and approach Bailey to see what information she might have about her parents' connection to the murder, but I still wasn't keen on involving her.

Maybe I could approach Mr. Hansfield and get some information out of him, but I wasn't sure how to go about that in a way that wouldn't make him immediately suspicious. I was a complete stranger to him, after all. I might be able to come up with another way to find out more about him, including his whereabouts on the night of the murder, but I'd have to think about it some more first.

I hadn't forgotten about Chester, and now I knew there was a chance he wasn't in Seattle with Vicky at the time of the murder. Justine had mentioned that Vicky was captured on the convenience store's surveillance footage, but what about Chester? Vicky and Chester were romantically involved, so I had to wonder if Glo was right. Would Vicky cover for Chester even if she knew he'd killed her brother?

There were still so many question marks in my mind. I needed to find more answers before Ivan or Lisa ended up under arrest. I didn't know if Ray had enough evidence to arrest either of them, but I wasn't keen to wait around to find out. Somehow I needed to find out more about the people on my suspect list.

With my hot chocolate long finished, I shifted Flapjack from my lap and got up to stretch. More than half an hour had passed since Brett had gone upstairs for a shower, and he had yet to reappear. Not hearing any sounds of movement coming from above, I decided to go in search of him. The second floor bathroom was empty, so I moved on to my bedroom. As soon as I stepped through the doorway, Bentley jumped up and trotted over to greet me. Brett, on the other hand, didn't stir. He was sprawled out on the bed, fully dressed, his hair damp from his shower, sound asleep.

I approached quietly, my heart aching at the sight of him sleeping. I'd known he was tired, but clearly he was more exhausted than I'd realized. Although tempted to touch him, I didn't want to disturb him. Being careful not to make too much noise, I switched off the overhead light and turned on the lamp on the dresser instead. I fetched my book from the bedside table and curled up on the window seat, wanting to stay close to Brett while he slept. Bentley settled back down on his dog bed and I read three chapters before I heard movement from across the room.

I set down my book and smiled as Brett sat up on the bed, scrubbing a hand down his face.

He blinked against the lamplight. "Marley?" He glanced at the bedside clock. "I fell asleep? I only meant to put my head down for five minutes."

"Clearly you needed more than five minutes."

"I guess so, but I didn't want to fall asleep on your birthday."

I left the window seat to sit next to him on the edge of the bed. "You're here. That's all I need to be happy. Speaking of which…" I wriggled my hand into the pocket of my jeans. "I have something for you."

My fingers closed around the small metal object in my pocket, the one I'd gone to Glover Street for earlier that day. I pulled it out but kept it hidden in my closed hand, a skittering of nervousness running through my stomach.

Curiosity replaced some of the sleepiness on Brett's face. "A present? It's not my birthday, and Christmas is still a couple of weeks off."

"It's not a birthday present or a Christmas present." I opened my hand and showed him the key resting on my palm.

His gaze shifted from my face to the key, and then back again. "The key to your heart?" He said it with a hint of the lopsided grin I loved so much.

"You already have that." Nervousness pattered through my stomach again.

The blue of his eyes seemed to deepen a shade. "To your house?"

I nodded, then forged ahead. "It's an I'm-crazy-in-love-with-you-and-want-you-to-live-here-with-me present."

His grin slowly reappeared. "Even though I'm always forgetting to put the cap back on the tube of toothpaste?"

I smiled. "I'll never understand why that's so hard to remember, but yes, even so."

He stared at me for a second, and it felt like he was looking through my eyes, straight into my soul. He placed his hand over mine, the key trapped between our palms, and then he kissed me, slowly and softly, leaving me breathless.

"Does that mean you accept?" I asked when I was able to speak again.

His adorable grin reappeared. "It does. I accept wholeheartedly. But if you need more convincing of that…"

He took the key from my hand and kissed my palm, then my wrist.

I smiled, almost lightheaded with happiness. "Feel free to convince me all you like."

Chapter 19

After arriving at The Flip Side early on Wednesday morning, I stood near the stone fireplace, enjoying the warmth from the crackling flames as I opened the recently delivered edition of the *Wildwood Cove Weekly*. Wally's murder had unsurprisingly made the front page.

I read through Justine's article, Charlene's influence obvious now that I knew Justine's feelings on the matter. Aside from mentioning that Wally wasn't well-liked, the article was quite bland, and didn't come close to naming anyone who might have had it in for the self-proclaimed Waffle King. The article also didn't reveal anything I didn't already know. I hadn't expected anything different, so I wasn't disappointed.

I was still trying to figure out a way to move my own investigation forward. Brett was on his way to Seattle and didn't expect to be back in Wildwood Cove until the late afternoon or evening. After that, he would probably spend some time at his parents' place, making sure his dad got settled. That meant I'd be on my own after work, with time to kill.

I needed to come up with a plan, but in the meantime I had plenty to keep me busy. Ivan had brought a garbage bag full of boughs to work with him that morning, clipped from the fir trees in his yard. I'd planned to cut some boughs from the trees in my own yard to use as decorations at the pancake house, but now Ivan had saved me the trouble.

Over the next half hour or so, I placed the greenery on the fireplace mantel and on the window ledges. Once that was done, I added the decorations I'd picked up at the craft fair. I placed Patricia's eagle on the mantel, right in the center, and hung an adorable set of stockings. At each end of the mantel I set a rustic lantern filled with red and gold baubles, a red bow and a sprig of greenery tied to the handle at the top.

I filled in the remaining spaces with cute snowman heads made from little bubble bowls sprayed with frosted paint. The eyes and coal-piece mouths had been painted on in black, the noses were made from tiny felt carrots, and each snowman was adorned with a top hat. What had really drawn my eye at the craft fair was the fact that the snowmen were lit from within with LED lights so they gave off a cheery, warm glow.

I added more of the snowmen to the window ledges and finally stood back to study the results of my work. I was pleased with the transformation. With flames popping and snapping in the fireplace and the new decorations adding holiday cheer, the pancake house looked cozy and festive. The only thing that didn't look so great was the carpet of needles on the wood floors, the result of working with the boughs. I quickly fixed that with a broom and dust pan and was soon ready to open the restaurant for the day.

The first diners arrived shortly after seven o'clock. Gary Thornbrook showed up about half an hour later and sat in his usual spot. It didn't take long for his buddy Ed to arrive and join him at the table near the back of the restaurant.

After confirming that they wanted their usual orders, I filled their mugs with coffee.

"I saw Sheriff Georgeson in town," Ed said as I finished filling his mug. "And a couple of deputies. Seems there's something going on."

"What kind of something?" Gary asked, shaking the contents of a sugar packet into his coffee.

Ed shrugged. "There was an ambulance too. Must be something serious."

"Whereabouts in town?" I asked.

"Pacific Street," Ed replied. "They were gathered outside the candy shop."

"Floyd Nuttal runs the candy shop." Gary stirred his coffee with a spoon. "He'd still be at home at this hour."

"I don't think it had to do with Floyd," Ed said. "That door that leads to the apartment above the store was open. Could be that's where the problem was."

"Who lives there?" I asked. "Not Mr. Nuttal?"

"Nope." Ed blew on his coffee before taking a sip. "He's got a house on Sea Breeze Drive. I thought that apartment above his shop was empty."

"It was until recently," Gary said. "That new guy's been living there the past couple of weeks."

I glanced across the room as an elderly couple entered the pancake house. "What new guy?" I had a feeling I already knew the answer to that question.

"The Waffle King's buddy," Gary said. "Lester or something."

"Chester," I supplied.

"That's it."

Leigh was looking after the elderly couple, but two orders of candy cane pancakes were ready to be delivered to another table. Ed and Gary didn't seem to have much more information, so I was able to tear myself away from them and fetch the pancakes.

My thoughts whirled around and around in my head as I worked. Had something really happened to Chester?

As the morning progressed, it seemed more and more certain that something grave had happened in town, whether it was to Chester or someone else. Almost everyone who came into The Flip Side was talking about the hubbub on Pacific Street. It was late in the morning when Patricia walked into the pancake house and I received more concrete news.

"Did you hear what happened?" Patricia asked as I poured her some coffee.

"I heard that *something* happened," I said.

"It's that friend of Wally Fowler's. Chester." She shook her head sadly. "It turns out he's dead."

I set the coffeepot down on the table. "How?"

"I don't know if this is fact or just rumor, but the word is that he was shot. Can you believe it? Two murders in less than a week."

I struggled to keep up with what she was saying, my own thoughts distracting me.

"They must be connected, don't you think?" Patricia said.

"It sounds like there's a good chance of that."

When I left her to her breakfast a few minutes later, I retreated to my office and sank down in the chair behind the desk. It would probably be best if the two murders were connected. Otherwise, that meant there were two killers loose in Wildwood Cove. One was bad enough, but if the same person had killed both men, then Chester didn't belong on my suspect list, even if Vicky had given him a false alibi.

What about the attempt to harm Glo with the SUV? Was that connected? I felt sure it must be, somehow. Too bad I hadn't seen the driver. If I had, all three cases might be solved by now.

My thoughts veered in Vicky's direction. The poor woman. First she'd lost her brother to foul play, and now her boyfriend. Who did she have left? Anyone?

I couldn't stick to my plan of pressing her for information after work. That would be too unkind considering this latest loss. I sat back and turned my chair in a slow circle, recalling the last time I'd seen Chester. He'd been drunk at the Windward Pub, complaining about being used. He'd also said he could take someone down.

Had he known something about Wally's murder?

Maybe he'd known the identity of the killer and had threatened to turn them in to the police. That would explain why he'd ended up as a victim. But he hadn't only said he could take someone down. He'd said if he went down, he wouldn't go alone.

That made it seem like it was possible he had something to do with Wally's death. Perhaps he was in on it with someone else.

Vicky?

I halted the chair's momentum, facing my desk and sitting up straight as a theory formed in my mind.

What if Vicky really did lie about Chester being with her in Seattle? She and Chester could have conspired to kill Wally together. Maybe Vicky purposely left town so she'd have an alibi, and then she lied to give Chester one too. Meanwhile, Chester carried out the nefarious deed here in Wildwood Cove.

It made sense. Vicky stood to inherit millions upon the death of her brother. She'd claimed she didn't know for sure if he'd left his estate to her, but that easily could have been another lie. With Wally out of the way, she and Chester could have lived a life of luxury together.

But why kill Chester?

So she could have all the money to herself.

I nearly jumped out of my chair, ready to seek out Vicky for more information. I stopped myself and sank deeper into my seat. I could be wrong, and if I was then Vicky didn't deserve to be hounded so soon after Chester's death.

There had to be another way to find out more about Chester and Vicky. I left the office for the kitchen, fueling my brain and body with a lunch of pumpkin pie crêpes and fruit salad. By the time I closed up the pancake house at two o'clock, I'd decided on a plan of action. I had to take care of a few tasks at The Flip Side before I could set out on my quest, however, and while I was busy cleaning the dining area, Sienna showed up, tapping at the front door and waving at me through the glass.

I glanced at the clock on the wall. It was past three, but Sienna must have come straight from school.

"Ahhh. It's much warmer in here," Sienna said with appreciation, rubbing her arms as I let her inside. "And I love all the decorations! Did you hear the news about the Waffle King's friend?"

"I did. Rumors were flying this morning, but it was your mom who told me he was shot."

"It's so creepy." Sienna shivered, and I didn't think it was from the cold this time. "Do you think the Hansfields might be behind this murder, too?"

"If they're responsible for Wally's death, then I think that's a good possibility. But I do have other suspects."

"Like who?"

I hesitated, wondering how much information I should share. I was still worried about Sienna getting too enthusiastic about sleuthing, but maybe that ship had already sailed so far from port that there wasn't anything I could do to draw it back in.

"Wally's sister, for one. We know she has an alibi for her brother's murder, but if she gave Chester a false alibi and they were in on the crime together—"

"Then maybe she bumped off Chester!" Sienna finished for me. "She inherited her brother's money and I heard he was loaded."

"He was worth millions."

"His sister probably promised Chester a cut of her inheritance if he killed her brother, but then she wanted to keep all the money for herself so..." She drew a finger across her throat.

"That's what I was thinking," I said. "Although, when I saw Vicky the other day she seemed really smitten with Chester."

"Maybe she's a good actress."

"She could be. I don't know nearly enough about her to say that's not a possibility."

Sienna followed me around the room as I swept the floor. "What I really came here to talk to you about is Bailey."

"What about her?"

"She was looking super sad this afternoon. I asked her again what was wrong and this time she broke down crying."

"Did she say why she was upset?"

"Oh, yeah. It was like once she started talking, she couldn't stop. I guess she's had everything pent-up inside for a long time." Sienna picked up the wire stand that held a collection of newspapers so I could sweep beneath it. "It turns out she got caught shoplifting at a store in town. She feels terrible about it. Her dad arranged things so she's doing volunteer work at the shop to avoid charges."

"Sounds like she got off lucky."

"Yep. But that's not all. Things haven't been great at home for her since the waffle guy came back to town. Her mom's been really upset and distracted with him back in her life. Plus, her dad's been working a lot and he's all worried about her mom, so Bailey feels like she doesn't even exist to them anymore. I'm guessing that's what drove her to shoplifting. Maybe she wanted their attention? And she thinks they're keeping secrets. They've been having a lot of whispered conversations that break off as soon as she enters the room."

I paused in my sweeping and leaned on the broom handle. "What kind of secrets?"

Sienna shrugged. "She doesn't know." She raised her eyebrows. "But maybe we do."

"Wally's murder."

She nodded. "And now maybe this other guy's murder too. Does that make sense?"

I tapped my fingers against the broom handle. "If Chester somehow knew or suspected that they were behind Wally's death, then they might have killed him to keep him quiet."

The enthusiastic light died out of Sienna's eyes. "Poor Bailey. What will happen to her if both her parents end up in jail?"

"Whoa," I cautioned. "Slow down. We don't know for sure that they had anything to do with the murders."

"But they're hiding *something.*"

I remembered how Glo had lied to me the other day. "They are, but we need to keep this to ourselves for now, okay? Rumors—even if they turn out to be untrue—could be devastating for Bailey."

Sienna mimed zipping her lips, her expression solemn now. "I won't say a word to anyone." She pulled her phone out of her jacket pocket and checked the screen. "I've got to run. Let me know if you find out something new about the Hansfields?"

She didn't wait for me to reply, and I was glad of that, not wanting to commit to anything. With a wave, she left the pancake house, and I resumed my cleaning.

As much as I would have preferred for Sienna to stay out of amateur sleuthing, I had to admit that her information was interesting. It strengthened my suspicion that Glo and Forrest Hansfield were guilty of something, and quite possibly murder. But I was equally as suspicious of Vicky now. Maybe that wasn't such a bad thing. I could pursue one avenue of investigation to start, and if that led to a dead end, I'd still have other suspects to look into.

It gave me hope to have some direction. Maybe now I could stop spinning my wheels and actually do something to help Lisa and Ivan.

"Was that Sienna's voice I heard?" Ivan asked when I stopped by the kitchen to say goodbye a short while later.

Tommy had already left for the day, and it looked as though Ivan was about to do the same, everything put away and the worktops spotlessly clean.

"It was." Worried he might ask why Sienna had stopped by, I hurried on to say, "I'm on my way out now. See you tomorrow."

I made a quick exit and figured I was lucky to do so. On my way out of the kitchen, I hadn't missed the glint of suspicion in Ivan's dark eyes. He was never keen on me sticking my nose into murder investigations, although I knew that was because he didn't want me coming to any harm. But with him and Lisa in trouble, there was no way I was backing down, so I slipped out the back door of the pancake house and hurried off on my search for clues.

Chapter 20

The Windward Pub was quiet when I arrived, only four of its tables occupied and no one sitting at the bar. I was relieved to see that the bartender was the same one who'd been working the other night when Brett and I had dinner there. Hopefully he'd be willing to talk to me, especially since he wasn't busy.

"What can I get you?" he asked when I approached the bar.

"An orange juice, please," I requested. I figured if I was going to fish information out of him, the least I could do was order something.

I settled onto a stool as he poured my juice.

"Do you remember when Chester Burns was in here a couple of nights ago?" I asked when the bartender had set the glass of juice in front of me.

"Sure." He frowned. "It's terrible what happened to him."

"It is." I took a sip of my juice as he ran a cloth over the bar, the dark wood gleaming. "He seemed upset when he was up on the stage."

"He had a bit too much to drink that night." The bartender flipped up his cloth to rest it over his shoulder. "But, yeah, he wasn't too happy."

"Because he thought someone had been using him."

He flashed a wry grin. "Woman trouble."

"Really?"

"So I assumed. After I got him down from the stage he was complaining about someone stomping on his heart."

My thoughts immediately jumped to Vicky. "But he didn't mention a name?"

"Nope." The bartender looked more closely at me. "What's your interest?"

"I'm just wondering if the person he was complaining about was the one who killed him."

"Geez. You could be right. But if this woman had already dumped him, why go to the trouble of killing him?"

I shrugged and took a long sip of my drink instead of sharing my theory with him.

"Too bad he didn't mention her name," he said. "Do you think I should be talking to the sheriff?"

"It probably wouldn't hurt," I said.

A burst of male laughter drew my attention to a booth across the room. Adam Silvester was seated there with two other men, all three smiling as they made their way through burgers and beers.

"That's Adam Silvester, right?" I said to the bartender, even though I already knew the answer.

"Yep. And it's a great day for him."

"How come?" I asked with interest, watching Adam out of the corner of my eye.

"Do you know about his kid?"

"I know she needs surgery that Adam can't afford."

The bartender nodded at the guys when one of Adam's buddies signaled for three more beers. "He couldn't afford it before."

"But he can now?" I guessed, noting the wide smile that hadn't faded from Adam's face.

"Yep." The bartender filled a pint glass. "Talk about a weight off his shoulders."

When the bartender left to deliver the beers to Adam and his friends, I drained the last of my juice and left some money on the bar. As I passed by Adam's booth on my way out of the pub, I couldn't help but wonder how he'd suddenly managed to come up with the money for his kid's surgery.

* * * *

I wanted to check in on Lisa before heading home, but I knew she'd still be at work and I didn't want to bother her there. I drove to her neighborhood, anyway, deciding to see if Joan was at home in the meantime. Adam Silvester and his sudden access to money remained on my mind, as did Chester and Vicky, but I wasn't sure what my next move should be. Maybe Leigh would know where Adam's money had come from. She was probably busy with her kids now that school had let out for the day, but I could ask her when she arrived at The Flip Side for work the next morning.

I had plenty to keep me busy until then. The mystery of Camelia's disappearance had never left my thoughts, even though I'd pushed it to the back burner of my mind temporarily. I wasn't sure how Joan would react to me bringing up the subject of her brother, and I hoped I wouldn't upset her.

As I climbed the steps to her front door, I crossed my fingers, hoping she'd be willing to talk to me about Harry.

When I knocked on the door, a volley of barking came from inside the house. Unlike the last time I'd been there, I heard Joan's voice amid the barking, trying to shush Angel. When she opened the door, the West Highland terrier wiggled out onto the porch to sniff at my legs, his tail wagging.

"Marley, nice to see you," Joan said. "What brings you by?"

"I was hoping to speak to you about something," I said, giving Angel a pat on the head and receiving a lick to my hand. "Something from the past. If you're willing to talk about it."

The smile faded from Joan's face and understanding showed in her eyes. "I figured this day would come."

"You know why I'm here?"

"It's about Harry, isn't it? Harry and Camelia."

"Yes," I said, a hint of uncertainty in my voice. I couldn't tell what she was going to say or do next.

She sighed, but then she gave me a sad smile. "You'd better come in."

I stepped inside with a sense of relief, but my uncertainty hadn't left me altogether. I really didn't want to upset Joan, but the subject of her brother had clearly brought up some sadness already.

We sat at her kitchen table, cups of tea in front of us, Angel lying near Joan's feet.

"You knew I'd ask you about Harry and Camelia eventually?" I asked once we were settled.

She nodded. "It was just a matter of time with you living in that house and being related to Grace. I figured you must have heard stories about Camelia. Now that you live in Wildwood Cove, it was inevitable that you'd eventually hear Harry's name in connection with hers."

"I don't want to upset you by digging up painful memories," I said. "But I find it so hard to accept when mysteries go unsolved, and this one involves my family, even if it's a somewhat distant branch of it."

"I understand," she assured me. "And I'm not upset. My memories from that time aren't the happiest, but I'm okay with talking about Harry, about everything that happened all those years ago."

"From what I've read and heard, the popular opinion seems to be that Harry was responsible for Camelia's disappearance and Tassy James's too."

Joan's hands tightened around her mug of tea as she nodded. "That's what most people believed. Still do, most likely. But it's not true."

She said those last words with conviction, but I had to wonder if that was simply because she couldn't believe that her older brother was a murderer.

"How do you know?" I asked, keeping the question as gentle as possible.

"Harry never would have harmed those girls." She gave me a tense smile. "I know you probably think I simply can't accept that my brother could have killed them, but there's far more to it than that."

I waited, eager to hear more, but forcing myself to be patient.

Joan sipped at her tea, her gaze wandering out the window to her backyard with its bare-limbed trees. "It was all so long ago, and yet at times it feels like it was just last week." She reeled her gaze back in, focusing on me. "I was only ten years old when it all happened. I knew Grace quite well. She was a bit older than me, but Wildwood Cove was a small town—even smaller than it is now—and we played together now and then, up until Camelia disappeared. Grace stayed well away from me after that."

When she saw the sad surprise on my face, she hurried to add, "I don't think that was as much her doing as her parents' influence. They believed as much as anyone that Harry was likely behind their oldest daughter's disappearance. It makes sense that they wouldn't have wanted their other child associating with his family, even once he was no longer in town."

She fell silent, her eyes distant, as if her mind was drifting away from the present and into the past.

"I found some of Camelia's diaries in the attic," I said once the silence had lasted several seconds. "It sounded like she was falling in love with Harry."

Joan's sad smile made a brief reappearance. "And he was in love with her. Completely." Some of the sadness left her smile. "I thought it was all so romantic. Camelia was so beautiful, and Harry was my favorite brother. There were five of us kids in the family. Three boys and two girls. I was the youngest."

I nodded, but didn't say anything, letting her continue.

"I saw the way he looked at Camelia, the way he treated her. There's no way he ever would have harmed her. He wouldn't have harmed any girl. Tassy worked at our house as a maid. One day she never made it home, and when Camelia vanished, it all seemed like too much of a coincidence. Harry knew both girls. He'd been seen with Camelia frequently in the weeks before she disappeared, and he walked Tassy home sometimes, especially if it was after dark. He seemed like the most likely suspect, at least to those who didn't know him like I did."

"The sheriff didn't seem to agree."

"Ah, but I'm guessing you've heard what people thought about that."

"He and your dad were buddies."

"And it's true. They were." She frowned, her eyes changing, taking on a hint of an angry glint. "And he would have turned a blind eye to the truth for my father's sake—that much I can't deny. He did it often enough."

Her statement surprised me. "What do you mean?"

"I never admitted this to anyone until I met my late husband, Emmanuel, but my father was a mean drunk. He kept up a good appearance as the mayor and an upstanding citizen, but he drank a lot, and he wasn't the nicest of men even when sober."

Sympathy and apprehension sat heavily in my stomach. "I'm so sorry, Joan. Was he violent?"

"Oh, yes. At times. He'd strike out at any of us, but if Harry wasn't the target and he was around, he'd step in. So he always took the worst of it."

I pushed my unfinished tea aside, no longer having an appetite for anything. "And the sheriff knew?"

"He did. Never did a damn thing about it, even when my father beat up Harry so badly that he ended up with a broken arm and a concussion."

I winced. "Didn't people get suspicious?"

"Oh, I'm sure there were plenty of people who were far more than suspicious. But my father would spin a story about Harry falling down the stairs or whatnot, and even if people didn't truly believe it, they pretended they did."

We sat silently for a minute until Angel raised his head and whined at Joan.

"It's all right, sweetie," she said, giving him a pat. "It's all in the past now."

I wasn't sure if I should voice my next question, but after a brief hesitation, I did. "And Harry never showed any signs of copying your father's violent behavior?"

"Never. Harry was the complete opposite of our father. He didn't harm Tassy James or Camelia Winslow. I knew that without a doubt even before I ever had confirmation of that belief."

"Confirmation?" I latched on to that word. "You have proof that Harry didn't kill the girls?"

"I never had proof that he wasn't involved in Tassy's disappearance, but, yes, there was evidence that showed my brother most definitely did not kill Camelia Winslow."

Chapter 21

"What kind of proof?" I asked, surprised and eager to hear more.

"Maybe you've heard that Harry left town shortly after Camelia was last seen."

"I did."

"Before he left he told me it was too difficult for him to stay here with so many people having already convicted him in their minds. Those people made it clear he was no longer wanted in town. That was the reason he gave me at the time."

"That must have been terrible for you," I said.

"It was. Especially when he told me he wouldn't be in touch for a good while. I begged him to write to me secretly, but he said there was no way for me to get letters without people knowing. And that was true. The lady at the post office was a terrible gossip, and my parents would have noticed if I'd received mail."

"Why would it have been bad for your parents to know he was writing to you? Wouldn't your mother at least have wanted to know where he was and that he was all right?"

Joan nodded, and for the first time her eyes grew misty. "It was terribly hard on our mother. But Harry insisted that he needed to keep his whereabouts secret, so he slipped away one night before our father got wind of his plans."

"And he was never heard from again. That's what Nancy Welch at the museum told me. So how did you end up with proof that Harry didn't kill Camelia?"

The mistiness faded from her eyes. "He was heard from again. He got in touch with me. I just never told anyone about it."

I pulled my cooling tea back toward me and took a sip, trying to understand. Some of my puzzlement must have shown on my face.

Joan patted my hand. "I'll explain. It's hard to get everything out at once."

I waited as she gathered her thoughts.

"I didn't hear from Harry for decades. It was only eight years ago that I received a letter from him. This isn't the house I grew up in, but he managed to find out my married name and my current address thanks to the wonders of the internet."

"It must have been a shock to receive a letter from him after so long."

"It certainly was. I wasn't even sure if I should believe it was really from him at first. But his handwriting hadn't changed much over the years, and he called me Jojo in the letter. No one else ever called me that. I'll admit, I broke down crying when I read the letter. Shook like a leaf too. He included his address and phone number. He was living in Raleigh, North Carolina, by then. I called him up and he invited me to visit. So I did. He didn't want me to tell anyone that we'd been in contact, though. So I kept it to myself right up until today. My husband had passed away by then, you see. Otherwise I would have told him, of course."

"What was it like to see him again?"

"Incredible. I'm afraid I blubbered quite a bit at first. Decades had passed, and he was well into his seventies by then, but there was no doubt he was my brother Harry."

"And when you visited him… Is that how you found evidence that he didn't kill Camelia?"

She nodded. "For the first time, I heard the truth. Some of it was hard to hear—some of it is still hard to think about—but other parts were a relief, like finding out that Camelia wasn't murdered. She lived until the age of sixty-nine. She died of a stroke one evening, sitting across the room from Harry."

I took in that information, connecting the dots. "They were together all that time."

Joan smiled, and this time there was no sadness in it. "They were. Madly in love right up until the very end. He had photos of the two of them throughout their lives. There's no doubt about it. Camelia was alive and well for decades after she vanished from Wildwood Cove."

I struggled to make sense of everything she'd told me. "So did they leave Wildwood Cove together?"

"They left separately, but with a plan to meet up in Seattle, which they did."

"But why would Camelia run away like that and leave her family to think she might have been killed? Why couldn't Harry let you or your mother know where he was?"

Joan's smile disappeared. "This is the part that was hard for me to hear, even though I think in a way I suspected it all along."

I waited as Joan paused and closed her eyes for a moment, as if steeling herself to say her next words.

"Camelia wasn't murdered, but Tassy James was," she explained. "Only, it wasn't Harry who killed her. It was my father."

I stared at her. "Are you sure? Harry told you that?"

She nodded. "And I believe him. Like I said, I think somewhere deep down I always knew. My father was a nasty piece of work, and he was... inappropriate with Tassy at times. My best guess is that he took that too far and she fought back. It's all too easy for me to picture him reacting violently in such a scenario."

I wrapped my hands around my mug, seeking some warmth, but it had long since cooled. "I'm so sorry, Joan." I couldn't even begin to imagine how terrible it had to be for her to know her father was a murderer.

"You're probably wondering how Harry knew this," she said.

"Did he witness Tassy's murder?"

"No. Camelia did."

I sat back in the chair, floored by that revelation. "How?"

"She'd arranged to meet Harry in the woods beyond our house. Harry was late and while she was waiting, Camelia saw my father strangle Tassy and bury her body. When Harry finally arrived, Camelia was distraught. They considered going to the sheriff with what she'd seen, but in the end they were both too scared."

"Because the sheriff would have protected your father."

"He would have," Joan confirmed. "My father wanted to protect our family's image, so Harry didn't get much official attention as a suspect. But Harry never doubted—and neither do I—that if Harry or Camelia had accused him of killing Tassy, he would have sacrificed Harry to protect himself. Nobody would have believed Harry over the mayor of the town. At first they tried to keep quiet about it, to pretend they knew nothing, but then Camelia got spooked. She didn't like the way my father looked at her whenever she was visiting the house. Whether he somehow suspected that she knew something, or he was eyeing her as a replacement for Tassy for his unwanted advances, they never knew for certain. Either way, they decided it would be safer for the two of them to disappear. So that's what they did. Camelia left with nothing more than the clothes on her back and some money Harry had given her. She didn't think she could get out of her house with a suitcase without her family knowing, and her parents would never have let her go off with Harry—or any other man—no matter what the reason. So she went in secret, taking no belongings. Then Harry followed soon after."

"But for Grace and her parents to be left wondering for the rest of their lives…" I said with an ache in my chest.

"I don't know for sure that Grace was left to wonder."

"How do you mean?" I asked.

"Harry told me that Camelia left a letter for Grace, letting her know that she was leaving of her own accord."

"So Grace knew Camelia was alive."

"I don't know for certain. By the time I learned all of this, Grace had long since passed away. To my knowledge, she never let on that she knew Camelia was alive, but maybe she did know and decided to keep that information to herself. In the letter, Camelia gave the address of a friend in Seattle and told Grace if she wrote to her there she'd get the mail eventually. But the friend never received anything from Grace. Camelia figured she was angry about her leaving like she did and was never able to forgive her enough to try to get in touch."

I couldn't reconcile any of that with the Grace I'd known. "Are you sure Grace received Camelia's letter? Was Harry sure?"

"No, I don't think he knew for certain. And to be honest, I wondered about that myself from time to time. Camelia didn't want to leave the letter out in the open, so she hid it in a secret hiding place that she and Grace had used in their younger years."

"Do you know where the secret hiding place was?"

"I haven't a clue, I'm afraid." Joan regarded me closely. "You don't think Grace ever found the letter."

"I can't say for sure, of course," I said. "But I have a strong feeling that's probably the case."

Joan shook her head. "That would be terribly sad. If Grace had still been alive when Harry got in touch with me, I would have told her everything. But it was far too late."

A wave of sorrow washed over me as I thought about Grace dying without ever knowing the truth. That couldn't be undone now, but maybe there was still a chance to set things straight. "Have your father and the sheriff from back then both passed away?"

"Oh, yes. Years ago. And I thought about trying to clear Harry's name, many times over the last few years, but I no longer have any evidence to back up his story and I don't want to publicly dredge up that part of the past if I have no proof."

"What about Harry himself? And all the photos that prove Camelia was alive long after she vanished?"

"When Harry got in touch with me, his health was failing. He passed away only weeks after I visited him. Before I was able to get back to Raleigh to collect his personal effects, a bad flood destroyed everything on the lower level of his house."

"Including the pictures," I guessed.

Joan nodded. "I searched and searched for any others, but there weren't any left. So I have no proof. Only a secondhand story from Harry."

My thoughts swirled about like dry leaves caught up in a sweeping wind. "But if we had the letter, that would help." I tried to grasp another one of my whirling thoughts. "If Grace had found it, surely she would have kept it. But it wasn't with Camelia's diaries or the newspaper clippings. It's possible she put it elsewhere, but I really believe she didn't find it."

"But how can we possibly find it?"

"If we knew where the secret hiding place was…"

"I have no idea."

"Neither do I, but I do have an idea about where I might be able to find out. I don't remember any mention of a hiding place in Camelia's diaries, but I only skimmed through the early ones. Maybe if I read them more carefully, I can find a clue." I grabbed hold of another thought as it swirled around. "And what about Tassy's body? If you know where she was buried, that's something you should tell Sheriff Georgeson."

Joan's face took on a pained expression. "I know. I should have said something as soon as I heard the story from Harry, but I was so overwhelmed at the time, and the man who was sheriff before Ray Georgeson… I'm pretty sure he would have laughed and written me off as a batty old woman."

"Ray won't do that," I assured her.

"No, I can believe that. He's a good man. But I don't know exactly where she's buried. The woods went on forever back then, and the house isn't there anymore. It was torn down to make room for new houses a few decades ago, and some of the trees were cleared too. Tassy could be under a house now."

Disappointment weighed on my shoulders. For a few moments, I'd had a spark of hope that we could at least find Tassy so she could have a proper burial, to bring at least a measure of closure to any of her family members who might still be alive.

I asked Joan if she knew if any of Tassy's relatives were still around.

"She had several siblings—at least six—most of them younger than her, so it's more than likely some of them are still alive. I don't think any of them live here in Wildwood Cove, though."

Ray could probably track them down. At least, I hoped so. But unless we could find Tassy's remains, there wouldn't be any reason to.

"I'll see if I can find Camelia's letter," I said. "But even if I can't, I think you should tell Sheriff Georgeson what you know. Maybe it won't come to anything, but maybe it will."

"You're right," Joan said. "I should have done so already, but better late than never, I suppose."

I didn't stay much longer. Our foray into the past had left us both somber and I was itching to get my hands on Camelia's diaries again. The letter's whereabouts was a mystery unto itself, one I knew I wouldn't be able to ignore any more than I could the recent murders. Maybe I wouldn't be able to find it—maybe it didn't even exist any longer—but I knew I wouldn't be able to accept those possibilities until I'd done everything I could to locate it.

As I left Joan's house and followed the narrow path to the sidewalk, the front door to Lisa's house opened and Ray emerged onto the porch. I halted my steps, apprehension settling over me. Ray nodded at me as he headed for his cruiser, speaking into his radio.

Lisa stood on her porch now, rubbing her arms, still in her work clothes but without a coat. As Ray drove off, I hurried over to Lisa.

"What's happened?" I asked with concern, noting the slight trembling of her lips as she pressed them together.

Tears welled in her eyes and overflowed onto her cheeks. "I'm going to end up in jail," she said with despair. "Now the sheriff thinks I killed Wally *and* Chester."

Chapter 22

I ushered Lisa inside and out of the cold, shutting the door behind us.

"What possible motive would you have for killing Chester?" I asked once we were in the house.

Lisa wiped at one cheek with the back of her hand. "To keep him quiet because he knew I killed Wally."

"But you didn't kill Wally. And if Chester knew you had, why would he have kept quiet over the past few days? He had no reason to cover for you."

"That's what I told Sheriff Georgeson but..."

She looked like she was about to crumple into a heap on the floor. I grabbed her arm and quickly steered her to the couch in the living room.

"What is it?" I asked, knowing there was something she hadn't yet told me.

"They found a bracelet in Chester's apartment. The sheriff showed it to me. It's mine, Marley. I didn't admit to that, but he already knows. I could tell."

I joined her on the couch. "But how would he know that? And how did your bracelet end up in Chester's apartment?"

Lisa dropped her head into her hands. "I don't know! I lost the bracelet yesterday but I don't know where or exactly when."

None of this was good, but I didn't want to add to Lisa's distress by letting on how discouraged I felt by her news. Instead, I forced myself to focus and carefully thought things over.

"I don't think you're tall enough to have committed Wally's murder, so does Ray still think Ivan was in on it too?"

"Yes." Lisa raised her head and wiped away another tear. "Especially since..."

"Since what?" I asked with apprehension.

"Sheriff Georgeson wanted to know if I have an alibi for Chester's murder. I do, but it's not one he bought."

"Why not?"

"Because my alibi is that I was with Ivan that night."

My eyebrows shot up. "The whole night?"

"It's not what you're thinking," Lisa hurried to say. "He cooked me dinner and then we were watching a movie at his place. I fell asleep on the couch and Ivan didn't have the heart to wake me since I haven't slept well all week, so he let me stay there."

I sank deeper into the couch cushions. The only person who could confirm Lisa's alibi was a suspect himself, and Lisa's bracelet was found at the second crime scene. I was surprised Ray hadn't arrested her already. Maybe he was waiting until he could prove the bracelet belonged to Lisa.

"The next time the sheriff shows up, he'll probably drag me off in handcuffs," Lisa said, her thoughts on the same page as mine.

I put a hand to her back. "I'm going to do everything I can to make sure that doesn't happen, but you should get a lawyer, Lisa. You shouldn't answer any more questions without one."

"I know, even though it makes me ill to think it's gone that far. I've got the names of a couple of criminal lawyers in Port Angeles. Ivan will need one too." She picked up her phone from the coffee table. "And I should tell him what happened with the sheriff. He'll probably be questioned next."

I put a hand on hers. "Maybe it's best if you don't contact him."

"But I don't want him taken by surprise."

"I know, but it might not look good if your phone records show that you contacted him right after you were questioned by the sheriff. It wouldn't prove anything, but it might look suspicious, like you were trying to get your stories straight."

Lisa reluctantly set her phone back on the coffee table. "This is awful. I don't understand how things got this bad."

"You really can't remember when you last saw your bracelet?" I asked. That seemed to be the most incriminating evidence.

"I had it on yesterday morning when I left for work, but when I went to bed last night, it was gone. I looked for it at the office today, but it wasn't there. I looked all over the house too. It's not the first time it's fallen off, but I felt it happen the other times."

"Where else did you go yesterday?"

"I went to the Beach and Bean for coffee and I picked up a few things from the grocery store after I left work."

"But you never went to Chester's apartment for any reason?"

"No."

"Can you think of anyone who might want to frame you for the crime?"

"Do you think that's what's happening?"

"It didn't cross my mind before, but with your bracelet showing up in Chester's apartment... I can't think of any other way to explain that."

Lisa thought for a moment, but then shook her head. "I can't think of anyone who would want to do that to me. Why would anyone hate me that much?"

"It might not be about hate. It might just be that you were a convenient target when the killer wanted to deflect suspicion." I paused as I turned things over in my mind. "When Ray asked you for an alibi, did he give you a timeframe?"

"Between ten last night and seven this morning."

So Chester must have been killed between those hours.

Lisa eyed her phone. "I'm worried about Ivan. If it's a bad idea to phone him, maybe I should go by his place."

"I'm not sure that's a great idea either. I'm sorry, Lisa. I don't want you making things any worse for yourself."

"Will you go see him?"

"Of course. I'll go over there now if you want."

She nodded. "Please."

"And while I'm gone, you should call one of those lawyers."

She agreed to do so. I gave her a hug and promised her I'd find a way to help her and Ivan. It was a promise I was determined to keep.

* * * *

I was worried I might find a sheriff's department cruiser parked outside Ivan's home when I arrived, but the only car in front of his single-story white house was his classic Volkswagen bug. As I waited for a response to my knock on the front door, I checked my text messages. Brett had arrived back in town with Chloe and his parents and was planning to stay at his parents' house for at least the next couple of hours. That was what I'd expected, and it meant that I had no reason to hurry home.

Before I had a chance to send a response, Ivan opened the door.

"I'm here on Lisa's behalf," I said. "Partly, anyway."

Alarm showed on Ivan's face. "Is she okay?"

"Yes," I hurried to assure him. "Well, mostly."

He stepped back to allow me inside. Once in the foyer, I detected a delicious aroma wafting down the hall from the kitchen at the back of the house.

"Have you eaten dinner?" Ivan asked as he shut the door.

"No, but don't let me interrupt if you're eating. And don't worry about me."

He led the way down the hall. When we reached the kitchen, he checked a pot on the stove while I told him about Lisa's visit from the sheriff.

The pot's lid clattered against the countertop as it slid from Ivan's grasp. "Her bracelet was at the crime scene?"

"To me it seems like someone is trying to frame her."

He let out a deep, growl-like sound. "Who?"

"I wish I knew."

My stomach growled, the delicious smell of whatever Ivan was cooking making my mouth water. He cast a brief glance my way before removing two dinner plates from a cupboard and setting them on the counter. His scowl was more menacing than ever as he spooned risotto onto both plates.

"You really don't have to worry about feeding me," I protested.

He directed his scowl at me. "You're hungry."

I couldn't exactly argue that point, especially since my stomach chose that moment to give another loud grumble.

Ivan added a piece of chicken to one plate and grilled eggplant to both.

"I can get you some tofu," he said, reaching for the refrigerator door.

"Please don't go to any trouble, Ivan. Really."

He glared at me, the force of his dark gaze almost making me take a step backward, but then he relented and handed me the plate without the chicken.

"Thank you," I said weakly, still recovering from the force of his glare.

I joined him at the kitchen table by the window that overlooked his backyard. It was dark outside now, but I knew if it were light out I'd see well-stocked birdfeeders and a neatly tended yard.

"Why would anyone frame Lisa?" Ivan asked once we were seated, glasses of water set before us along with our meals.

I shared my thoughts on the matter, including the fact that the killer might have targeted her simply because she was already a suspect.

Ivan nodded as he sliced his knife through the piece of chicken. "That sounds likely. Surely Lisa wouldn't have any enemies."

"She doesn't think so, and neither do I."

I put the first forkful of mushroom risotto into my mouth and the taste momentarily distracted me from our conversation. "This is amazing, Ivan. By far the best risotto I've ever tasted."

He gave the compliment only a grunt of acknowledgment, but I thought his scowl eased slightly for a second or two.

I steered my thoughts back on track. "The sheriff didn't come by to question you this afternoon?"

Ivan shook his head. "Probably just a matter of time."

I agreed that was likely the case. "Lisa wanted to make sure you knew what was happening, but I didn't think it would be good for her to contact you herself. I don't want anyone thinking you were trying to get your stories straight before you got questioned again."

Ivan gave that a curt nod of acknowledgment.

"So I promised her I'd come by and see you," I continued. "But I also wanted to know your thoughts on everything. Do you have any idea who killed Wally and Chester?"

Ivan was in the midst of chewing, so he didn't reply right away. I took the opportunity to taste the grilled eggplant.

My eyes widened as the delicious flavors hit my taste buds. "This is incredible too. You should put together a cookbook, Ivan. All your recipes are amazing."

That suggestion was met with a noncommittal grunt and he quickly got the conversation back on course. "I don't know who killed those men." His eyes narrowed at me. "You must have suspects."

"I do," I confirmed. "There's Glo Hansfield, for starters." I filled Ivan in on her motive. "But apparently whoever killed Wally was tall enough and strong enough to force his head down into the bowl as he poured the liquid nitrogen."

Ivan nodded. "Makes sense. And Glo Hansfield is short."

"Exactly. That's the problem with her as a suspect, but I'm thinking her husband could be involved. He's nearly a foot taller than his wife."

Ivan stared off across the room for a few ticks of the clock on the wall. "Forrest Hansfield," he said after a moment. "He's an accountant. He has an office in town."

"Does he?" I tucked that information away for the time being. "There's also Vicky Fowler. She inherited Wally's millions, and she's not overly distraught that he's dead. But she has an alibi for his murder, and she seemed to be in love with Chester, even though their romantic relationship only started recently. But there's something more." I told him what the bartender had shared with me about Chester complaining that someone had trampled his heart.

"Vicky?" Ivan asked.

"That's what I thought, but there's still that alibi."

"For Wally's death, but not Chester's," Ivan pointed out.

"True." I ate some more risotto. "Do you think Chester could have killed Wally and then Vicky killed Chester?" I shook my head as soon as the words were out of my mouth. "I still find that last part hard to believe. The last time I saw Vicky, she genuinely seemed to be in love with Chester, or at least well on her way to being in love with him."

"Relationships change," Ivan said. "Sometimes abruptly."

I conceded that point, but I still had trouble picturing Vicky killing Chester. Although, if she'd lied to cover for Chester and then found out that he'd killed her brother, maybe she'd lost all warmth for Chester and sought revenge for Wally. That was something to consider.

Ivan speared the last of his chicken with his fork. "Who else?"

I told him about Adam Silvester and how he'd recently come up with the money needed for his daughter's surgery.

"Killing Wally and Chester wouldn't have helped him financially unless someone hired him to commit the crimes," Ivan pointed out.

I remembered something I'd heard days before. "That's true, but the day after Wally's death, Vicky discovered that a bunch of cash was missing from the waffle house."

"But Wally's death didn't look like a robbery interrupted."

"Good point." I thought that over as I finished off my eggplant. "But if Adam killed Wally out of anger because he refused to lend him or give him the money he needed, maybe he took the time to look around the waffle house after the murder and found the cash."

Ivan took a long drink of water and set his glass down. "Could be. But then why kill Chester?"

"Because he knew something that incriminated Adam?"

Ivan's frown deepened, but he said nothing.

"I need to take a closer look at all those suspects if I'm going to figure out who's responsible."

"Investigating leads to danger," Ivan said, his dark gaze pinned on me again.

I tried not to squirm in my seat. "You and Lisa are my friends, and Lisa could be arrested at any time now. I know you don't want that to happen any more than I do."

Ivan's glower was positively frightening now. "I won't sit back and let you put yourself in danger."

I opened my mouth to object, but he cut me off.

"I know you won't stop investigating, so we'll do it together."

As my surprise wore off, a smile tugged at the corners of my mouth. "Partners in crime?"

"Truth-seeking, not crime."

"Right."

I almost mentioned that Sienna wanted in on the investigation as well but stopped myself. I knew Ivan had a soft spot for the sixteen-year-old and I didn't want him thinking I'd encouraged her to get involved in crime solving.

"All right, partner," I said instead. "What's our next move?"

Chapter 23

I helped Ivan clean up after our delicious dinner, but once that was done, neither of us were content to sit back and relax for the rest of the evening. Instead, we drove into the center of town in my car, searching for an opportunity to find out more about Vicky or Forrest.

The waffle house was dark when we drove past. Ivan thought Vicky was living in the apartment above one of the shops down the street, but those windows were dark as well. Continuing along the street, Ivan directed me to Forrest Hansfield's office and there we had more luck. Despite the fact that it was nearing seven o'clock, the lights were still on, a warm glow spilling out through the Venetian blinds. I wasn't so sure that Forrest would be as welcoming as the lit window appeared, but I didn't let that deter me.

It took some convincing to get Ivan to remain in the car. His presence would be great if I needed an intimidation factor, but to start I wanted to try a gentler approach.

I'd parked across the street and part way down the road from Forrest's office but still within view of it. I shut the driver's door quickly behind me, wanting to keep as much heat in the car as possible for Ivan while he waited. Tucking my hands up into the sleeves of my jacket, I dashed across the quiet street and jogged along the sidewalk.

For a split second I wondered if the door would be locked, but it opened easily. The middle-aged brunette at the desk in the small reception area looked up, clearly surprised to have a visitor.

"Can I help you?" she asked, her eyes flicking toward her computer screen. Checking the time, probably.

Before I could answer, the door at the back of the reception area opened and Forrest Hansfield appeared, an overcoat buttoned up over his suit and a briefcase in hand.

"Marilyn, I'm…" He trailed off when he saw me. "Are you here for an appointment?"

He sent a confused glance at his receptionist. She gave him a discreet shake of her head in return.

"No, and I'm sorry for stopping by so late," I said quickly. "I saw the light on and hoped you might still be here. I've been looking around for an accountant, and my friend Lisa Morales recommended you, Mr. Hansfield."

The lines of confusion furrowing across his brow deepened. "Is she a client of mine?"

"Lisa Morales? I'm not sure, but if not she's heard good things about you."

"The name doesn't ring a bell, but maybe she knows one of my clients." He nodded toward his receptionist. "Please feel free to make an appointment with Marilyn and we can discuss things further."

He moved past me, heading for the door.

"It's terrible what's been happening in the neighborhood, isn't it?" I said, hoping to keep him from leaving.

He paused with his hand on the doorknob, a frown turning down the corners of his mouth. "Yes. Terrible."

"Were you working late the night Wally Fowler was killed?"

His hand dropped from the doorknob and he turned to face me. "Why do you ask?"

His sudden suspicion sent a prickling sensation up the back of my neck, but I tried my best to keep my expression free of anything but innocence and curiosity.

"I was just wondering if you'd seen anyone out and about, since the waffle house isn't too far from here."

"I was at home with my daughter that evening, which is where I should be now."

With barely a nod of dismissal, he made a swift exit.

I was disappointed that I hadn't managed to get anything further out of him, but maybe that one tidbit of information he'd provided would be useful to some degree.

Marilyn cleared her throat and I realized I was still staring at the door.

"So would you like to make an appointment?" she asked.

"Maybe I should do that another time," I said, trying to think of an excuse. "I forgot to bring my phone and my schedule's on it. I wouldn't want to accidentally double-book."

"No problem. You can stop by or give me a call anytime." She handed me one of Forrest's business cards.

"Thank you." I tucked the card in my pocket.

"I was here the evening the Waffle King was killed." She'd lowered her voice, even though we were alone in the office, as far as I knew. "My home computer died and I needed to do some work for this online course I'm taking, so I was here until nearly ten."

"Did you see anything?"

"No." She shuddered. "Thank goodness. It's spooky enough knowing the guy was killed just down the street. I wouldn't have wanted to see the killer skulking about. What if he came after me next? You know, to eliminate any witnesses."

The front door opened and I glanced over my shoulder, expecting to see Forrest returning for something he'd forgotten. Instead, a tall and muscular woman stepped inside, bringing a blast of frosty air along with her.

"Marilyn," the woman said in greeting, her gaze skipping past me to the receptionist. "Is Forrest in?"

"You just missed him, Jill. He's on his way home."

Jill nodded and thanked Marilyn before ducking back out into the night.

"Anyway," Marilyn said when she was gone, "like I was saying, feel free to make an appointment once you know your schedule."

I backed toward the door. "Thank you. Good night."

I set off along the sidewalk, the shops lining the road all closed for the night. Street lamps cast pools of light along my path, but shadows filled the recessed shop doorways. I was about to head for the curb so I could cut across the street when a strong hand grabbed my arm.

I let out a gasp of surprise as I was yanked into the shadows filling a narrow gap between two buildings. Despite the darkness, I recognized Forrest as he shoved me up against the brick exterior of one of the stores.

"You think I don't know what you're up to?" he practically growled at me.

I struggled to get away from him, but both his hands now gripped my shoulders, holding me against the building.

"My wife told me all about you. You're trying to ruin my family and I'm not going to let that happen!"

A large figure loomed out of the darkness, grabbing Forrest and hauling him away from me.

Air whooshed out of my lungs in an exhale of relief. I rubbed at a sore spot on my left shoulder as I stepped out from between the buildings.

Ivan stood beneath the nearest streetlamp, holding Forrest by the collar.

"Don't you threaten Marley." The chef's voice boomed through the otherwise quiet night.

"She's trying to destroy my family!"

I couldn't help but feel a hint of satisfaction at the fear in Forrest's eyes.

"I'm not trying to ruin anyone," I said. "I'm just looking for the truth."

Forrest tried to step toward me. Ivan tightened his grip on the accountant's collar, keeping him in place.

"Did you kill Wally Fowler?" Ivan asked.

"You're crazy, the both of you," Forrest said, his voice dismissive now. "Let me go or I'll call the sheriff."

"And how will you explain dragging a woman off into the darkness?" Ivan said, but he released his hold on Forrest's collar.

"Keep your nose out of my family's business," the accountant blustered, backing away from Ivan. "You'll be sorry if you don't."

With that warning, he turned and fled, jumping into a car parked halfway down the street and roaring off seconds later.

I realized that my heart was thumping out a booming beat in my chest.

"Are you okay?" Ivan asked.

"Yes," I said after gulping in some cold night air. "Thanks for stepping in."

Ivan glared off down the street in the direction Forrest's car had gone. "If he's the killer, you need to be extra careful now."

I rubbed my shoulder again. "I know. And now it's all too easy for me to picture him shoving Wally's head into that bowl of liquid nitrogen."

We returned to my car and I cranked up the heat before driving in the direction of Ivan's neighborhood.

"Did you learn anything useful?" he asked.

"I'm not sure. He said he was at home on the night of Wally's murder and his receptionist confirmed that he wasn't in the office. If I could talk to his daughter without making her suspicious, we might be able to find out if he really does have an alibi or not."

"Best not to poke at that hornet's nest," Ivan advised. "He's already angry enough to hurt you. If he finds out you're involving his daughter…"

"Don't worry. I'm well aware of the risk."

I pulled to a stop in front of Ivan's house.

He unclipped his seatbelt but didn't move to get out of the car. "Don't go investigating on your own, no matter what clues you're looking for."

"I won't," I assured him. "And I'll be careful."

His frown didn't ease up, but he nodded before getting out of the car.

When I arrived home, I made sure all the doors and windows were locked. My encounter with Forrest had left me spooked and I was glad for Bentley's company, especially since Brett was still at his parent's house. With lights blazing all over the main floor, I got busy festooning the inside of the house with Christmas decorations, trying not to think about the bad turn the evening might have taken if Ivan hadn't been there to save me from the angry accountant who very well might be Wally and Chester's killer.

* * * *

Brett ended up spending the night at his parents' place, wanting to be there in case his mom needed help caring for his dad. I'd assured him over the phone that I didn't mind, even though I wanted nothing more than his company after the evening I'd had. I made sure to keep all hints of unease out of my voice and didn't mention my encounter with Forrest. If I had, Brett would have hurried over to be with me, and I didn't want him to feel like he needed to be away from his parents on his dad's first night out of the hospital.

I didn't sleep well and couldn't stop yawning as I got ready to open The Flip Side the next morning. When everything was done save for flipping the Closed sign to Open, I made myself a strong cup of tea while Ivan and I filled Tommy in on our adventure the night before.

"Sounds guilty to me," Tommy said once he'd heard the tale about Forrest Hansfield. "Does the sheriff suspect him?"

"I have no idea," I said, "And I don't want to ask. I'd only get a lecture."

Blowing on my tea, I carried my cup with me out of the kitchen, just in time to greet Leigh as she arrived.

"Have you heard Adam Silvester's good news?" I asked once we'd exchanged good mornings.

"About having the money for his daughter's surgery? I found out this morning while I was dropping the girls off at daycare. It's fantastic news."

I followed Leigh into the break room where she shrugged out of her winter jacket and hung it in her locker. "Any idea how he suddenly came up with the money?"

"No," she said. "I thought maybe a family member was helping him out, but I don't actually know for sure." She eyed me as she tied back her bleached-blond hair. "I'm guessing your interest has something to do with the murders."

"A bunch of cash went missing from the waffle house the night Wally was killed," I explained. "And earlier that day when Wally was here, Adam was giving him a death glare."

Leigh shut the locker. "So you think Adam killed Wally and stole the cash to help pay for his daughter's medical bills?"

"It's a possibility."

"I hope it's not true. I really like Adam, and his poor daughter already lost her mom. She took off soon after Tabitha was born." She tipped her head to the side. "But…"

"But what?"

"One of the mothers at daycare this morning was saying that Adam had asked Wally for a loan after the bank turned him down."

"I'm guessing Wally turned him down too."

"Apparently. That doesn't surprise me, considering what Wally was like, but it does seem cruel. Wally had millions and Adam did so much for him back when they were in school."

"I heard they were buddies back then."

Leigh shrugged as we made our way out of the break room. "I think Adam thought they were buddies. For Wally, I'm betting it was more of a relationship of convenience. Adam was always really good at math, and Wally struggled with it. My understanding is that Adam was always helping Wally with his homework. Maybe even doing assignments for him. I'm not sure if Wally would have graduated without Adam's help."

"Then it must have stung all the more when Wally turned down Adam's request for help."

"Probably. I guess Adam finally saw Wally for who he really was."

"That would explain the death glare."

But could it also have driven Adam to murder?

Leigh disappeared into the kitchen to say good morning to Ivan and Tommy while I wandered over to the fireplace to enjoy the warmth from the dancing flames. As I sipped at my tea and thought over my conversation with Leigh, my gaze landed on the carved driftwood eagle I'd purchased from Patricia at the craft fair. It looked perfect on the mantel, and since I'd put it on display a couple of customers had asked where they could find ones like it. I made a mental note to suggest to Patricia that she leave some business cards at the pancake house for any customers who inquired about her sculptures.

Shifting my thoughts back to Adam, I recalled how I'd seen him on the sidewalk near the hardware store on the night of Wally's death. He'd seemed distracted, and he was heading in the direction of the waffle house. Had he been on his way to ask Wally for a loan? And when Wally turned him down…

I drained the last of my tea and turned away from the merry crackling of the flames in the fireplace. I didn't want Adam to be the killer. That would be terrible for his poor daughter. But I couldn't ignore all the evidence pointing his way. He had to stay near the top of my suspect list.

When I ducked into the kitchen to drop off my tea mug, Leigh was in the midst of telling Ivan and Tommy about our discussion about Adam. I only stayed around long enough to contribute a comment or two, and then I was back out through the swinging door. It was time to open the pancake house for the day. Any more investigating would have to wait.

Chapter 24

As I changed the sign on The Flip Side's front door, a smile spread across my face. Brett was out on the promenade, heading my way.

"How's your dad doing?" I asked once I'd greeted him.

"The trip home exhausted him, but he's resting comfortably now."

"Did you get any sleep last night?" I checked his face for signs of exhaustion, but he looked better than he had a couple of days ago.

"I did. I only got up twice to check on Dad." He pulled me into a hug. "I missed you, though."

"The feeling's mutual." I would have kissed him then, but the first customers of the day—an elderly couple who frequented the pancake house—were approaching the front door.

"Have you had breakfast?" I asked Brett once I'd greeted the couple and told them to sit wherever they liked.

"Not yet."

"You need to try the eggnog French toast," I told him.

"I'm not going to argue with you there."

Business was slow at the moment, so I told Brett to get settled in the office and fetched him a plate of French toast and a cup of coffee. Unable to resist temptation, I brought along a plate of gingerbread crêpes for myself. Ivan had infused the batter with molasses and spices so the crêpes tasted like my favorite holiday treat—ginger cookies. Filled with eggnog whipped cream and drizzled with chocolate, the gingerbread crêpes were my favorite of the holiday items we'd added to the menu for December.

As we ate, I thought about telling Brett everything that had happened the day before, but I stopped myself before the words came out of my mouth. He had enough to worry about as it was, and I didn't want to add to that.

"How was your day yesterday?" Brett asked as he cut a piece off his French toast.

"It was all right," I said, maybe a bit too quickly. "I'm guessing you're working today?"

He washed down a bite of French toast with a sip of coffee, his blue eyes on me the whole time. "I am, but what happened yesterday?"

I hesitated.

"Marley, now you're worrying me."

"There's nothing to worry about," I rushed to assure him. "But you have enough going on at the moment. I don't need to bother you with the details of my snooping."

"I thought we agreed you wouldn't hold back?"

"True," I admitted, but I didn't go any further.

He gave one of my ringlets a gentle tug. "I want to know. If it interests you, it interests me."

"All right," I relented with a smile, knowing I'd feel better with him in the loop.

I told him everything, from the discovery of Lisa's lost bracelet at the scene of Chester's death to my frightening encounter with Forrest.

Brett's eyes darkened at that part of the tale. "You should tell Ray."

I frowned at that suggestion.

"Really, Marley. He should know about it. If Ivan hadn't been there…"

"I know, but Ray will be ticked off if he knows I've been poking around." I could tell he was going to keep arguing the point, so I quickly told him what I'd learned about Adam that morning.

"Adam Silvester," Brett said, thinking.

"Do you know him?"

"No, but I think I know who you mean. He works at the grocery store, right?"

"I don't know."

"Speaking of groceries," Brett said after he'd swallowed the last piece of his French toast, "I'm going to swing by the store after work. My mom gave me a list of things she needs. I'll drop everything off there and check in on my dad, but then I'll head home. I should be there by six-thirty, so maybe we can have dinner together?"

I couldn't help but smile. "Home. I like the sound of that."

"So do I."

I was still smiling when I walked him to the front door a few minutes later.

"Why don't you give me your mom's grocery list?" I suggested. "I'll be finished work before you, and I'd like to stop by your parents' place for a few minutes anyway."

"You don't have to do that. The store doesn't close until six, so I'll have time."

I convinced him that I wanted to take care of the task and he handed over the list. I walked him out of the pancake house and down the promenade so I could kiss him goodbye out of sight of all the diners currently enjoying their breakfasts.

Once I'd seen him off, I hurried back inside, escaping the cold air that was cutting through my clothes. As the door shut behind me, I caught sight of a familiar face across the dining area. Glo's cousin Jill had arrived in my brief absence and was now seated at a small table near the back of the restaurant.

The pancake house likely wouldn't get busy for a while yet, so I decided to do some work in the office until the breakfast rush got underway. I stopped by the kitchen to tell Leigh where I'd be, and on my way out, I noticed Jill staring at me. She was all the way across the room, yet I could feel the frosty touch of her gaze against my skin. Unsettled, I turned my back on her and continued on my way to the office.

I tried to shake off the uneasiness that had burrowed into my bones, but I had trouble focusing on my computer screen. Had Forrest and Glo told Jill about what they saw as my interference in their lives? They must have. I couldn't think of any other reason why Jill would show such animosity toward me. I'd never officially met the woman, and I hadn't had any real interaction with her.

By the time I left the office to give Leigh a hand during the breakfast rush, Jill was gone, and I was glad of that. I didn't want her causing a scene in the middle of my restaurant. Maybe she wouldn't have, but that wasn't something I could have counted on.

Fortunately, all the rest of The Flip Side's patrons were in a much better mood than Jill, and the day passed quickly as I chatted with customers, served meals, and cleaned tables. When the last diner had left the pancake house shortly after two o'clock, I indulged in a plate of candy cane pancakes, enjoying the peppermint flavor and the crunch from the crushed candy sprinkled on top. The pancakes tasted extra delicious when eaten with pure maple syrup poured over them, and the candy cane flavor had a way of bringing back happy Christmas memories from my childhood. I tried not to linger too long over my delicious snack, and once I'd cleaned up my dishes, I tidied up the restaurant and headed to the bank.

Once I'd finished my banking, I consulted the shopping list Brett had given me. It wasn't a long one, so I decided I could pick up the groceries on foot rather than heading home to get my car first. I grabbed a shopping basket from the stack inside the grocery store and worked my way up and down the aisles, adding an item to my basket here and there.

When I reached the dairy products, I saw Vicky staring at the array of cheeses available, a shopping cart parked next to her holding only a few items.

"Vicky?"

She startled when I said her name, and I suspected she'd been staring at the cheeses without really seeing them.

"How are you doing?" I asked her.

She tried to produce a smile but the result was feeble at best. "I'm...all right." Her gaze drifted back to the display of cheeses. "It's hard to decide what to buy when nothing seems appetizing these days."

I rested a hand on her arm. "I'm so sorry, Vicky. Is there anything I can do for you?"

She blinked rapidly, as if fending off tears. "Have coffee with me?" She sniffled and then shook her head. "Sorry, that sounded pathetic. It's just... I've been so lonely without Wally and Chester."

A wave of intense sympathy forced me to blink away some tears of my own. "It's not pathetic." I glanced at the groceries in my basket. "I need to deliver these to my boyfriend's parents, but how about we meet up after that?"

"I really don't want you to feel you have to. I shouldn't have said anything."

"It's fine," I assured her. "I want to."

This time her smile was stronger, though it still trembled. "Thanks."

"Do you want to meet at the Beach and Bean?"

"How about at the waffle house? I don't much like being out in public these days. Too many people stare at me and whisper behind my back."

I winced. I might not have been guilty of staring at her, but I had put her on my mental list of murder suspects. "Then I'll stop by the coffee shop on my way and get us both something."

She agreed to that arrangement and as I left she finally settled on a block of cheddar cheese to add to her grocery cart.

I had misgivings about being alone with the woman since I couldn't be certain that she wasn't involved in the murders, but I felt so bad for her that I couldn't have turned her down. Hopefully we'd stay close to the restaurant's front windows so we'd be in plain view of passersby. Deciding to make sure that happened, I headed for the checkout counter and paid for the items in my basket. The two bags of groceries I ended up with weren't exactly light, but Brett's parents lived less than a ten minute walk away, so that didn't worry me. What *did* worry me was the sight of Jill standing by a display of paperback novels and puzzle books.

Wildwood Cove was a small town, so it wasn't all that strange to see the same person twice in one day, but I had the unsettling feeling that it was no coincidence we were both in the store at the same time, mostly because of the fact that she was once again staring at me with hard eyes. When I met her gaze, she didn't flinch, clearly not bothered by the fact that I knew she was watching me.

I thought I did a good job of appearing unconcerned, but when I reached the end of the street, I couldn't keep myself from checking over my shoulder to see if she was following me. She wasn't, as far as I could tell, and that brought me some relief. Even so, I picked up my pace and didn't slow down again until I'd reached Brett's parents' house.

* * * *

I didn't stay at the Collins' house for long. I spent a few minutes visiting with Frank, but as happy as he was to receive a visitor, he tired quickly. When I set off for the center of town again, I found myself glancing over my shoulder every couple of minutes, expecting to find Jill trailing me or glaring at me from across the road. I didn't want to let her get to me, but she was an intimidating woman, with her unfriendly eyes and muscular frame. If she wanted to hurt me, I had no doubt that she could. Hopefully it wouldn't come to that, but I remained on alert, not about to let her sneak up on me if she did decide to do more than glare at me.

When I reached the Beach and Bean, I ordered the mocha Vicky had requested and bought a hazelnut steamed milk for myself. With the takeout cups in hand, I headed along the street to the waffle house. As I approached the front of the restaurant, I spotted Sienna by the front door. She held a small paper bag in one hand and shaded her eyes with the other so she could peer through the glass door of The Waffle Kingdom.

"Sienna? Are you looking for Vicky?"

"Oh, hey, Marley." She stepped back from the door. "My mom sent me over with some cookies for Vicky, and I'm working up the nerve to knock on the door." She lowered her voice. "I told my mom it was crazy to send me to see a murder suspect, but she said that was nonsense because the whole town knows Vicky has an airtight alibi."

"For Wally's murder, anyway," I said.

"That's what I told her! I mean, Vicky could still be guilty of killing Chester, but my mom doesn't believe it."

Movement inside the waffle house caught my eye. Vicky had emerged from the back of the restaurant so I waved to her.

"She seems genuinely cut up about Chester's death, though," I said to Sienna as Vicky headed toward the door. "But we're having coffee together, so you don't have to be alone with her."

"Thanks. And you shouldn't be alone with her either," she said as Vicky unlocked and opened the door.

"Have you met Sienna Murray?" I asked Vicky.

"My mom, Patricia, talked to you the other day," Sienna put in.

"Oh, right," Vicky said. "I remember."

"She sent you these cookies." Sienna held out the bag to her. "Freshly baked."

"That's very kind of her. Thank you." Vicky accepted the bag and stepped back. "Come on in, both of you."

"Your mocha," I said, handing over the drink once the door was shut.

"Thanks." Vicky gestured at the nearest table. "Please, sit down. Sienna, can I get you something to drink? There's some soda in the back. Pretty much any kind you can think of. We were all stocked up for the opening."

Sienna still didn't look too comfortable with the idea of hanging out at the waffle house, but she requested a cream soda and joined me at the table while Vicky disappeared into the back, leaving the cookies and her mocha behind. She returned seconds later with Sienna's drink and a plate.

"These look delicious," she said as she slid the cookies from the bag onto the plate. "Please help yourselves."

I took one of the chocolate chip cookies and bit into it. Like everything Patricia baked, it was delicious.

Sienna popped open her can of cream soda. "Are you still planning to open the Waffle Kingdom?"

Vicky shook her head and nibbled at a cookie. "That was never my dream. Besides, the one Wally opened in Seattle last year was a flop and this one probably would have been too." She smiled wistfully. "No, my dream is to one day open a chocolate shop."

"Really?" I said with surprise.

"I worked in a small chocolate factory for years," she said. "I was thinking of striking out on my own when Wally inherited his money and got it into his head that he wanted to open a chain of waffle houses."

"Wildwood Cove has a candy shop but not an actual chocolate shop," Sienna said, her former discomfort replaced with enthusiasm. "I bet it would be really popular."

"Maybe," Vicky said, her smile fading. "But I haven't decided if I'll stay in town."

"Where will you go if you don't stay?" I asked. "Were you living in Seattle before?"

"Yes, that's where my son is."

"I didn't realize you had a son," I said.

"He lives with his father most of the time." She shrugged, the movement weary. "I don't know what I want to do. It's hard to make plans right now. I still haven't completely grasped the fact that Wally and Chester are gone." Tears glistened in her eyes and I expected her to start crying. Instead, she rubbed her forehead. "Chester. Right."

"What is it?" I asked.

"I found Chester's phone in the office earlier. He must have left it here by mistake before he…" She swallowed hard. "Before he died. I don't know if the sheriff will want it, but I figured I'd better tell him about it."

"That's probably a good idea," I agreed.

"Does it have any clues on it?" Sienna asked.

"Clues?" Vicky sounded confused. Before Sienna could clarify, she shook her head. "The battery was dead. It's the same kind of phone as mine, though, so I plugged it into my charger a few minutes ago."

"Have you heard anything from the sheriff recently?" I asked. "Has he made any progress with the investigations?"

Vicky took another small bite of her cookie before responding. "He hasn't told me much at all." Her eyes grew damp again and she fished a tissue out of her pocket. "I wish I could stop seeing Chester in my mind, the way he was when I found him." Her breath hitched. "But every time I close my eyes I see him."

"You found his body?" Sienna looked horrified.

Vicky wiped at a tear and nodded. "I couldn't reach him by phone or text, so I went by his apartment and found the door unlocked. He was lying on the floor, covered in blood." She scrunched her eyes shut. "It was awful."

"I'm so sorry you went through that," I said.

"Why would anyone want to hurt Chester?" she asked.

"Maybe he knew who killed Wally?"

"He would have said something if he did."

I tried to phrase my next question as gently as possible. "Were things still good between you and Chester when he died?"

"Of course. I loved him."

"Enough to lie for him?"

Her gaze cut toward me as sharply as a knife. "What do you mean?"

"Chester was in Wildwood Cove the night Wally died, wasn't he?"

I expected her to at least try to deny it, but instead she broke down into sobs, surprising me and startling Sienna.

"He knew he might be a suspect if the cops found out he was in town," Vicky said once her sobs had subsided. "So he asked me to say he was with me."

"And that didn't make you at all uncomfortable?" I asked.

Vicky sniffled. "I didn't see the harm in it because I knew he couldn't have killed Wally. There's no way he would have. I'm sure of it."

Since Chester was dead now, maybe she was right about that.

"Um, would it be all right for me to use your washroom?" Sienna asked, shifting in her seat as if anxious to get away from the table.

"Of course. It's just past the office." She gestured vaguely over her shoulder toward the back of the restaurant.

"Thanks." Sienna left us and headed in that direction.

Before she disappeared from sight, she sent a conspiratorial grin over her shoulder and gave me a thumbs up. Vicky had her back to her and didn't notice. I wanted to jump up and stop Sienna from doing whatever she was about to do, but I couldn't without alerting Vicky. So instead I gulped down some steamed milk and hoped Sienna wouldn't get up to too much mischief.

Chapter 25

I tried to keep Vicky engaged in conversation, but her heart clearly wasn't in it. Not wanting to give up, I asked if she had any remaining family aside from her son. She replied that she had a couple of distant cousins in New England and another somewhere in Central America.

"I hardly know them," she said. "So I've really only got my son now."

"What happened with the missing cash? Did you ever find it?"

"No, there's still no sign of it. It's not like I need it, since Wally left me everything he owned, but it's strange how it disappeared."

"Have you seen Adam Silvester around lately?" I asked, wanting to see how she reacted to his name.

To my surprise, a hint of happiness lit up her face. "Of course. Why do you ask?"

"He was in need of money until recently. I wondered if there was a chance he could have taken the cash."

"No way. Not Adam. He's a good guy. Besides, he has the money he needs now because I wrote him a check the other day."

I hadn't expected that. "To pay for his daughter's surgery?"

Vicky nodded. "He wanted it to be a loan, but I couldn't do that. In the end I convinced him to accept it as a gift for Tabitha."

"That was very generous of you."

"Not really. I have the money and Adam was always nice to me when we were growing up." Her eyes filled with tears. "He's the only friend I've got left."

Her half-finished cookie resting forgotten on the table, Vicky's gaze drifted to the window behind me. She'd taken a few sips of her mocha but seemed to have forgotten about it as well. When Sienna slipped back into her seat, she fiddled with her soda can, her legs jiggling beneath the table. She shot a pointed look my way and I detected a light of excitement in her eyes. She clearly had something she wanted to tell me, something she didn't want Vicky to hear.

"Is there anything I can do for you, Vicky?" I asked, deciding to wrap up our visit.

"No, but thank you. I really appreciate you coming by. You too, Sienna. Please thank your mom for the cookies."

Sienna pushed back her chair. "I will."

"Go ahead and take your drink if you're not finished," Vicky said with a nod at the can of cream soda.

Sienna and I said some parting words to Vicky and left the waffle house together.

"I feel so bad for her," I said, casting a last glance through the window once we were on the sidewalk.

"Me too," Sienna said. "I mean, if she's not a murderer." She gave a little hop as we walked along the street. "Guess what."

"You were snooping."

"And I found something juicy." She wrinkled her nose. "That's a bad pun."

"Pun?"

"You'll see what I mean in a minute."

We waited for a car to drive past on Wildwood Road and then we dashed across to the other side, setting off along the grassy verge toward our neighborhood.

"You know how Vicky said Chester had left his phone in the office?" Sienna said after she'd taken a swig of her cream soda.

"Yes," I said slowly. I could guess where this was going.

"I decided to take a quick look and found it on the desk."

"This is where I should tell you to keep your nose out of the whole murder thing, but I guess that would make me a hypocrite."

"And boring. Come on, you want to know what I found, don't you?"

"I do," I admitted, but not without a touch of guilt. "But after this, both of us should avoid snooping through other people's property. If either of us were to get caught by the wrong person…"

"Okay, no more snooping. Can I tell you what I found out?" She had a hop in her step again, and I suspected she was about to burst from keeping her discovery to herself.

"What did you find?"

"An email." She practically shoved her phone into my hands. "I took a picture of it."

Sure enough, the photo displayed on her phone showed the text of a short email. I zoomed in on it and read it over.

I got the tickets! It's time to start our new life of sunshine and riches. Costa Rica, here we come!

The author had signed off with xoxo, but no name. There was no name associated with the sender's address either, although the address itself contained the name Juicy Mama, followed by a string of numbers.

"Juicy Mama," Sienna said, making a face. "Gross. What kind of nickname is that?"

I handed her phone back to her, thinking over what I'd read.

Sienna shook her soda can, the remains of her drink sloshing about inside. "So? Don't you think the email is suspicious?"

"Possibly."

"Possibly?" She gaped at me in disbelief.

"Hold on. When was that email sent?"

Sienna checked her phone. "Friday morning."

"The morning after Wally's death."

"See?" Sienna said. "Suspicious, right?"

"Okay," I conceded. "You might have something there. Whoever wrote the email thought they were about to start a new life with lots of money. Quite possibly Wally's money."

"Exactly. So this Juicy Mama person—ugh—thought she was going to get Wally's money, and she sure doesn't seem cut up about his death. It sounds like she and Chester were in cahoots."

"It does sound like that's possible," I agreed cautiously, not wanting to jump to any conclusions too quickly. "But that's probably not the only explanation."

"But the most likely one. And don't you think Vicky must have sent the email? She's inheriting Wally's money and she had a thing going on with Chester. So they wanted to take off somewhere sunny with Wally's millions and killed him so they could do that."

"And, like we thought before, Vicky went out of town to make sure she had an alibi. Meanwhile Chester killed her brother. Then Vicky lied, saying Chester was with her, so they'd both have an alibi."

"Yes! But Vicky didn't really want to share her millions with him," Sienna said. "So that was the end of Chester."

I frowned and slowed my steps as we reached my driveway. I still had the same problem with that theory. "But don't you think she seems genuinely upset that Chester's gone?"

Sienna shrugged. "Like I said before, maybe she's a good actress. Or, it could be that she regrets killing him. Either way, she's guilty."

"We don't know that for sure." When I saw the light of excitement in her eyes dim, I quickly added, "But it's definitely possible. And when Vicky gives Chester's phone to Sheriff Georgeson, he'll see the email."

"So the case could be solved any day now." Her enthusiasm made a quick comeback.

"Let's hope so."

We parted ways, Sienna heading farther along the road and me following the driveway to my house. I hadn't quite reached the front steps when I heard a vehicle turn off the road. Recognizing Brett's pickup truck, I waited for him to park and get out of the vehicle.

"Good timing," I said with a smile.

He kissed me and put an arm around my shoulders as we headed for the front door. "I stopped to visit my dad for a minute or two. Thanks for taking the groceries by. My mom really appreciates it and my dad was happy to see you."

"I was happy to see him too. And your mom."

Once inside, we greeted the animals. Then I got busy preparing dinner while Brett took Bentley out for a walk. He joined me in the kitchen once he was back, and I told him about my afternoon.

"Sounds like Ray really needs to have a look at Chester's phone," Brett commented.

"He should," I agreed. "Vicky said she was going to give it to him. Although, if she's guilty and she realizes there's evidence on the phone, maybe she'll change her mind."

Brett stopped stirring the veggies he was sautéing and fetched his phone from the kitchen table. "I'll send Ray a text to let him know she has it."

"Good idea."

He returned to the stove once the text was sent.

"I'm worried about Sienna," I said after a moment.

"Because she's turning into an amateur sleuth?"

I nodded. "I don't want anything bad to happen to her."

Brett pulled me close and kissed the top my head. "Now you know how I feel."

He was grinning, but at the same time I knew he was serious.

"But Sienna's sixteen."

"True, but you said she agreed to no more snooping."

"She did."

I just hoped that was an agreement she'd stick to.

* * * *

Later that evening, I curled up on the couch with Camelia's diaries while Brett watched a movie on the television. I started with the earliest diary, reading every entry, searching for even the tiniest of clues that might point to Camelia and Grace's secret hiding place. I was more than halfway through the second diary before a surge of excitement zipped through my bloodstream.

I sat up straight and snapped the diary shut.

"Did you find a clue?" Brett asked. I'd filled him in earlier on what I was doing.

"The secret hiding spot's in the house, like I was hoping. Upstairs." I was already off the couch.

Flapjack didn't move from his spot on the back of the couch, but Brett and Bentley followed close behind me. I hurried up the stairs to the second floor tower room. When I'd inherited the house, the hexagonal room was being used for storage, full of broken furniture and odds and ends. I'd since cleaned it out and turned it into a library, leaving only an antique chair and the bookshelves that stood against the walls without windows or doors. At this hour, the windows showed nothing but darkness, and I had to flip on the overhead light to see where I was going.

I decided to start by checking the floorboards. When Brett realized what I was doing, he joined in, and soon we'd tested every board. Not a single one was loose.

"Maybe there's a secret door or something?" I said, determined not to give up.

We moved around the room, tapping and pressing different parts of the walls. Again we had no luck.

"Are you sure the hiding spot's in this room?" Brett asked.

"The diary said the upstairs tower room."

Almost hidden by the room's open door was a small closet. I opened it, excitement still humming through my bloodstream. I tugged on the string hanging from the ceiling and the single bare bulb in the closet flicked on. I'd removed the dusty old clothes I'd found in the closet when I moved in and had donated them to charity. I hadn't yet put anything in their place so I had easy access to the back of the closet.

Inside the small space, narrow slats of weathered wood paneling covered the walls. I ducked beneath the single shelf that ran the width of the upper part of the closet so I could reach the back wall. Starting from the right, I tapped each of the wooden slats, searching for any that might be loose. It only took me four tries to find one.

I pried the slat away from the wall with my fingernails until the top half was bending slightly away from the wall, far enough that I could see behind it.

"Anything?" Brett asked from over my shoulder.

"I found a loose panel, but there doesn't seem to be anything behind it." I couldn't keep my disappointment from creeping into my voice.

"Let's remove it completely."

I moved aside so he could duck under the shelf and pull at the slat. It didn't take much for the entire panel to break away from the wall.

I crouched down to check near the baseboard, but there was nothing hidden there. I jiggled the neighboring panels, but they held fast. Not wanting to give up, I tried every other piece of paneling and every floorboard in the closet. None of them was the least bit loose.

Backing out of the closet, I wiped my dusty hands on my jeans, my spirits plummeting. "I was sure we'd find the letter." I sounded as glum as I felt.

Brett put an arm around me. "Maybe it's not here to find. Jimmy lived here for decades. Could he have found it at some point?"

"I don't think so. I'm sure he would have mentioned it if he had."

Returning to the closet, I ran my fingers along the edges of the panels neighboring the vacant spot. I hoped desperately that my fingers would touch paper, but I had no more luck than the first time. My nose twitched, tickled by the dust in the closet, so I left the enclosed space before I started sneezing.

"I'm sorry, Marley," Brett said. "I know you really wanted to find the letter."

I nodded, but didn't know what to say.

As I switched off the light in the closet, the doorbell rang. I looked to Brett, surprised.

"Not expecting anyone?" he guessed.

"No." I didn't usually have visitors this late.

We headed downstairs, Bentley racing to the foyer ahead of us. I opened the front door to find Lisa on the porch, huddled inside her jacket, her breath forming little clouds in front of her face.

"Lisa, come on in." I quickly shut the door behind her to stop the icy draft that was wafting into the house.

"Hi, guys." She gave Bentley a pat while he wagged his tail and licked her hand.

"What is it?" I asked, noting how anxious she looked.

"I just...can't sleep. I keep thinking the sheriff's going to turn up at any moment to arrest me." She glanced at Brett. "Sorry, I don't mean anything against him, but I'm not in a good situation."

"Don't worry about it," he assured her. "Come on in and sit down."

"I was really sorry to hear about your dad," Lisa said to Brett as we led her to the family room. "How's he doing now?"

"He's home and on the mend."

"I'm so glad to hear it."

When we reached the family room, Flapjack stood up on the couch and stretched, arching his back with his front paws outstretched. Lisa sat down and he immediately claimed her lap, purring as she ran a hand over his fur.

"Do you want to stay the night?" I asked her.

"Could I? I know it's terrible of me to impose..."

"You're not imposing at all. Of course you can stay."

"Thank you, Marley." She closed her eyes. "I just want all of this to be over."

"It will be soon," I said.

I hoped desperately that I'd told her the truth.

Chapter 26

Clouds moved in during the night, nudging up the temperature and bringing a rain shower or two. By the time I reached the pancake house in the morning, the clouds were scudding away, revealing more and more blue sky. I got off to a slower start than usual, spending some time with Lisa in the morning before she'd headed home to get ready for work. She'd managed a few hours of sleep, but she still had dark rings under her eyes, and I knew that likely wouldn't change until she could stop worrying.

She was still afraid that Ray would appear at any moment to snap handcuffs on her, or to demand a sample of her DNA, backed by a warrant, so he could prove the bracelet found in Chester's apartment belonged to her. I wished I could tell her that wouldn't happen, but I knew as well as she did that it was a real possibility.

Brett was working at a new job site, renovating a kitchen and bathroom for Mr. and Mrs. Jepson, who owned one of the beachfront houses farther along the cove. He'd told me before setting off that he was going to stop by his house after work to pack up more of his clothes.

That left me with a smile on my face, despite my concerns for Lisa. I'd known he was moving in, of course, since he'd accepted my offer, but somehow transferring more of his belongings made it seem more real.

I'd worried momentarily about Chloe, since she lived at his house, but Brett assured me that he wasn't going to force her to move anytime soon. If she wanted to get a roommate, Brett would be fine with that. If he decided to sell the house, it wouldn't be for a while yet.

During a lull at the pancake house later that morning, I fingered the seahorse pendant around my neck, knowing how lucky I was to have a man like Brett in my life. Thinking about my necklace reminded me of the one Chester had given Vicky. I cast my mind back to the previous afternoon, trying to remember the details of my visit to the waffle house. I was fairly certain that Vicky had still been wearing the necklace. If she'd killed Chester, would she have kept that reminder of him hanging around her neck?

I carried a plate of gingerbread crêpes and a serving of pumpkin waffles to a waiting couple, and cleared dishes from a recently vacated table. As I worked, my thoughts returned to Vicky.

As I'd told Sienna, it was possible that Vicky had killed Chester after conspiring with him to kill Wally, but I was still having a hard time accepting that theory. I couldn't shake the feeling that Vicky's grief was sincere. But she was the one who'd inherited Wally's money, and—as far as I knew—the only person who could have expected to inherit it. So who else would Juicy Mama be?

I wished the email had contained more clues as to the sender's identity. If Chester was in love with Vicky, why would he have planned to take off to Costa Rica with another woman?

I smiled at a group of customers as they left The Flip Side, relieved that the workday was nearing its end. I loved working at the pancake house and chatting with customers, but today I was so distracted that keeping my mind on food orders was a struggle.

When the last diner had left, I went through my usual afternoon routine of tidying up the dining area and taking care of a few office tasks. I checked my phone as I was getting ready to leave and noticed that Sienna had sent me a series of text messages.

Talked to Bailey. Her dad was home all evening the night Wally died. So Forrest Hansfield had an alibi.

Not snooping! Sienna's next message read. *Just asked a few questions.* She'd followed that text with another.

Uh-oh! Bailey thinks her mom's cousin killed Wally and she's freaking out. She wants to confront her. Not good! Going with her.

I grabbed my jacket, pulling it on before tapping out a rushed message. *Try to stop her! I'll meet you if you tell me where.*

By the time I grabbed my tote bag, Sienna had already replied. *We're heading for River Drive. More soon.*

I hurried out the door, locking the pancake house behind me. I wished I'd brought my car to work that morning so I could get to Sienna and Bailey faster, but I hadn't so I'd have to make do on foot. Setting off at a jog, I passed through the center of town and into Wildwood Cove's southern residential neighborhoods. I rushed by Leigh's house without slowing my pace, continuing on for another two blocks before switching to a walk.

Sienna had sent me another text message with Jill's address.

Come around back. Bailey's going in!

I was on the right street now, and within seconds I identified Jill's house. I let myself into the yard through a squeaky wooden gate and followed a path around to the back of the house. The grass was neatly tended but beyond that I didn't notice anything about the yard. As soon as I was behind the house, I saw Sienna waving to me through a large window. I hurried up the steps to the back porch and Sienna met me at the door, taking my arm and practically pulling me inside.

"Bailey's freaking out," she whispered as she shut the door behind me.

Sounds of someone moving about came from deeper in the house.

"Where's Jill?" I asked, not hearing any voices aside from our own.

"She's not here."

"Then how did you two get in?"

"Bailey knows where Jill hides her spare key."

So technically we weren't breaking and entering, but we were still in Jill's house without her permission. Getting caught wouldn't be a good idea.

Sienna led me down a hallway to a room that apparently doubled as an office and exercise room. Barbells and free weights took up most of the space, and a desk sat against one wall. Bailey was seated before the desk, shuffling through the contents of an open drawer.

"Bailey, this is Marley," Sienna said.

Bailey barely glanced up from what she was doing. She shoved the drawer shut and moved on to the one below it.

"I told Bailey you've been looking into the murders."

Bailey finally paused and focused her attention on me. "Do you have any proof?"

"No," I replied. "I'm not even sure yet who committed the crimes."

"I am."

She returned to her investigation of the drawer's contents. It appeared to hold mostly papers, thumb drives, and miscellaneous office supplies.

"What makes you so sure Jill was involved?" I asked.

Bailey flipped through a sheaf of papers before stuffing them back in the drawer. "My parents have been keeping secrets lately. I know my mom did something she doesn't want anyone to know about. She hated Wally. He killed my aunt years ago and she can't—couldn't—stand the sight of him. You suspect my mom too," she said almost accusingly, her blue eyes on me.

"That's true," I conceded, "but she's not tall enough to have killed Wally on her own."

"That's what Sienna told me. So you thought maybe my dad helped her. Only he was home that night with me. So if my mom had help, it must have been from Jill." She slammed the drawer shut and turned on the desktop computer with a jab of the power button. "Jill's tall enough and strong enough." She pointed at all the weights in the room. "She's a freaking bodybuilder. She could probably kill just about anyone with her bare hands."

"That doesn't mean she would," I said.

I didn't disagree with anything Bailey was saying, but I didn't want to feed the furor that had apparently taken over her.

"Except she hated Wally too," Sienna said from beside me.

"Exactly." Bailey glared at the computer, probably because it was taking its time booting up. "Jill and my mom have always been close. Jill was seriously mad when Wally Fowler moved back to town, and she'd do anything to protect my mom."

Maybe Jill really did belong at the top of the suspect list.

"What are you hoping to find?" I asked as Bailey manipulated the mouse, opening the computer's web browser.

Sienna was the one to answer. "More evidence that Jill's the one who sent the email to Chester about going to Costa Rica."

"*More* evidence?"

Sienna gestured for me to follow her out into the hall. I did so, and she pointed to the foyer. I took only a few steps before I saw what she wanted to show me. Sitting off to the side of the front door was a suitcase. I tested its weight. It definitely wasn't empty.

I set the suitcase down. "Okay, so it looks like Jill's going on a trip. Do we know where to?"

"We will if Bailey finds airline ticket receipts," Sienna said as we returned to the combination study and weight room.

"I'm not sure this is a good idea," I said to both girls. "If Jill comes home and finds us all here…"

Bailey didn't budge. "I'm not leaving until I find the evidence."

"We don't know that there will be evidence," I pointed out.

Bailey ignored me and Sienna appeared unconvinced.

"Jill has a daughter who's away at college," Sienna said. "So she's a mother. Plus, her last name is McDonald."

It took only a second for me to realize the significance of that. "So her initials are JM. You think that's where the nickname Juicy Mama came from?"

Sienna shrugged, but I could tell she did believe that.

Maybe it was true. I had to agree that plenty of evidence was pointing at Jill, although all of the puzzle pieces still didn't quite fit together in my mind. If she'd wanted revenge on Wally, would she have dated and killed Chester?

And guilty or not, I didn't want to know what would happen if Jill found us in her house. Bailey might be related to her and she might have used a key, but that didn't mean Jill would be pleased to know we were in her house, going through her papers and computer.

Bailey released a sound of frustration. "I'm trying to get into the Juicy Mama Gmail account, but I can't figure out the password."

"Did you try her birthdate?" Sienna asked.

"I don't know her birthdate, other than the month." She yanked open one of the desk drawers and rifled through it again. "I bet I can find it."

I tried to think of other connections between Jill and the crimes. "Was Jill ever seen with Chester that you know of, Bailey?"

"No, but that doesn't mean she wasn't seeing him."

I remembered Chester's visit to the antiques shop. "Does she have pierced ears?"

"Yes." Bailey paused in her search. "Does that mean something?"

"Possibly. I saw Chester buying a necklace and a set of earrings at the antiques shop. He gave the necklace to Vicky, but she doesn't have pierced ears. Maybe he didn't realize that at the time and returned the earrings."

Sienna picked up my train of thought. "Or he gave them to the other woman he was seeing—Jill."

To my surprise, Bailey's face crumpled. She scrunched her eyes shut as tears leaked out and rolled down her cheeks. "She did it, didn't she? And my mom was in on it. My mom's an accessory to murder." Sobs shook her whole body.

Sienna hugged her. I patted Bailey's back, a rush of sympathy for the teenager almost bringing tears to my eyes too.

"We don't know that for sure," I told her.

"*I* do." She continued to sob in Sienna's arms.

"We should get you home, Bailey," I said.

"I can't go home. I have to find proof."

"We should leave that to the professionals." I wasn't oblivious of the fact that I sounded like Ray.

Bailey shook her head, adamant. Sienna released her from her hug and Bailey pulled a letter out of an envelope.

"I can take you to talk to the sheriff if that will make you feel better," I offered, eager to get the girls out of the house.

"As soon as I find proof." Tears still rolling down her cheeks—silently now—she tried a new password for the email account.

I was about to suggest she try getting into the account from another computer when the lock on the front door clicked.

Chapter 27

All three of us turned our heads toward the hallway. The front door opened and closed. Keys jangled and something clunked against the floor. I glanced around the room, desperately searching for a place for the three of us to hide. One of the girls might fit under the desk, but there were no other hiding places. Sienna and I stared at each other, horrified.

Footsteps headed along the hallway. I glanced at Bailey. She didn't appear the least bit worried. Her face had taken on a fiercely determined expression, her blue eyes icy. She fixed her gaze on the doorway, and I turned my attention there too.

Jill strode along the hallway. She almost made it past the door before she glanced in the room and saw us. She did a double take, her brown eyes going wide.

"What the hell is going on here?" She noticed her cousin's daughter sitting at the desk. "*Bailey?*"

My heart thudded in my chest. I stepped in front of Sienna, as if that would somehow protect her from the fury now radiating off Jill.

"And you!" Jill pointed at me. "What are you doing in my house?"

Bailey stood up. "We're looking for evidence."

Jill stared at her, angry and bewildered. "Evidence?"

"Evidence that you're a murderer."

Jill gaped at Bailey for another second before swinging around to face me. "You," she spat out, jabbing a finger at me. "You put her up to this, didn't you?"

"No," I said, surprised but relieved to find I sounded calm and confident.

"Like hell you didn't. Forrest told me all about you. You're trying to throw him and Glo under the bus, to have them blamed for things they didn't do."

"That's not true."

"No?" She loomed over me, glaring down at me. "I've been watching you and I've asked around. Lisa Morales is a friend of yours. She's a suspect, and you're trying to get her off the hook by framing Glo and Forrest."

"I'm not trying to frame anyone. If anyone's being framed, it's Lisa."

Jill snorted, sounding unnervingly like an angry wild animal.

From behind me, Sienna grabbed my hand. I gave hers what I hoped was a reassuring squeeze.

Beside me, Bailey raised her chin. "We know you killed Wally on Mom's behalf. You probably killed Chester too. And now you're taking off for Costa Rica."

"Costa Rica? Where did you get a crazy idea like that?"

"From the email you sent Chester," Bailey said with a note of cold triumph. "And your suitcase is all packed."

"I'm going to a bodybuilding competition in Chicago, and I never sent an email to Chester."

"A likely story," Bailey shot back.

"That's it." Jill produced a cellphone from her pocket. She pointed at Bailey. "I'm calling your mother." She pointed at me next. "And then I'm calling the sheriff to deal with you. You'll be arrested for breaking and entering."

Bailey held up a key. "We didn't break and enter."

Jill grabbed the key from her. "Your mother will deal with you. The sheriff will deal with this busybody." She glared at me with that last statement.

My stomach sank. It looked like I'd end up in handcuffs before Lisa did.

"If you call the sheriff, he might arrest you," Bailey said.

"He has no reason to arrest me!" Jill shouted.

Bailey burst into tears again and some of Jill's ire drained away.

"Bailey, I didn't kill anyone and neither did your mom."

Bailey sniffled. "But she had reason to kill Wally."

"Yes, she did, and I'm not all that sorry he's dead, but we had nothing to do with the murders."

"Mom's hiding *something*." Bailey hiccupped and wiped at her tears. "I know she is."

Jill heaved out a sigh. "She slashed Wally's tires."

"She did?" I said with surprise. Then I realized how much sense that made. "She slipped away from the ladies' night at the hardware store to do it."

Jill clearly still had no kind feelings toward me, but she nodded.

Sneaking away to slash the tires explained the dark smudge I'd seen Glo trying to rub off her hand after she came in through the store's back door.

Bailey wiped away another tear. "But why didn't she say so? She made me come clean about my shoplifting, so why didn't she face up to what she did?"

"She was probably afraid it would make her look too suspicious," I said.

Jill nodded again. "Your mom slashed the tires right around the time Wally was killed. She had motive and opportunity, and the tire slashing shows she was capable of taking out her anger on Wally, in some form at least. Your dad and I told her not to say anything. We thought it would be for the best."

Bailey stared at her hands, now clasped in her lap. "So you and mom didn't hurt anyone?"

"No. I swear we didn't."

Bailey raised her eyes. "Please don't call the cops. Sienna and Marley are only here because I'm here."

Jill addressed me, her eyes hard again. "If you and your little friend leave *right now*, I won't call the sheriff. But if I ever see you with so much as a toe on my property again, the outcome will be very different."

Sienna still had hold of my hand, so I tugged her toward the door.

"Bailey, do you want to come with us?" I asked. I wasn't completely comfortable with the thought of leaving her behind.

She nodded and lowered her eyes. "Sorry," she mumbled to Jill before following me and Sienna to the front door.

We hurried out of the house and down the street, not slowing until we reached the corner.

"Do you believe Jill?" Sienna asked Bailey as we came to a stop.

Her friend nodded. "I think so."

She hugged herself and shivered, and I realized for the first time that she didn't have a coat.

As if reading my thoughts, Sienna said, "She left her house in a rush after I told her about the email. She didn't stop for a coat or anything else."

I slipped out of my own jacket and put it around Bailey's shoulders.

"Thanks," she said through chattering teeth.

"We should get you home," I told her.

She didn't outright agree with the suggestion, but she also didn't protest.

I led the way along a side street. We hadn't gone far when an old and rusting car approached us from behind and pulled up to the curb, the front passenger widow lowering.

"Hey, there," Justine said, leaning over from the driver's seat to speak to us through the open window.

"Hi, Justine," Sienna replied with a wave.

Justine's gaze landed on me. "Isn't it a bit cold to be going around without a jacket?"

"It is," I said, without bothering to explain the circumstances.

She motioned us closer to the car. "Climb in. I can give you a ride if you're not going far. My daughter's with my stepmom, but I don't need to pick her up for another half hour."

"I'd like a ride," Bailey said, still shivering despite wearing my jacket.

"Thanks, Justine." I opened the back door so Bailey and Sienna could get in.

Once I'd buckled up in the passenger seat, Justine pulled away from the curb.

"Where to?" she asked.

Bailey provided directions to her house. It only took a minute to get there in the car.

"Are you going to be okay?" I asked as Bailey opened the back door.

"I think so." She handed me my jacket over the seat. "Thanks." She directed the last word at all of us.

"I'll text you later, okay?" Sienna said as her friend got out of the car. Bailey nodded and shut the door.

Justine set the car in motion again. "Where to now? Home, Sienna?"

"Yes, please. And Marley lives near me."

Justine turned onto Main Street and followed it northward.

My thoughts remained with Bailey. For her sake, I hoped everything Jill said was true. I believed her about the slashed tires. Hopefully that's where Glo's involvement ended. I thought there was a good chance that was the case.

That took me back to the Vicky-and-Chester-in-cahoots theory. Although I had trouble getting past the idea of Vicky's grief being nothing more than a show, in other ways that theory made more sense than the one involving Jill and Glo, especially when it came to the suggestion in the email that Chester and the sender would enjoy a life of riches in Costa Rica.

Unfortunately, I didn't feel any closer to actually proving anyone's involvement in the murders. That wasn't good news for Lisa or Ivan. I wasn't looking forward to telling them that I still couldn't prove their innocence and I was all too aware that time was running out.

"Do you think Bailey will be okay?" Sienna asked me as Justine turned onto Wildwood Road.

"I hope so. I think there's a good chance Jill was telling the truth."

"What's going on?" Justine asked with clear interest.

I hesitated, remembering that Justine was a reporter, not sure how much it would be wise to tell her. Before I could decide what to share or hold back, Sienna spoke up.

"We thought Bailey's mom and her mom's cousin might have killed Wally and Chester, but that doesn't seem like it's the case anymore."

"Really?" Justine glanced at Sienna's reflection in the rearview mirror. "What made you think that?"

"I saw an email on Chester's phone. It sounded like he and some woman had been planning to take off for Costa Rica with lots of money."

"And you thought that woman was Bailey's mom?"

"Her mom's cousin," Sienna said. "But it looks like we were wrong."

I shifted in my seat, wondering how to get the message to Sienna that she probably shouldn't share too much with Justine. Maybe Charlene wouldn't let Justine print anything that would upset or humiliate the Hansfields, but I couldn't be sure about that.

"Vicky's the one who's inheriting Wally's money," Justine said. "Could she be the one who sent the email?"

"That crossed our minds, but we really don't know who sent it," I said, hoping that would put an end to the conversation.

Justine gave no indication that she'd heard me. "I heard a rumor that Chester and Vicky had a romance going on. It seems likely that she'd be the one planning to take off to Costa Rica with him."

Sienna leaned forward between the two front seats. "We thought about that too. Marley thinks Vicky seems genuinely sad about Chester's death, though. But I figure maybe she's just a good actress."

"She is," Justine said. "So I've heard, anyway."

"I'm still not convinced," I said.

"Lisa Morales is still a suspect."

"It wasn't Lisa," I said with conviction.

"You're probably right," Justine conceded. "Lisa's too nice to kill anyone."

"Plus, she doesn't have kids," Sienna added.

"What's that got to do with it?" Justine asked.

"Whoever sent Chester the email has the handle Juicy Mama."

"I'm sure the sheriff will figure it out," I said quickly, hoping to put an end to the conversation.

I didn't like the expression on Justine's face. I suspected she was already writing a story in her head, one that would include information that Ray might not want the public knowing at this stage of the investigation.

She smiled and tucked her hair behind one ear. "I'm sure you're right."

I was about to point out my driveway when icy fear shot through my veins.

Dangling from Justine's ears were the earrings I'd seen Chester buy at the antiques shop.

Chapter 28

My heart rate jumped into overdrive as a string of thoughts rushed through my head.

"That's Marley's place." Sienna pointed to the entrance to my driveway.

"Actually, keep going," I said to Justine, forcing myself to sound calm and completely normal. "I'd like to talk to Sienna's mom for a few minutes."

That way the teen wouldn't be left alone in the car with a murderer.

"She's out," Sienna said. "I don't think she'll be home until this evening."

I scrambled to come up with a new plan. "Then I'll get out near the Jepsons' place. My boyfriend's working there."

Justine pulled to a stop across the street from the Murrays' driveway and Sienna climbed out, thanking Justine for the ride.

"See you, Marley."

I waved to her and watched as she jogged across the road. My fear lowered by a single notch once she was safely out of sight, but I could still barely breathe. My heart was thumping painfully hard against my rib cage. Time seemed to have slowed, each second ticking by sluggishly.

Justine drove forward again, but then she pulled back onto the shoulder of the road and stopped.

"Would you mind getting out here, Marley?" she asked with a smile.

"Um, sure." I wasted no time opening the door, feeling equal parts wary of why she'd stopped and eager to get away from her. "Thanks for the ride." I forced a smile and climbed out of the car. "See you around."

I was almost ready to let out a sigh of relief when the driver's door opened. The friendly smile had vanished from Justine's face.

My heart nearly stopped, stuttering with fear, when she pointed a gun at me over the hood of the car.

"Sorry to interfere with your plans," Justine said, her expression now cold, "but you'll have to wait to see your boyfriend. Indefinitely."

"What's this about?" I had to force the words out of my dry throat.

"Oh, I think you know," Justine said. "You figured it out, didn't you?"

My gaze darted to the left and right, hoping to find that we weren't alone. Aside from the two of us, the road was deserted.

"I don't know what you're talking about," I said slowly, struggling to stay calm while my whole body trembled.

"Cut the act." Justine practically spat the words across the hood of the car. "I saw it in your eyes. You figured it out just a moment ago. What tipped you off?"

"Your earrings," I replied, not wanting to make her any angrier.

"How could my earrings tell you anything?"

"I was at the antiques store when Chester bought them. He bought a necklace at the same time and gave it to Vicky. I thought maybe he'd returned the earrings because Vicky's ears aren't pierced. But he didn't, did he? He gave them to *you*."

"He bought them here in town?" Her face flushed with rage. "That idiot! He ruined everything!"

Shards of fear cut through me at her anger.

"Did you know he was seeing Vicky?" I asked, hoping to keep her talking until I could figure out a better way to keep her from harming me.

"He wasn't seeing her. Not really. It was all part of the plan."

"The plan to get her inheritance," I said, the full picture becoming clearer in my head. "Or at least part of it. Did you really think Vicky would hand Chester a bunch of money because he wooed her with some jewelry?"

"It was a good plan. It just needed patience. Vicky was falling for Chester already. It wouldn't have been long until she fell head over heels. It was easy to get her to provide Chester with an alibi. Once Wally was dead, Chester was supposed to ask Vicky for money for a business of his own. It's not like she's financially savvy. I'm sure she would have handed it over."

That was likely true, considering what she'd done for Adam.

"And then you and Chester were going to take off for Costa Rica."

She didn't bother to confirm that statement.

"Come over here," she ordered. When I hesitated, she snapped, "Now!"

Unable to tear my eyes away from the gun, I complied, moving around the front of the car with measured steps. When I approached Justine, she took two steps away from the car.

"Ditch your phone."

I carefully pulled the device out of my tote bag and tossed it over the hood of the car. I felt sick as I let it go. My only possible lifeline was gone.

Justine nodded at the driver's seat. "Get in."

"Why?" I asked.

"You do realize I've got a gun pointed at you, don't you?"

"Think this through, Justine," I said as I slowly settled into the driver's seat.

"I already have. Put your hands on the steering wheel where I can see them."

Again, I obeyed the order.

"Don't move or I'll put a bullet through your head."

She shoved the door shut with her foot and hurried around the front of the car, keeping her weapon pointed at me through the windshield. She yanked open the passenger door and slid into the seat beside me.

She jutted her chin at the keys dangling from the ignition. "Drive."

My predicament was only getting worse. I desperately tried to think of a way to disarm Justine, but I didn't see how I could without getting shot.

"Justine…" I started, hoping to stall her.

"Drive!"

Her voice was filled with fury, but I also detected a note of panic. That scared me more than her anger. I didn't want her acting more rashly than she already was.

I started the engine and put the car into motion. "Where are we going?"

"You'll find out when we get there. Just keep driving."

I did as instructed, wishing a car would pass by. Not that it would do much good. I didn't know how I could get anyone's attention without putting myself in even more danger.

Although I didn't know our final destination, I could guess what would happen when we arrived there. I was the only one who knew Justine was involved in the murders. I didn't doubt for a second that she was planning to get rid of me. There were miles of forest outside of town. It could take a long time for anyone to figure out what had happened to me, if they ever did.

Memories of my conversation with Joan fluttered to the forefront of my mind. Tassy was buried out there in the woods somewhere, her remains never discovered. The thought of Tassy steeled my resolve. There was no way I was going to end up like that. There was no way I wasn't going home to Brett that night.

"Chester must have really loved you to kill his best friend for you," I said.

"How do you know *I* didn't kill Wally?"

I kept my eyes on the road, not wanting to see the gun. "You're not tall enough."

Although I wasn't looking at her, I sensed Justine stiffen as a car drove past us in the opposite direction. She relaxed again once the other vehicle was out of sight.

"He didn't want to do it at first, but I can be very convincing." She sounded smug. "That night they were alone in the kitchen and an opportunity presented itself, so Chester took advantage."

"And shoved Wally's face into the liquid nitrogen."

"I have to give him credit. I didn't think he was capable of such creativity. I figured he'd use a knife or something. But Wally wanted Chester to help him figure out how to use the liquid nitrogen to make ice cream so he could show off at the grand opening. The Waffle King pretty much set up his own death."

She was so matter-of-fact about it that a chill crept up my back and down my arms.

"Keep going straight," she directed.

Instead of taking the turnoff toward the highway, I continued following the road along the curve of the coastline.

"But you killed Chester before he had a chance to get any money from Vicky. What went wrong?"

"He got *some* money, just not nearly enough. He watched Vicky open the safe one day and memorized the combination. Wally had nearly thirty thousand bucks sitting in there. Chester stole it and wanted the two of us to take off without waiting for more money." She let out a derisive huff. "I've already had to start over once after my divorce. I'm not doing that again. The whole point of this was to have lots of money, to have a better life for me and my daughter. Thirty grand wasn't going to cut it."

Her daughter.

The thought of that poor kid sent a wave of sadness crashing over me. I did my best to shake it off. I needed to stay focused.

"So you shot Chester," I said, hoping she'd keep talking.

"I didn't *want* to shoot him. I didn't want to kill him at all, but when I got ticked off about the money he realized I cared more about it than I did about him. After he tried to run me down with his car, I knew I had to get rid of him. My plan was to smother him while he was drunk, but he fought back so I had to use the gun."

I struggled not to shudder at her callousness. "But why frame Lisa?"

"That was nothing personal. I knew she was already under suspicion and I saw her lose her bracelet at the coffee shop one afternoon. The opportunity was too perfect. I planted it at Chester's apartment. Then I told the sheriff I'd heard about the bracelet found at the scene and hinted that it sounded like one Lisa wore."

Anger mixed in with my sadness and fear. She had no remorse for all the terrible things she'd done.

I gave up on keeping her talking. The road dead-ended in less than a mile. If I was going to do something to help myself, I had to hurry up and act. I saw the Jepson property up ahead where Brett and his fellow workers were busy with renovations. I wished I had some way of reaching him, but I was on my own.

I tightened my already-fierce grip on the steering wheel. Short of crashing the car—which could get us both killed—I couldn't think of a plan that wouldn't get me shot.

A flicker of movement caught my eye. Up ahead, a deer darted across the road. I glanced Justine's way. The deer had captured her attention too. The gun drifted to one side. I pounced on the opportunity and grabbed Justine's wrist, smashing her hand against the dashboard.

She let out a cry of rage as the gun dropped to the floor by her feet. She shoved me hard and my shoulder slammed against the door. The car swerved. I barely kept it from crashing into the ditch.

Justine ducked down to retrieve the gun.

With a squeal of tires, I turned the car into the nearest driveway without slowing, hoping to get us closer to help.

Justine had the gun again. As she pointed it toward me, I latched on to her wrist, throwing off her aim. She tried to yank her arm out of my grip and I lurched over to her side of the vehicle. I had one hand on the steering wheel, but the car swerved wildly, leaving the long driveway for the grass.

I was about to hit the brakes when a loud bang exploded around us. The front passenger window shattered. My ears ringing, I yanked Justine back my way and the gun slid from her hand and fell into the footwell on my side of the car. She threw herself over my legs to get it from the floor. Her body weight pinned my foot down on the gas pedal.

"Justine!" I yelled at her, the car gaining speed fast.

We zoomed past a white Victorian and I swerved just in time to miss a gazebo.

I wasn't as lucky with a garbage can. The car struck it with a clang and it flew across the yard.

Justine was still scrambling around for the gun near my feet. I tried to jerk my foot off the pedal, but it remained trapped. I yelled at Justine again, this time more frantically.

She bolted upright, the gun in her hand.

The car gave a massive jolt as it left the yard for the beach. We bounced up into the air, the car flying forward.

I saw the ocean ahead of us, rushing toward the windshield.

Then the car smacked into the water.

Chapter 29

The impact rattled my bones. My body slammed against the steering wheel before I was thrown back against my seat. I stared straight ahead, shocked by all that had happened in the last several seconds.

Icy water tickled at my ankles, jerking me back to the reality of our situation. We were in the ocean and the car was sinking.

Bitterly cold water trickled in around the edges of the doors. Neither of us was wearing a seatbelt and Justine was slumped forward against the dashboard, blood running down her face from a gash on her forehead. No airbags had deployed. Maybe the old car didn't have any.

I couldn't see the gun. A gushing sound drew my attention to the right. The car was now low enough in the water that the ocean was pouring in through the broken window.

Desperate to get my legs out of the numbingly cold water, I knelt on the seat. I tried to open the driver's door but the pressure from the water kept it shut tight.

"Justine!"

She didn't stir.

The freezing water was up over the seats now and it was cascading over Justine as it poured in through the window. I grabbed her and heaved her my way. I could hardly move her. There was no way I'd get her out the window.

I needed to find help.

The water was nearly up to my chest now. Every inch of my body was either going numb or screaming with pain from the cold. I climbed over Justine's legs and drew in as deep a breath as I could. I plunged head first into the onslaught of water, nearly gasping at the shock of the cold. My fingers grabbed the edge of the window frame and I fought my way out of the car. I was almost free when my right foot got caught on something. I kicked and flailed, panic tightening its vise around my already-burning chest.

My foot kicked free and I almost sobbed with relief.

Where was the surface?

Everything was dark. No, not completely dark.

I fought my way toward the light, desperate for air, knowing I couldn't hold my breath much longer.

My lungs burned.

My body demanded that I breathe in.

Just as I opened my mouth, I broke through to the surface. I gasped in great gulps of air, then choked on a mouthful of salty water. Coughs racked my body as I desperately tried to get oxygen into my lungs. I was flailing in the water; my clothes heavy and pulling me down, down, down.

The water closed over my head again.

Someone grabbed me beneath my arms and hauled me back to the surface.

I'd drawn in three desperate, wheezing breaths of air before I realized someone was swimming with me, towing me on my back.

"You're okay, Marley. I've got you."

I wanted to cry at the sound of Brett's voice, but I was too focused on trying to keep oxygen going into my lungs while coughs still shook my body.

We paused in the water and I got my first look at Brett as he found his footing in the shallows and scooped me into his arms.

"You're going to be okay," he said.

I shivered as he splashed toward shore.

"Justine," I said, my teeth chattering together. "She's still in the car."

Two men ran toward us. Brett passed me into the arms of one of them.

"There's still someone in the car," I heard him yell as he splashed back out into the ocean. "Get Marley inside!"

The man not holding me charged into the water after Brett.

"Are you okay, Marley?"

I didn't want to take my eyes off the spot in the ocean where Brett had disappeared beneath the surface, but I glanced up at the man who held me in his arms.

"Pedro?"

"Can you stand?" he asked.

I nodded and he set my feet down on the sand.

"Let's get you inside."

I checked over my shoulder for Brett and saw with relief that he was towing Justine to shore, his colleague waiting to help him get her out of the water.

A crowd was gathering on the beach. A woman hurried toward me and Pedro and I recognized her as Mrs. Jepson.

"You poor thing. Are you hurt?" she asked.

"No. Just cold," I said, my teeth still chattering.

"We need to get you into dry clothes right away." She put an arm around my shoulders and hurried me up to her house and in through the back door.

She steered me to a powder room and supplied me with fluffy towels, a plastic bag, and a purple tracksuit. Moving as quickly as I could, I peeled off my soaked clothes, dried off, and donned the tracksuit. I stuffed my soaked clothes into the plastic bag and rushed out to the back porch.

Justine was now lying on the ground near the porch steps, winter jackets piled over her. Brett was kneeling next to her. She opened her eyes and made a choking sound before coughing up water. Brett helped her onto her side, settling her in the recovery position. She moved a couple of her fingers, but not much else.

"She had a gun," I warned Brett.

He glanced up sharply and then returned his attention to Justine, checking beneath the jackets covering her.

"She doesn't have it now."

Pedro switched places with Brett, taking over Justine's care. Brett reached me in three swift strides but stopped short of touching me.

"I want to hug you but I don't want to get you wet again." He settled for kissing my forehead.

"You need dry clothes," I said.

"Yes, I do. And you need to be inside where it's warm."

A siren cut through the air, drawing closer every second.

"Help's almost here for Justine," Brett said.

"She killed Chester and she was going to kill me too."

A shadow passed across Brett's face. He related that information to Pedro and then bundled me into his truck. We passed an ambulance as it turned into the Jepson's driveway and in under a minute we were home.

Brett changed into dry clothes while I put the kettle on. When he reappeared in the kitchen, dressed in jeans and a sweater, I abandoned the cocoa powder I'd taken from the cupboard and practically barreled into him. He hugged me and I pressed in close to him, seeking out some warmth, but he was as cold as I was.

"Are you okay?" he asked. "You aren't hurt?"

"I'm fine," I assured him. "Thanks to you. I'm lucky you used to be a lifeguard.

He kissed me and then studied a sore spot on my forehead that was likely bruised. "You're not dizzy or feeling sick?"

"No."

"It's a good thing you weren't in the water very long. You should be okay as long as you keep warm."

"You need to do the same," I reminded him.

"I will." He took over the job of making hot chocolate.

While he made the drinks, I dried my hair and changed into clothes of my own, dressing in layers with leggings under my sweatpants and two long-sleeved shirts under my coziest hoodie. I added thick socks and warm slippers before returning to the kitchen.

Brett pressed a mug of hot chocolate into my hands before pulling the hood of my sweatshirt up over my head. "You need to keep in all the heat that you can."

We settled on the couch, under a couple of blankets. I snuggled up close to Brett and he wrapped an arm around me. Bentley sat by his feet and leaned against his legs, watching us with his brown eyes. I would have liked to have Flapjack on my lap for extra warmth, but he was snoozing on the kitchen windowsill and now that I was beneath the blankets, I didn't want to get up from the couch to get him.

Brett phoned Ray, but the call only lasted seconds.

"He's at the scene now," Brett explained once he'd hung up. "He'll come by soon."

I took a long sip of my hot chocolate and relished the warm trail it left as it worked its way down to my stomach. "Do you want to know what happened?"

"Yes. Every detail. But I can wait so you don't have to tell it twice." He rested his cheek against the side of my head. "I was working on the second floor of the Jepson house and saw the car go flying into the water. I was horrified, and that was before I knew you were inside."

"I might have drowned if you weren't there." I shivered, partly because I was still chilled and partly from the memory.

Brett pulled me closer to him. "When I saw you there in the water, struggling..." His words grew thick with emotion before trailing off.

I tipped my head back so I could see his face. He was fighting to stay composed, and I knew that today's incident had piled on top of everything else he'd been through lately. I brushed a curl of hair off his forehead, wishing I could wipe away all his recent pain just as easily.

He swallowed before speaking again. "I don't ever want to lose you, Marley."

I rested my head against his chest. "I'll always do everything I can to make sure you don't."

We lapsed into silence, but it was peaceful and comforting. I drank more hot chocolate and Brett drank his as well.

"Are you warm enough?" I asked after a while.

"I am. What about you?"

"Getting there."

I raised my head as the doorbell rang.

Brett put a gentle hand on my shoulder to keep me on the couch. "I'll get it."

Bentley trotted after him and I focused on my hot chocolate so I wouldn't think too much about my frightening ordeal. I wrapped both hands around the mug, absorbing as much warmth as possible. The hot liquid felt good going down and I'd nearly emptied the mug by the time Brett and Bentley returned to the family room with Ray following behind them.

I couldn't help but tense at the sight of the sheriff. He wouldn't like the fact that I'd once again tangled with a killer. I was relieved to see that his expression was serious but not angry.

"How are you feeling, Marley?" he asked as he sat in the armchair across from me and set his hat on a side table.

"Cold, but otherwise okay."

"Your head's all right?"

I gently touched the sore spot on my forehead. "Yes. Nothing serious."

Ray studied me from his seat. "Are you feeling up to telling me what happened?"

I nodded.

Brett took a seat beside me again and I set my empty mug on the coffee table so I could hold one of his hands with both of my own. He gave my fingers a reassuring squeeze and I drew strength from his presence.

"Where's Justine?" I asked before starting my account of the day's events.

I had to be sure that wires hadn't ended up crossed, that she hadn't been allowed to leave the Jepsen property a free woman.

"My deputies escorted her to the hospital to get checked out. She won't be going anywhere without them."

I released a deep sigh of relief and Brett gently squeezed my fingers again.

Ray flipped open a notebook and clicked his pen. "Whenever you're ready, Marley..."

Chapter 30

I fell asleep on the couch after Ray left. When I woke up, the room was dark except for a glow of light emanating from the hallway. I sat up and glanced around, finding myself alone. Brett had tucked another blanket around me at some point, but he was nowhere to be seen now. Disentangling myself from the blankets, I found Brett's cellphone on the coffee table and checked the time. It was nearly midnight.

My own phone was still out by the road somewhere but searching for it would have to wait until morning. I figured Brett had gone up to bed, and I decided to join him instead of spending the rest of the night on the couch. The light over the stairway was on, and when I reached the foot of the steps, I heard faint noises up above. I paused, listening and trying to figure out what was going on, but all I could make out was a scuffle and a quiet thud.

As soon as I reached the second floor, I saw that the light in the tower room was on, the door half open. I pushed it open wider. Bentley was curled up in the middle of the floor, but he jumped up when he saw me, his tail wagging as he skittered across the hardwood floors to greet me. Flapjack was snoozing on the window seat and didn't so much as stir upon my arrival.

Brett had his back to me, but he turned and smiled as I ran my hand over Bentley's fur.

"How are you feeling?" he asked.

"Warm, and it's wonderful."

His smile faded and a crease formed between his eyebrows. "Did I wake you?"

"No, I didn't hear anything until I reached the stairs." I rubbed my sleepy eyes. "What are you doing?"

"I had a brainwave after you fell asleep."

I put a hand to my mouth to cover a big yawn. "Please tell me this has something to do with Camelia and Grace's secret hiding spot."

"It does."

That brought me more fully awake.

"All Camelia said in her diary was that the hiding spot was in this room, right?" Brett said.

"Right."

"So maybe the hiding spot has nothing to do with the actual structure of the room."

I tried to guess what he was getting at. "The furniture?"

Brett grinned at me. "Exactly."

My gaze swept around the room. "There were a few pieces of broken or damaged furniture in here when I moved in, but decades have passed since Camelia wrote her diary. Whatever furniture was in here back then could be long gone."

"Could be. Or not."

I could tell by his grin that he'd found something.

"Where is it?"

His grin took on a hint of deviousness. "Maybe I should let you look for it."

I tried my best to glare at him, although it wasn't an easy task when I was looking into his gorgeous blue eyes. "It's the middle of the night and I'm half asleep. You're in danger of making me grumpy."

He pulled me over to him. "Maybe I think you're cute when you're grumpy."

I growled—only half annoyed—and shoved at his chest. "Brett!"

Bentley added his voice to the mix with a loud woof.

Brett laughed. "All right. I'll show you what I found."

He reached up to the top of the nearest bookcase and pushed at the molding along the front edge. I drew in a quick, surprised breath when the top of the piece of furniture lifted up like a lid.

A smile spread across my face. "A secret compartment! Is the letter inside?"

"I haven't looked yet. I thought you should do the honors."

I didn't want to stand on the room's antique reading chair so Brett wove his fingers together to create a step. I was full of expectation as he boosted me upward, but when I got a look in the compartment, my smile disappeared and my spirits plummeted. The compartment was empty.

"Anything?" Brett asked.

"Nothing."

He lowered me to the floor.

"I was so sure it would be there." I couldn't hide my disappointment.

"So was I."

I tugged at the trim along the bottom of the case, but it didn't budge. I moved on to the next bookcase, my hopes rising again. Bentley followed me, his tail wagging.

"I already checked the others," Brett said. "This is the only one with a hidden compartment."

As he spoke, I tested the tops of the other bookcases. He was right, not that I'd really doubted him.

"I'm sorry, Marley. I didn't mean to give you false…"

I spun around to face him when he trailed off. "What is it?"

He was examining the first set of shelves again. "This reminds me of a bookcase one of my great aunts showed me years ago." He ran a hand down the gleaming wood and tugged at one of the side panels. It swung open, revealing another compartment, stretching nearly the full height of the bookcase, several small hooks inside.

"For storing jewelry and other small valuables," Brett said.

Whatever might have been stored there at one time, there was nothing left. I tested the other side panel and it too opened.

"Empty," I said with a frown.

"Try the bottom again."

"It wouldn't budge the last time."

"I know, but I had the same problem with the side panels earlier. The top had to be open before the sides would open."

I brightened. "So maybe the sides have to be open before the bottom opens?"

I dropped to my knees and tugged at the piece of trim while Bentley nosed at my hands, trying to get in on the action. This time the piece of trim slid out toward me, revealing a shallow drawer.

My eyes widened when I spotted a folded, yellowed piece of paper lying inside. I picked it up carefully, afraid it might disintegrate in my hands, disappearing before I could read the words written upon it.

"Bentley, no," I said, moving my hand out of his reach as he tried to press his nose to the letter.

I got to my feet slowly, never taking my eyes off the paper.

Brett stood next to me as I carefully unfolded the letter. Despite the passing of decades, the tidy, inked handwriting was still easily legible.

Hardly breathing, I read the letter silently as Brett looked over my shoulder.

Dear Gracie,

I want you to know that I'm safe and that I've left of my own free will. I'm with Harry, and we're going to get married. I know some people think bad things about him, but they're wrong to. Harry's a good and gentle man, and I love him deeply. I wish I didn't have to go, to leave you and Mom and Dad, especially without saying goodbye, but Harry and I didn't see any other option. It was too dangerous for us to stay in Wildwood Cove. I can't explain why, not without putting you in danger too, so I hope you'll trust that we're doing what we have to do. One day, when it's safe again, I'll get back in touch. For now, please keep this to yourself. If Mom and Dad find out, they'll search for me and Harry, and if they do that the wrong people could find out where we are. I'm enclosing the address of a friend in Seattle. You can write to me there and I'll get your letters eventually. I'll understand if you hate me for leaving like this, but I hope you won't. I'm praying that you'll look in our secret hiding spot and find this letter.

With love,

Camelia

When I finished reading the letter, I realized I had tears in my eyes.

"She never did get in touch with her family again. She thought Grace was too angry to send her any letters through her friend."

"And Grace never looked in the hiding spot," Brett said.

"Like everyone else, she thought Camelia had left unwillingly. Grace never had reason to think her sister would have had a chance to prepare before disappearing. It probably never crossed her mind to look here." I raised my eyes to meet Brett's. "It's so sad."

"It is," he agreed.

I leaned against him and he rubbed his hand in slow circles on my back.

"I need to show this to Joan," I said.

"Tomorrow." Brett kissed the top of my head. "For now, let's try to get some sleep."

Chapter 31

It took weeks to find the remains buried in the woods. The search didn't start immediately after Joan and I presented everything we knew to the sheriff's department, but once the ground had thawed and everything was organized, the search finally began, starting in the forest at the edge of what was once the Sayers family's property. It was ground-penetrating radar that located the remains. The grave was fairly shallow, and not far from the spot where the Sayers' house had stood.

News of the find spread rapidly, but I already knew about it by the time word passed from diner to diner at The Flip Side. Ray had contacted Joan soon after the discovery of the skeleton, and she'd called me right away.

Once the pancake house was closed for the day, I set off on foot for Joan's house, wondering if she'd have any further news. Although I was in a hurry, I paused when I reached Main Street, distracted by the sight of someone familiar. Ivan had just emerged from the law office where Lisa worked. He held open the door and Lisa followed him out onto the sidewalk. He took her hand and she raised herself up on tiptoes to kiss him. Before they turned and walked away from me, I saw a bright smile on Lisa's face. I noticed a hint of a smile on Ivan's face too.

They disappeared around the corner at the end of the street without ever noticing me and I made no effort to get their attention. It had only been days since Lisa had told me they were now a couple and I wanted to leave them to enjoy their time together.

Continuing on my way, I hurried to Joan's house and greeted her with a hug.

"Have they confirmed that it's Tassy?" I asked.

"No," Joan said as she hung my jacket in the foyer closet. "All they know so far is that they have a female human skeleton."

"It might take time to identify her," I said. "But hopefully they will."

We were about to sit down in Joan's living room when movement outside the window caught our attention. Ray had pulled up in his cruiser. As we watched, he headed up the walkway to the front door. We met him there, Joan opening the door before he had a chance to knock.

"Do you have any further news, Sheriff?" Joan asked once he was inside.

"I'm afraid not. I just wanted to let you know that this investigation will take time. Rumors will probably fly around town now that we've found the remains, but at this point we're unable to officially identify the deceased."

"There was nothing to identify her at the scene?" I asked.

"Unfortunately, no. I was in contact with Cecelia McEnroe—Tassy James's youngest sister—last week. According to her, Tassy always wore a gold chain with a small dragonfly pendant. She never took it off. The James family was poor, and it was the only thing of value Tassy owned. She inherited it from her grandmother."

"But you didn't find the necklace with the remains?"

"No. There's no necklace."

"But it could still be Tassy," I said, not wanting to give in to disappointment. "She could have lost the necklace during a struggle when she was killed."

Ray nodded. "Any number of things could have happened to it. If it's Tassy we've found, we should be able to get a firm identification eventually."

I glanced at Joan. She'd gone quiet, and I noted with alarm that her face had paled.

I put a hand to her arm, worried she might be about to faint. "Joan? Are you all right?"

"Yes." The word was barely audible. She took a step away from us. "I'll be right back."

She disappeared up the stairway to the second floor.

I looked to Ray, but he appeared as puzzled as I was.

Seconds later, we heard Joan's footsteps on the stairs again, this time heading our way. She stopped in front of us, her right hand in a fist. She held it out and uncurled her fingers. Sitting on the palm of her hand was a gold chain attached to a tiny, delicate gold dragonfly.

"Tassy's necklace," I said with surprise.

"Where did you get it?" Ray asked.

Joan stared at the necklace as if it were an alien object, one she couldn't quite believe she was holding. "It was my mother's." Her voice was hoarse. "My father gave it to her as a birthday gift a few months after Tassy disappeared."

We were all silent for several seconds before Ray spoke.

"I can ask Cecelia McEnroe if she can identify it as belonging to her sister."

Joan nodded, her face stricken. She relinquished the necklace to Ray, sliding it into the plastic evidence bag he held open. He left moments later with a promise to be in touch with Joan again before too long.

"I'm so sorry, Joan," I said, squeezing her hand.

She swallowed hard and her face regained some of its color. "I already knew it was my father who'd killed Tassy, but knowing he took that necklace from the poor girl and gave it to my mother..." She shook her head and put a hand to her chest. "Will you join me for a margarita, Marley? I think I'm in need of one."

"Of course."

"Do you think this proves my father's guilt and Harry's innocence?" she asked as she mixed our drinks in the kitchen.

"I don't know if it would in a court of law," I said. "I guess it could be argued that it was Harry who took the necklace from Tassy and it ended up in your father's possession in some innocent way." When Joan's forehead furrowed, I hastened to add, "I don't believe that, and I think it would be a bit of a stretch to argue that, but I don't know what would happen at a trial. I'd like to think that all of the evidence, as circumstantial as it might be, would lead to justice."

"But there won't be a trial. My father's dead and Harry's dead. I just want people to know that Harry was no killer."

"I think most people believe that already."

Charlene had written a piece about Tassy and Camelia for the local paper, with input from Joan. She'd covered the story well, and it had captured the town's interest. Before Charlene wrote the story, Joan had managed to track down a couple in Wisconsin who'd known Harry and Camelia for years. They'd come up with pictures of the couple and had send them to Joan, so she now had proof that Camelia had lived for many years after leaving Wildwood Cove with Harry.

"Maybe Charlene will write another story now that the remains have been found," Joan said. "If I tell her about the necklace, maybe that will help to clear Harry's name even more in the public eye."

"I'm sure it will."

That thought seemed to comfort her, at least to some degree.

She handed me one of the margaritas she'd prepared and held up her own glass.

"To Tassy James," she said. "May she now rest in peace."

I clinked my glass against hers. "To Tassy."

Recipes

Candy Cane Pancakes

1½ cups all-purpose flour
1½ cups milk
2 teaspoons baking powder
½ teaspoon baking soda
2 tablespoons butter, melted
1 large egg
½ teaspoon peppermint extract
½ teaspoon vanilla extract
3 6-inch candy canes, crushed

Melt the butter and set aside to cool. In a bowl, mix together the flour, sugar, baking powder, and baking soda. In a separate bowl, beat together the egg, milk, melted butter, vanilla, peppermint extract, and half of the crushed candy. Make a well in the dry ingredients and add the liquid ingredients. Ladle the batter into a greased skillet and cook on medium heat until bubbles form on top. Flip and cook the second side until golden brown. Sprinkle with the remaining candy and top with pure maple syrup. Serves 4.

Gingerbread Crêpes

1 cup all-purpose flour
1½ cups milk
2 eggs
¼ cup brown sugar
½ teaspoon vanilla extract
2 tablespoons molasses
½ teaspoon ground cinnamon
¼ teaspoon dried ginger
¼ teaspoon ground cloves
Butter for greasing the pan
Chocolate sauce

Sift the flour and brown sugar into a mixing bowl. Add the cinnamon, ginger, and cloves. In a separate bowl, whisk together the eggs, milk, molasses, and vanilla. Make a well in the dry ingredients. Pour in half the liquid ingredients. Whisk until smooth. Add the remaining liquid ingredients. Whisk until smooth again.

Heat crêpe pan or small skillet over low heat for several minutes. Grease lightly. Increase to medium heat. Leave for one to two minutes. Pour ¼ cup of batter into the pan. Tilt and swirl to coat the pan. Cook until lightly browned. Flip with a spatula and brown the other side. Remove from pan. Makes approximately 12 to 16 crêpes.

Place a dollop or two of eggnog whipped cream (recipe to follow) onto the crêpe, fold the crêpe and drizzle with chocolate sauce.

Eggnog Whipped Cream

½ cup whipping cream
3 tablespoons eggnog

Whip the chilled cream in a mixing bowl until soft peaks form. Add the eggnog one tablespoon at a time and continue to whip until medium peaks form.

Eggnog French Toast

1 cup eggnog
3 large eggs
½ teaspoon vanilla extract
¼ teaspoon ground cinnamon
8 slices white bread
2 tablespoons butter

In a mixing bowl, whisk together the eggnog, eggs, vanilla, and cinnamon. Pour the mixture into a shallow baking dish. Dip the bread slices into the mixture, soaking for 20 seconds each side. Using a slotted spatula, let the excess drip off.

Melt 1 tablespoon of butter in a skillet over medium-low heat. Cook the bread slices in the skillet until golden brown, then flip and continue to cook until the second side is also golden brown. Add more butter to the skillet as needed. Serve with pure maple syrup or dust with confectioner's sugar. Serves 4.

Acknowledgments

I'd like to extend my sincere thanks to several people whose hard work and input made this book what it is today. I'm forever grateful to my agent, Jessica Faust, for helping me bring this series to life and to my editor at Kensington Books, Martin Biro, for helping me shape this manuscript into a better book. Thank you to Sarah Blair for always reading my early drafts and cheering me on, and to Jody Holford for providing feedback and being such an enthusiastic Marley and Brett fan. Thanks also to my wonderful friends in the writing community, and to all the readers who have returned for another of Marley's adventures in Wildwood Cove.

If you enjoyed *Yeast of Eden*, be sure not to miss the first book in Sarah Fox's brand new Literary Pub mystery series!

WINE AND PUNISHMENT

Booklover Sadie Coleman knows that in life, as in fiction, the right setting can make a world of difference. The small town of Shady Creek, Vermont, seems like the perfect place to start over after losing her Boston job to a merger and her relationship to her ex's gambling addiction. She's bought and redecorated the old grist mill pub, transforming the Inkwell into a cozy spot where tourists and regulars alike can enjoy a pint or a literary-themed cocktail, or join one of several book clubs.

Little by little, Sadie is adjusting to the rhythms of her new home. Fall in Shady Creek is bookmarked by the much-anticipated Autumn Festival, complete with a pumpkin catapult competition and pie bake-off. Unfortunately, the season also brings an unwelcome visitor—Sadie's ex, Eric, who's angling for a second chance...

Before Sadie can tell Eric to leave, he's found dead near the Inkwell. When the local antique shop catches fire on the same night, it's clear the town is harboring at least one unsavory character. Now, with her Aunt Gilda, her friend Shontelle, and the pub's patrons all in the mix, Sadie must uncover the truth...before a killer declares last call.

A Kensington hardcover and e-book on sale January 2019!

Turn the page for a sneak peek!

Chapter One

The crisp autumn breeze rustled through the colorful maple trees flanking the old grist mill. I stood back from the red-trimmed stone building, near the edge of the road, so I could get a full view of the property. A creek flowed along in front of the mill, gurgling and splashing, turning the old red water wheel, and a wooden bridge led the way from the wide footpath to the flagstone walkway that ended at the building's main door.

Beyond the mill a forest of sugar maples, beech trees, and conifers formed a serene backdrop, birdsong audible even from where I stood. Overhead, the bold blue sky was cloudless, and the early October sunshine brightened the entire scene before me.

It was postcard-perfect.

I'd thought that the moment I'd first laid eyes on the grist mill four months earlier. Now, with the fall colors at their most intense, I often found myself stopping to soak in the view of my new home and to revel in the fact that it was really mine.

That wasn't my purpose at the moment, however. In only four days, the town of Shady Creek, Vermont's annual Autumn Festival would get under way. Although I was new to town, the importance of the upcoming event hadn't escaped me. The residents had made it clear that the festival was Shady Creek's event of the year, and for any local business not to participate was simply unthinkable.

That's why I stood by the road, shading my eyes from the sun, assessing the picturesque building with a critical eye. I lived on the upper floor of the renovated mill, while the main level was dedicated to my literary-themed pub, the Inkwell.

I'd only had possession of the property for three months, and I was determined to make a success of the business. To do that, I needed the townsfolk on my side, and showing anything but enthusiasm for the Autumn Festival would be akin to shooting myself in the foot. Not that I wouldn't have been enthusiastic. I was looking forward to the festival. I was also looking forward to making a good impression on the town of Shady Creek.

"You're looking awfully serious, Sadie."

I dropped my hand from my eyes as Melanie Costas, one of the pub's employees, arrived at my side. Her bleached-blond and electric-blue hair was spiked straight up, and the silver stud in her nose glinted in the sunlight.

"Don't tell me there's something wrong with the building," she said, squinting through the sunlight at the mill.

"No," I assured her. "At least, I sure hope not. I'm thinking about how to decorate for the Autumn Festival."

"You and the whole town." Mel shaded her eyes as I had done moments ago. "Got any ideas?"

I tucked my red hair behind my ear as I thought about my response. "Pumpkins and decorative gourds, of course. Maybe some bales of straw, and a fall wreath for the main door. A scarecrow too, as long as it's not a creepy one."

"I could put together a scarecrow for you," Mel offered as we started along the pathway toward the bridge.

"Really?"

"Sure. I've made a couple before. And I promise it won't be creepy."

I smiled as we crossed the creek, the water babbling cheerfully beneath the bridge. "That would be fantastic."

Mel was a talented artist, so I knew she'd come up with something great, and that was one item I could take off my to-do list.

"I'll go to the pumpkin patch tomorrow morning," I said, opening the pub's large red door and holding it for Mel. Before following her through it, I flipped the wooden closed sign hanging on the outside of the door so the open side faced outward.

"How's the catapult coming along?"

"Er," was all I could come up with as the door fell shut behind me.

"That bad?" Mel said with a grin.

"With Damien out of town the past couple of days, progress has . . . stalled."

Mel shrugged out of her green military surplus jacket. "I'll come early tomorrow to lend a hand," she promised.

"Thank you. We're going to need all the hands we can get."

Although the entire Autumn Festival was a highly anticipated event in Shady Creek, the most popular part of it was the pumpkin catapult competition held at the end of the nine-day festival. Local businesses and other groups formed teams, with each one building its own catapult. Distance and accuracy were important when it came to catapulting the pumpkins, and the winning team would receive a trophy and, more importantly, bragging rights for the next twelve months.

I'd never anticipated that I'd need construction skills when I'd purchased the pub, but participation in the competition was expected. Luckily, Damien—another of my employees—did carpentry on the side and had designed the catapult for the Inkwell's team. Actually, building the contraption had yet to get past the initial stages, however.

I wasn't overly concerned. Damien would be back to work on the catapult the next day, and I figured that as long as we had one good enough to allow us to participate in the competition, that would suffice. I had enough on my plate without worrying about winning a contest that was all about having fun.

"How about the book clubs?" Mel asked. "Are you having more luck with them?"

"Definitely." I couldn't help but smile. "The first one is tomorrow night. Six people have signed up."

"Sounds like a great start."

That was my thought exactly. The idea of hosting book clubs at the Inkwell excited me to no end, and so far, the local response had pleasantly surprised me. The next night's romance book club had the most people signed up at the moment, but there had also been interest in the mystery book club starting up in a couple of weeks, and I was hoping to organize another one for science fiction and fantasy readers.

As Mel disappeared into the back of the pub, where the kitchen and tiny cloakroom were located, I remained by the front door, surveying the main room. When I'd purchased the building and business, the pub had been quite ordinary, aside from the beautiful historic building that housed it. It was a place for townsfolk to gather and chat over a pint or two, but it wasn't much beyond that. As soon as it had passed into my possession, I'd made sure to change that.

I'd long dreamed of owning my own bookstore, but when I'd arrived in Shady Creek, trying to escape the ruins of my former life in Boston, I'd fallen in love with the renovated grist mill as soon as I'd seen it. When I found out that it was for sale, it seemed like a sign from the universe, and I'd used nearly all of my savings to purchase the mill and business, setting my life on a new course that I'd never anticipated.

Briefly, I'd considered transforming the pub into a bookstore, but once I'd realized that it was a favorite gathering place for the locals, I changed my mind, and instead incorporated my passion for books into the existing business.

I'd been a bibliophile for as long as I could remember; since before I could even read the words on the pages. My dad had read to me every night as a young child, and his home library—though housed in a small room—had seemed like such a magical place to me while growing up. Once I could read on my own, I'd devoured story after story, working my way through books by C. S. Lewis, Enid Blyton, Kit Pearson, and many others. I'd feasted on series like Nancy Drew and the Baby-Sitters Club, and once I'd discovered Agatha Christie's novels, I was hooked on mysteries for life.

My dad had passed away a few years ago, and I still missed him all the time, but I knew I'd never lose the love for books he'd instilled in me. That's why it seemed so right to work books into my new business, even if not in the way I'd imagined while growing up and dreaming of one day having my own bookshop.

Once the purchase of the mill was finalized, I renamed the pub and gave it a literary theme, with drinks named for famous books and fictional characters. I was hoping to add some literary-themed food to the menu soon too, and my extensive collection of books lined the shelf that ran along the upper portion of the exposed stone walls, adding coziness to the pub's rustic charm. The wide plank floors and wood beams were original to the building, and vintage metal-banded barrels had been incorporated into the structure of the bar at the far end of the room, like stout pillars. The lighting in the pub wasn't bright, but I thought the warm glow added to the charm of the place.

Before my arrival in Shady Creek, I'd never imagined myself as a pub owner, but I was enjoying my new role, despite the stresses that came with learning the ropes of the business and staying afloat financially. So far, I was managing, if not exactly prospering.

Behind me, the front door opened, letting in a current of cool air tinged with wood smoke.

"Enjoying the view again?" a man said from over my shoulder.

I turned to see Harvey Jelinek—one of the Inkwell's regulars—grinning at me.

"Hi, Harvey," I greeted as he shut the door behind him. "I can't seem to help myself."

"I don't think anyone's going to blame you for that. It's a great place."

"It is, isn't it?" I smiled as we headed for the bar. "What can I get you?"

"Just a coffee." He took up his perch on his favorite stool at the end of the bar. "I'm meeting Rhonda here in a bit, and then we're heading to Rutland to have a late lunch with my sister."

"That sounds nice." I grabbed a clean mug and the coffeepot I'd put on to brew earlier.

"It will be as long as my sister doesn't hassle me and Rhonda about when we're getting married."

I filled the mug and slid it across the bar to Harvey. "You two are engaged?"

"No. That's just it. We're not at that point. But my sister doesn't always know how to mind her own business."

"Family can be like that," I said with understanding.

While my Aunt Gilda and my younger brother, Taylor, had supported me every step of the way, my mother and older brother hadn't held back when it came to expressing their negative views about all the changes I'd made to my life in the past four months. Words like "rash" and "shortsighted" had been tossed about. But what had stung the most was my mother's declaration that my new life would fall to pieces within the year, that I'd soon come to see the foolishness of my recent decisions. She was steadfast in her opinion, but I was just as resolute that she was wrong. At least, most days I was.

Two more of the Inkwell's regulars came into the pub then, thankfully distracting me from the unpleasant turn my thoughts had taken. I greeted the newcomers and pulled pints of beer for them as they settled onto stools at the bar. Mel emerged from the back and immediately joined the conversation about football that the patrons had struck up.

I was completely out of my depth with that topic, so I wandered down to the far end of the bar and called out a greeting to Rhonda Hogarth, who'd just arrived, carrying a cardboard box. Rhonda lived in the nearest house to the mill—a weathered old Queen Anne—and was the daughter of the man who'd sold me the pub. She was also one of the first friends I'd made in Shady Creek.

"What have you got there?" I asked her after Harvey greeted her with a kiss on the cheek.

She tipped the box my way so I could see the mason jars inside. Each one was decorated with colorful artificial leaves.

"Decorations," she said. "I got the idea from Pinterest and thought you might like some for the pub's interior during the festival. They've got LED lights inside."

She passed me one of the jars for closer inspection.

"These look great," I told her, turning the jar in my hands. I reached inside and flicked on the small light. The leaves glowed, highlighting their autumn colors. "I love them. How much do you want for the lot?"

Rhonda set the box on the bar and brushed her short dark hair off her forehead. "They're a gift."

"Let me pay you something," I protested.

"Nope. You know how I love this place. It makes me happy to lend a hand. That's all the payment I need."

"You're amazing, Rhonda. Thank you."

I took the box in my arms and hugged it to me as Harvey got up off his stool. He put some money on the bar for his coffee and rested his arm across Rhonda's shoulders.

"We'd better be off now," he said.

"Enjoy your day," I said to them as they went on their way.

I spent the next while wandering around the pub with the box of jars, placing the decorative light holders here and there. When I was done, I stood near the bar to admire the effect. I needed more decorations to make the place look truly festive, but the mason jars were a good start.

As the afternoon progressed, the number of patrons in the pub grew. Many were locals, but there were also several unfamiliar faces. With leaf-peeper season underway, busloads of tourists arrived daily, bringing smiles to the faces of all local business owners, including myself. I knew this would be the most prosperous season for the Inkwell, and the more visitors who came in for a drink or two, the more likely I'd be able to make the payments on my business loan in the upcoming months.

After exchanging a few words with one group of tourists, I cleared empty pint glasses from a vacated table.

"Don't you need to leave for your aunt's birthday dinner soon?" Mel asked when I reached the bar.

I glanced up at the Guinness wall clock. "Yes. I'll go get ready once Damien is here."

I continued on into the kitchen and deposited the glasses in the dishwasher. When I returned out front, Damien was making his way behind the bar, shrugging out of his black leather jacket.

"It looks like we're getting a good crowd," he remarked as he passed by me and into the back.

He reappeared a moment later without his jacket, wearing his usual outfit of jeans and a T-shirt, the tattoos on his muscular arms visible. Originally from England, Damien had an accent I loved listening to, but though we'd been working together for weeks now, I wouldn't have called us friends. The truth was that I wasn't entirely sure if he liked working for me or not. He'd come with the pub, so to speak, and had proved to be a valuable source of information and advice on many occasions, but I didn't think he had a whole lot of confidence in me as his boss.

I, however, had plenty of confidence in him and Mel. I didn't often take off during business hours, but that evening I was making an exception for a special occasion, and it was a relief to know I didn't have to worry about leaving the Inkwell in the hands of my employees.

A flash of red caught my eye, and I waved when I saw my friend Shontelle Williams threading her way through the tables toward the bar, unbuttoning her cherry-colored coat. Shontelle, a single mother of an eight-year-old girl, owned the gift shop across the village green from the Inkwell and had quickly become my closest friend in Shady Creek.

"Shouldn't you be getting ready?" she said, eyeing my jeans and V-neck sweater when she reached the bar.

"I'm just about to head upstairs."

I turned toward Mel, but she made a shooing motion with her hands before I could say anything.

"Go," she said. "We've got everything under control."

Shontelle hooked her arm through mine and steered me toward the door marked private.

"Call me if you need me," I said over my shoulder, barely getting the words out before Shontelle nudged me through the door.

I hastened up the creaking stairs that led to my apartment, Shontelle's high heels clacking on the steps behind me.

"Did you remember to pick up the cake?" she asked as I opened the door at the top of the stairs and stepped into my cozy living room.

"Yes, it's in the fridge." I went straight to my bedroom and grabbed the blue wrap dress I'd left hanging on the back of the door.

My white, long-haired cat was lying on the corner of my queen bed, watching me with his blue eyes. I paused to stroke his silky fur.

"Hello, Wimsey. Did you have a nice snooze?"

He purred and closed his eyes. I gave him a quick kiss on the top of his head and kicked off my shoes.

"Guess who I saw on my way over here," Shontelle called from the other room.

"I have no idea." I shed my clothes and slipped into the dress.

"That delicious Grayson Blake."

I poked my head out the bedroom door. "Don't you mean Grumpy-Pants Blake?"

"What did you do to make him grumpy?"

"Why do you assume *I* made him grumpy?" I asked, heading for my dresser and the jewelry box sitting on top of it. "I strongly suspect he was born that way." I switched out my silver stud earrings for a set of small hoops.

Shontelle appeared in the doorway and leaned against the frame. "I've never known him to be anything but a courteous gentleman. And one tall glass of delicious."

"Hrmph," was all I had to say to that.

I slipped past Shontelle and headed for the bathroom, where I set about touching up my makeup. My friend's opinion of the craft brewery owner matched that of my Aunt Gilda and pretty much every other woman in Shady Creek. Heck, I hadn't heard a man say anything negative about him either. Sure, he was attractive, and he brewed award-winning beers, but my business—and only—dealings with him hadn't been pleasant experiences. I found him brusque and as prickly as a porcupine. If not for the fact that his beers were so popular with both the tourists and locals, I wouldn't have bothered to sell them at the Inkwell.

Pushing thoughts of the brewery owner out of my mind, I added some color to my lips and fastened my red hair into a twist at the back of my head.

"All ready?" Shontelle asked when I emerged from the bathroom. She'd retrieved the cake from the fridge and held the bakery box in her hands.

"Almost."

I slipped into a pair of heels, grabbed my handbag, and pulled on my coat. I reached for the door but then spun around, almost smacking Shontelle across the face with my bag.

"Sorry!" I hurried into the kitchen. "I'd better feed Wimsey before we go."

Wimsey came trotting out of the bedroom when he heard the spoon clanking against his food dish. I set his dinner on the kitchen floor and gave him a quick scratch on the head as he dug into his food, purring away.

"Okay, this time I'm ready," I said as I returned to the door.

I locked up, and we headed down the stairs. As we reached the landing halfway down, Mel opened the door to the pub. She cast a quick glance over her shoulder and then slipped through the door, closing it behind her.

"Everything okay?" I asked, continuing down the stairs, noting that Mel appeared uncharacteristically hesitant.

"There's someone here looking for you."

"Who?" I made a move to go around her.

She put out an arm to block me. "I'm not sure it's someone you want to see."

I halted, suddenly apprehensive. "Who is it?" I asked again.

Mel gave me a sympathetic look. "It's your ex."

Meet The Author

Sarah Fox is the author of the Music Lover's Mystery series and the *USA Today* bestselling Pancake House Mystery series. When not writing novels or working as a legal writer, she can often be found reading her way through a stack of books or spending time outdoors with her English Springer Spaniel. Sarah lives in British Columbia and is a member of Crime Writers of Canada. Visit her online at AuthorSarahFox.com.

Printed in the United States
by Baker & Taylor Publisher Services